Fire Storm

A Novel
By
Marlow Kelly

D1091912

Copyright

Fire Storm
Published by Viceroy Press

COPYRIGHT 2018 by Marlow Kelly

ISBN 978-0-9952301-7-0

Cover art by Melody Simmons

Edited by Corinne Demaagd
From CMD Writing and Editing
https://cmdediting.com

For news of Marlow's next release sign up for Marlow's
Newsletter at: www.marlowkelly.com

Dedication

For my husband, Steve
You are my rock

Chapter One

Ben North clutched a hand to his chest in an effort to control his racing heart. The woman sat at his kitchen table, displaying her magnificent, naked breasts. He hadn't seen a bosom that superb since he'd served in Vietnam.

Her knee-length skirt had ridden up to her thighs, exposing her shapely legs. He should send her on her way, but the chance to spend time with a beautiful woman would be gone soon enough. He was two weeks away from his seventieth birthday and had more days behind him than ahead of him.

Besides, it would be rude to tell her to leave. To get to his cabin on Molly's Mountain, she'd had to drive past protesters and negotiate a steep, narrow trail that, at times, teetered on the side of a cliff.

"Don't you want me?" the woman at the table purred.

He wasn't sure if he could pleasure her. It had been years since his last sexual adventure. He cleared his throat. "Of course, I do, but are you sure? What about your husband?"

She stuck her bottom lip out in a pout. "He's having an affair."

"And I'm your revenge?" He had no time for her weasel of a husband, and there was poetry in the idea of him being used as an instrument for retribution.

Her gaze slanted to the floor as she swallowed and then licked her dry lips. "You're not the only one, but yes, you're payback."

There was something in her manner that was off. She could be lying, or maybe she felt guilty over her adultery. Yes, that was it. She wouldn't lie about having other boyfriends, but still, it was a surprise. "You have other lovers?"

She nodded and met his gaze, seeming direct and honest.

He'd always thought of her as uptight and unyielding. Maybe she showed the world the strict and conservative side of her nature, but in the privacy of the bedroom, she was a wild woman. He liked that idea.

She smiled, straightened her back, thrusting her chest forward, and then curled her index finger, beckoning him closer. "I want you to lick my breasts and suck on my nipples."

His cock sprang to life, which was comforting. Maybe he would be able to satisfy her. He stepped closer and knelt on the floor in front of her, ignoring the pain in his arthritic knees.

As he leaned in, she held up a hand to stop him. "Before you start, I need to get something out of my purse." She plucked her bag off the floor and placed it in her lap. She was probably looking for a rubber. That was the way of it these days. You couldn't have sex without protection, even if there was no chance of pregnancy.

She pulled out her compact mirror and lipstick and then placed her bag back on the ground.

He smiled. She wanted to make sure she looked good. Maybe she would primp her hair or touch up her makeup. He leant closer. He loved watching a woman put on lipstick. It was a feminine and intimate gesture. One he didn't realize he'd missed until this moment.

She pursed her lips as she opened the compact, held it level with his face, and blew.

He coughed when a fine, white powder flew into his nose and eyes. He tried to wipe it away, but it just smeared.

She blew again.

A chemical taste coated his tongue. He spat as he pulled away, trying to rid his mouth of the dry, bitter substance. Then the world tilted and swayed. The floor seemed to buckle under him. He cried out and grabbed the table, trying not to fall over.

A pretty she-devil with the largest breasts he had ever seen moved toward him. Horns grew out of her fair hair. "Where's the gold?"

He held his arms wide in an effort to prevent the walls from crushing him. "Why are the walls moving?"

"They're not moving. You're hallucinating. It's a side effect of the drug I blew into your face. I know you found a can of gold coins because I heard you telling Jack. Where is it?"

Jack? Jack Morgan was his oldest friend. Jack would chase the devil away the same way he'd chased away Ben's other demons. He tried to move to the door. He needed to get out of the house, to feel solid ground beneath his feet. But the floor slanted into an abyss. He gripped the table, scared he'd slip into the dark, inky blackness. "Help me!" he screamed at the devil-woman.

She smiled. Her evil eyes shone with blue fire. "I'll help you if you tell me about the gold."

He'd been tricked. The devil knew Ben's weakness and had disguised himself as a beautiful woman.

"You'd better get out of here before she kills you," the chair said.

The world righted itself, and he started for the door, ignoring the fact that chairs couldn't talk. The furniture levitated, drifting around the room. His mouth was dry, so dry he thought his tongue would crack. Blood pounded in his ears. He took another step but didn't have the energy to continue. He tried to inhale, but his lungs wouldn't expand. And now the damned furniture was spinning.

"Just tell me where the gold is!" the she-devil shouted.

"It's on Morgan land," he yelled. He didn't want to tell but was compelled to reveal everything. The devil controlled his mind.

"Where?" she insisted.

He opened his mouth to speak, but a crushing pain in his chest made him double over. He fell to his knees. Tim—he was supposed to meet him tomorrow and tell him about the gold. Now it was too late. He was a thief. He'd stolen from the Morgans, and the devil had come to claim him.

"Where is it?" The she-devil was on the ground next to him. "I need to know," she yelled, grabbing him by the collar.

Her words stabbed at him, coalescing into a dark, sharp knife that pierced his heart. The spasm extended through his chest and down his left arm. His world exploded into a white light of pain, and then nothing.

Chapter Two

Officer Dana Hayden gripped the steering wheel of her patrol car as she negotiated the treacherous and narrow dirt road to Ben North's cabin that was perched on the side of Molly's Mountain. She couldn't drive too fast since the dirt trail meandered around the mountain, sometimes teetering on the edge of a shear drop.

The homes west of Hopefalls were geographically isolated. The only way to reach them was to drive through the town. There were no other roads to this part of the county. Ben's only neighbors were the Kootenai National Forest and the Morgans, who owned the adjacent ranch.

She'd been to Molly's Mountain a number of times to deal with trespassers. Ben was embroiled in a particularly nasty lawsuit, one that had captured the attention of the press. Third Estate Mining Corporation claimed to own the mineral rights to Molly's Mountain and were using Montana's Eminent Domain Laws to force Ben from his land. Activists supporting both sides were camped out at his gate on the Hopefalls Highway. From there, it was a twenty-five-minute drive to the cabin.

Strictly speaking, the properties west of Hopefalls came under the jurisdiction of the Elkhead County-Granite City Police Department, and she had no power to arrest anyone, but she could talk to people as a private citizen. She'd been motivated to act as an intermediary for Ben since the town of Hopefalls had suffered a spate of vandalism. The graffiti painted on the side of the police station, town hall, and post office suggested a link to Ben's supporters. What had started off as defacement had escalated into arson when someone set fire to the mayor's shed. She'd had very few problems when she spoke to the protesters face-to-face, so she'd been unable to pinpoint a culprit.

Ben hadn't been grateful for her efforts. He was crotchety and gruff, but there was a spark in his eye that told her he was intelligent and alert, and she had instantly taken a liking to him.

She parked on the grassy ledge in front of the rundown cabin. Her boss, Police Chief Levi Booley, had parked his new Jeep Renegade close to the front door. Positioned beside it was the mayor's newer model Ford Explorer, which meant she had to park next to a sharp precipice. She inhaled as she took in the view. The morning sun cast a long shadow over the western side of the mountain. Forests gave way to wide meadows with more snow-capped mountains in the distance. It was stunning, but it was also a long way down, and heights had never been her thing. She wasn't exactly scared; she just had a healthy respect for Newton's law of gravity.

She climbed out of the patrol car, flinching as the skin at her waist caught between her Kevlar vest and gun belt. As a newly appointed officer for the town of Hopefalls, she'd been back in uniform for only two months. She couldn't get used to the stiff starched white shirt and wearing two belts— her gun belt and a belt to hold up her navy polyester pants. The gun belt was bulky and awkward, but necessary since it carried most of the tools needed for the job: two sets of handcuffs packed neatly into two handcuff cases, an expandable baton, a flashlight, Taser gun, her portable radio, and two spare, fully-loaded magazines, which ensured she carried at least forty-six rounds of ammunition.

As she ascended the three steps to the front door, her hand automatically went to her SIG Sauer. Booley had been cryptic when he'd phoned the station. He had refused to tell her the nature of the call, but claimed the area was secure.

She stood at the entrance and blinked, allowing her eyes to adjust to the dark interior. Ben lay near the door, flat on his back, his arms by his side. A revolver lay on the ground next to him. His face was white, bloodless, and his eyes cloudy and opaque. She could tell at a glance he was dead.

Whenever she encountered a body, her first instinct was to look away, but she resisted. Before moving back to Hopefalls, she'd worked with the Spokane Police Department for twelve years and had served six years as a beat cop before her promotion to detective. She knew the drill.

"There you are." Police Chief Booley stood in the center of the room, a tall rangy man with sharp eyes and a ragged face that revealed a lifetime smoking habit. "It took you long enough to get here." He wore muddy work boots, jeans, and a white cowboy hat. A lit cigarette dangled between his fingers.

Paul Harris, the mayor of Hopefalls, paced near the fireplace. He wore his usual uniform, a suit and tie. As always, his hair was perfectly combed, not so fussy as to be feminine, but not rugged either. His wife, Zoe Harris, sat on the old, duct tape-patched couch. She dabbed at her eyes with a crumpled tissue. Her short fair hair and gel nails were perfect, as always. Her eye makeup and mascara were also flawless despite the fact she'd been crying.

Dana bit her lip and counted to ten. Damn it, Booley had over thirty years' experience. He should know better than to contaminate the scene. He should've asked Mr. and Mrs. Harris to wait in the car instead of letting them trample all over the cabin. They needed to clear the room.

"Have you already called the Granite City-Elkhead County police? Or do you want me to do it?" It was her way of reminding her boss there were procedures to follow.

Booley gritted his teeth. "Yes, I called them."

She gave a curt nod as she snapped on a pair of latex gloves, hoping he would take the hint and extinguish his ash-trailing, evidence-tainting cigarette. "Then I'll have to ask you all to wait outside while I preserve the scene."

Booley's face flushed. "I'm your boss. I can do whatever I want."

Dana ignored his outburst. Her job was to protect the citizens of Hopefalls within the confines of the law, and she didn't care whose toes she had to step on to do that. "We need to secure the area and allow the Granite City-Elkhead County police to investigate. I need the three of you to wait outside. Who found the body?"

Zoe raised her hand.

Dana softened her tone. "Why were you here?"

Zoe sniffled. "I deliver food to the elderly."

"Did you touch Ben?"

The mayor's wife shook her head. "As soon as I saw him, I drove down the trail until I got a cell phone signal and told Booley that Ben was…that is to say I called…" She dabbed at her eyes. "I stayed in my car until Paul and the chief got here."

"They arrived together?"

"We drove up in my car," Booley snapped.

Dana paid no attention to the chief. Instead, she gave Zoe a sympathetic smile. "You'll have to wait until the Granite City-Elkhead County Police Department arrive. They'll want to question you."

The mayor, who had been silent to this point, marched past her and out the door. "I'm taking my wife home. They can find us there. There's no need for all this fuss. We know who did it."

"We do?" Dana ground her teeth together. She wanted to blast Booley and the mayor. She didn't like having a civilian tell her who'd committed the crime, even if he was, technically, her boss. The three of them had stomped all over Ben's cabin, leaving footprints, fingerprints, DNA, and cigarette ash. She doubted Booley would want to explain to the Granite City-Elkhead County police the evidence was tainted.

Booley pointed to the gun on the floor next to the body. "That's a limited-edition Colt six-shooter. It was made in 1984 and jointly purchased by Jack Morgan and Ben North. The two had a falling out, and Jack Morgan kept the weapon. It's worth thousands of dollars."

Zoe rose and walked toward Dana, not looking at Ben. "I'll wait outside."

Dana nodded as the mayor's wife inched past her. Of the three of them, only Zoe Harris's behavior was understandable. She was distressed and probably in shock. She had found the body, so her presence in the cabin was justifiable. The other two should've known better.

Dana pushed the thought aside, grabbed her notebook from her back pocket, and started documenting the crime scene. It didn't matter what Chief Booley or Mayor Harris said. She would work the case and hand her notes to the detective in charge of the investigation.

Ben North lay on the floor a few feet from the door. His lips were a faded shade of blue. She had viewed more dead bodies than she cared to remember, but she never got used to seeing a soulless corpse. Everything Ben had been was gone. All that was left was an empty husk. She forced herself to focus. In her experience, a body never fell neatly. After being shot, people normally landed in a crumpled heap on the floor. They did not lie there as if they were waiting to be placed on a stretcher. Ben's body had been moved.

Booley hunched down next to Ben, puffing on his cigarette, blowing smoke over the corpse.

Dana snapped the book closed, her patience at an end. "Sir, please extinguish that outside."

Booley grunted and walked past her, knocking her shoulder as he passed through the door.

She ignored his juvenile antics and flipped open her notebook, concentrating on the task at hand.

A trace of a white, powdery substance covered Ben's face. A chair near the small kitchenette lay on its side. Where was the food Zoe had delivered? She'd said she left as soon as she saw him. Ben was lying near the entrance. Zoe would've knocked, opened the door, and seen Ben. Then she would have driven back down the mountain to call for help. She probably hadn't actually stepped into the cabin until Booley and the Mayor arrived.

Dana continued with her notes. The kitchen cupboards and drawers were all open. Someone had been searching for something. From her position at the door, she couldn't see if the loft had been ransacked, but the living area seemed to be untouched. Maybe the assailant had found whatever they were looking for in the kitchen and hadn't gone through the rest of the house.

Booley's heavy footsteps thudded through the door. He didn't bump into her as he entered, which was a relief. Booley was a jerk. Dealing with his attitude was a challenge at the best of times. She didn't need the distraction while working a case.

"So you think Jack Morgan killed him?" Dana hadn't met Jack and didn't want to. It was better for her peace of mind if she stayed away from the Morgans. It helped their ranch was on the other side of Molly's Mountain, away from Hopefalls and in Elkhead County.

Booley stood over Ben. "It's doubtful. Jack's suffering from Alzheimer's. He's in a care home in Granite City, but he has a son, Timothy."

"Tim Morgan? The same Tim Morgan who killed Aunt Alice?" She backed through the door but stopped before she stumbled down the steps.

Booley nodded.

An invisible vice tightened around Dana's chest. Tim Morgan had devastated her family when he'd caused the car accident that had taken Aunt Alice's life. Unable to deal with his sister's death, her father had moved the family to Spokane, a place where she, at thirteen, had been an outsider. It was the beginning of a dark time for her, one that had lasted until she'd joined the Spokane police force in her twentieth year.

Dana straightened her shoulders. "I need you to leave the scene now."

"Sounds like you mean business." Booley smiled, revealing yellow nicotine-stained teeth.

"Yes, sir." She took one last look at the body. Although four wounds punctured the chest, there was very little blood. Damn. No blood meant Ben was already dead when he was shot. No, she couldn't draw any conclusions. All she could do was wait for the medical examiner's report and go from there.

She marched to her car, opened the trunk, and took out some crime scene tape. She would seal off the scene and preserve any remaining evidence. She wouldn't allow anyone to pass except the crime scene technicians and the Granite City-Elkhead County police. This was their chance to get Timothy Morgan. Nineteen years ago, he'd gotten away with killing Aunt Alice.

He wouldn't get away this time.

Chapter Three

Tim Morgan rode his ATV across the wild, overgrown fields of Wind Valley Ranch, heading for the forested wilderness of Molly's Mountain. It was late morning. The sun had shifted to the south so it wasn't in his eyes. Ben North, his neighbor, had called him yesterday morning and left a voicemail demanding to see him urgently. Ben had probably heard about his plans to sell Wind Valley and wanted him to change his mind.

If that was the case, he understood. This land was part of him, part of his past, but it would never be his. He needed to sell the ranch. There was no other choice. It hadn't been an easy decision, but he could no longer delay the inevitable. He'd sold off the livestock and equipment when his father, Jack, had first become ill. That money was gone.

Alzheimer's had stolen his father's mind to the point where he didn't recognize his own son. Tim had placed him in Shady Pines Care Facility, which was expensive but worth every penny. It comforted him to know his dad was getting the best care possible.

The mountain loomed ahead of him, dark and forbidding, a stone sentinel that guarded the valley. The wide basin that formed Wind Valley Ranch lay in the middle with the peaks of Wind Ridge behind him. The Cabinet Mountain Wilderness lay in the distance to the west. There were no vehicles allowed in the remote area unlike in Wind Ridge, where trails crisscrossed the forest, linking holiday cabins to the Hopefalls Highway.

A cow moose trotted across the open field on his right, and he stopped, enjoying the view of the long-legged creature as it loped through the field. In another place and time, he might have taken a shot. But he didn't hunt anymore. It was too much like being a soldier, and he'd worked long and hard to leave death behind. He liked to think he would never kill again, but he couldn't discount the possibility. Life had a way of kicking him in the teeth when he least expected it.

When he'd left the Rangers, he'd taken all the psychiatric help the VA could provide. He wasn't a psychopath. He still had empathy and cared for the people in his life, but killing had become easy, and some changes just couldn't be undone. In combat, he'd been able to separate his emotions from his actions. He took comfort in the fact that he'd only ever fought in a sanctioned conflict. He didn't have any desire to end a life, nor was he filled with remorse for the lives he'd taken. He'd done his duty and made his peace with it.

With the moose disappearing into the distance, he turned the throttle and continued onto Molly's Mountain. Normally, in early spring, the ground would be saturated and muddy from snow melt, but this year it was just a little damp. Winter had been unusually dry and mild with just one blizzard.

Evading pine trees, he reached Molly's Creek, the official boundary that separated Wind Valley Ranch from Molly's Mountain, and shut off his off-road vehicle. The waters of the stream cut deep into the earth. There was no way his ATV could negotiate the rivulet without getting stuck.

He slung his backpack over his shoulder and then clipped a can of bear spray to the strap. He waded through the ice-cold creek, ignoring the discomfort of having wet feet. He planned to jog through the forest and up the mountain to Ben's cabin. Running had always been his favorite form of exercise. He wasn't in top physical condition, not like when he'd been a Ranger. Nowadays, he was lucky if he managed one run a day, and even that got cut short if he had a particularly busy schedule.

His job as a salesman, representing Tillman's Organic Feed, relied on his ability to reach out to new and existing customers. He'd created his own position and introduced Tillman's products to stores and feed supply outlets for a percentage. The work suited him. When he'd first left the US Army 75th Ranger Regiment, he'd struggled with finding his own identity. It had taken a lot of therapy for him to understand and accept that he was happier when he spent time with people. He was, at heart, a social animal. He might have massive debts and no chance of having a permanent home, but every day he went out and talked to people about their business, their families, and their hopes for the future. He never tried to make a sale, he made friends, and that was the key to his success. His customers had become his community. But deep inside he wished for more. He wanted a wife and children, a real home.

Tim halted at the sound of someone crashing through the woods. He stood still, listening. Ben had a lot going on. Activists were camped at the entrance to his property night and day. A head of blue hair appeared near the skinny trunk of a lodgepole pine. Tim stayed still, watching. The boy, who was probably fifteen or sixteen, marched along, staring at the ground. He wore ear buds, the faint sound of a bass rhythm a startling contrast to the birdcalls and breeze that echoed through the forest.

A roar sounded. Tim froze. Two hundred yards behind the kid was a grizzly bear. She stood ten feet tall. Behind her were two small cubs. "Damn, shit, fuck." There was nothing more dangerous than a momma grizzly with cubs.

Unaware of the danger, the teen with blue hair bobbed his head to the music. A small part of Tim wanted to back away and leave the kid to his fate, but he wouldn't. He couldn't imagine a worse way to die than being eaten alive.

Don't panic. Think it through. He unclipped the can of bear spray, making note of the wind direction. A slight breeze blew directly in his face. That wasn't good. If he had to discharge the spray there would be blowback. He strode toward the kid, resisting the impulse to run and scream a warning. The bear hadn't charged, and he didn't want to do anything to provoke her. Maybe the roar had been a signal, telling them to back off. That was good. They would leave the area, and she could go back to caring for her offspring.

The teen removed his headphones as Tim approached. "Hey."

He didn't reply. He kept his focus on the grizzly. His pulse pounded in his ears.

The teen followed his line of vision. "Fuck." Blood drained from his young face and his lips trembled.

Tim snagged his arm and pushed the boy behind him. "About three hundred yards downhill is an ATV." With his spare hand, he fumbled in his pocket and withdrew a set of keys. He thrust them at the kid. We are going to walk—not run—to the vehicle. I'll cover us while you start her up. We'll move as one unit. If we stick together, our shape will seem larger and she won't charge. Understand?"

The kid snatched the keys from Tim's hand and stepped back out of his line of sight.

He eased away from the bear, careful not to make a sound. Then glanced behind him in time to see the kid racing downhill. *Shit.*

The bear charged. Tim held his ground. If he shot the spray too soon, it would disperse before the bear reached him. The smell of rotting flesh mixed with garbage stung his nostrils as the bear neared. He discharged a one-second burst, aiming at the ground in front of her. She didn't stop. He held his breath and aimed at her face. He gave a six-second blast. It shot twenty feet through the air. It hit the bear with a hot, burning cloud, billowing out, creating a chemical haze. Droplets blown back by the breeze hit his cheeks. He didn't wait to see if she slowed or veered away. He could taste the spray in his mouth, feel it burning his eyes and lungs. He turned and sprinted downhill. There was a chance she would ignore her pain and decide he was a good meal to feed her cubs. He was a fast runner, but there was no way he could outrun her. Any minute he expected to feel a clawed paw swipe across his back and break his spine.

He raced down the mountain and splashed across the creek, praying the kid hadn't stolen his ATV.

The boy was in the driver's seat trying to start the engine.

"Get out of the way," he shouted.

The kid scrambled to the back seat. Tim turned the throttle. The ATV roared to life. He accelerated, bumping over the uneven ground toward the safety of his childhood home.

Chapter Four

Tim forced himself to blink as he parked the ATV in front of the house. He needed to produce enough tears to wash the remnants of the bear spray from his eyes. It had been a tough drive back. The blowback had caused his face and hand to itch and burn.

He crashed through the kitchen door, turned the taps on at the kitchen sink, running the water until it was warm. Then he poured some dish detergent into his hands and scrubbed his face. Once he had washed off any residual chemicals, he ran the cold water, and contorting his body, bent over the sink and tilted his face up to flush his eyes. He really needed a shower, but that would have to wait until he'd dealt with the kid. After about two minutes, he turned off the tap. He straightened and faced the blue-haired teen who stood at the kitchen door, looking as if he was ready to bolt.

"I'm Tim Morgan. What's your name?" Tim growled.

"Logan—Logan Hayden." He fidgeted with the bottom seam of his shirt.

Tim's face still burned so he grabbed a large mixing bowl from a cupboard and a jug of milk from the fridge. Thank God, he'd purchased groceries last night. He poured the milk into the bowl. "Logan Hayden, you win the award for being an absolute bastard. I told you to stay with me. The minute you ran, she charged. If we'd backed up carefully and stuck together, we might have seemed bigger, more of a threat, and she might not have attacked. But no, you had to take off."

The kid's face reddened, and he stared at the ground. "Sorry."

Tim plunged his face into the bowl. The intense burning faded. He held his head in the milk as long as he could and then came up for air. Logan looked ashamed and scared. There was nothing wrong with being scared, especially when it came to bears.

Tim's lips, nose, and eyes still stung so he dunked his head in the bowl again. At fifteen, he'd been an arrogant asshole until life had kicked him in the nuts and taught him about humility.

He pointed to a tea towel that lay on the counter by the sink. "Pass me that."

"I'm really sorry." Logan crossed the kitchen and gave him the cloth.

"Let's forget about it. When I was your age, I made far worst mistakes than running from a bear."

He backed up to the door.

Tim patted milk droplets from his face. "Are you with the protesters camped at Ben's gate?"

"No." He crossed his arms over his chest. The abruptness of his answer, along with his posture, suggested he was being defensive. But Tim knew false bravado when he saw it, especially when it came from a teenage boy.

"How did you get out here?"

He shrugged. "I walked."

"From where?" Wind Valley was remote.

"Hopefalls."

It would've taken him all morning to walk from town. And he didn't have any supplies. "Did you drop your pack?"

"No."

Tim clamped his mouth shut to avoid lecturing the kid. But the fact that Logan had walked all the way out here without water, food, or any way to protect himself was beyond stupid.

"You must be thirsty. Grab a glass from the cupboard above the sink and help yourself to water." He dipped the edge of the towel into the bowl of milk and dabbed his still burning face.

Logan crossed the room, poured himself a glass of water, and downed it in one swallow.

22

"Did you say your last name was Hayden? Do you live on Maple Street?" He couldn't be one of those Haydens.

Logan finished drinking his second glass and then nodded.

Tim threw the towel on the table. "Oh, shit." He was a member of Alice Hayden's family. This was not going to be good. He thought they had left the area. His dad had said they'd moved away.

He'd avoided Hopefalls for years. It wasn't hard. Yes, he had to drive through town to reach Wind Valley, but he never stopped. He never got gas, shopped in the hardware store, bought groceries, or ate at the diner. The only person he kept in touch with was Victoria Anderson, his second-grade teacher who was also a family friend.

"It's Friday. Why aren't you in school?" Tim's job allowed him a certain latitude when it came to his schedule. He'd shuffled his customers around so he could take the day off and meet Ben. Damn it, he was going to miss his meeting with North. Plus, there were protesters camped at Ben's gate that needed to know about a momma grizzly in the area.

"I skipped school. I'm not learning nothing anyway."

"You're not learning anything." He thought about giving the kid a mouthful, but instead plunged his red-hot face into the milk. Logan wasn't his responsibility, and Tim had enough on his plate without dealing with a fifteen-year-old kid who was skipping school.

After a minute, he came up for air. "Do you have a license?" There was an old truck in the barn. Maybe Logan could drive himself back to town.

"I'm getting my learner's permit next week. You're that Tim Morgan, aren't you?"

He didn't answer. He could hear the accusation in the kid's voice. He would've liked to tell him to walk back to town, but couldn't, not with a bear in the area.

"I'll give you a ride. Are your parents home?"

"There's just Mom. She's a cop. She's at work now."

That was fucking great. He would give everything he owned if it meant he never had to walk into the Hopefalls police station again, but he had no choice. He cursed as he turned on the cold tap and washed the milk residue off his face. He would drop off Logan and report the bear.

At fifteen, Tim had run away rather than face his problems. He wasn't a kid anymore, and he wouldn't run away. Besides, he hadn't done anything wrong.

Chapter Five

Detective Ramirez from the Granite City-Elkhead County Police Department sat on the corner of Dana's desk. She ignored him as she tapped at her computer keyboard, completing her report. Once it was done, she would go on patrol, grab a sandwich for lunch, and stay occupied and out of the way. It had been a long morning and the way things looked it would be an even longer afternoon.

It was hard to step back and not interfere with the investigation, but that was exactly what she had to do.

It was good that the Granite City-Elkhead County Police Department had taken over the case. They were larger with more amenities at their disposal. It also meant Booley, the mayor, and his wife couldn't interfere with the investigation any more than they had already.

The Hopefalls Police Department was small, consisting of just four members, Dana, Xavier Robinson, who was also a patrolman, Shelly, the civilian clerk, and Chief Levi Booley.

Ramirez snagged a cookie from a plate on the desk. "These are good. Did you bake them?"

Dana shook her head and continued to type. "No, Shelly did."

Shelly looked up from her stack of filing, glaring at Ramirez. "Dana doesn't cook." Shelly was five feet tall, middle-aged, with a rounded figure. She was the backbone of the station, doing everything from taking calls to record keeping and clerical duties. She ruled her domain with a combination of motherly love and draconian fear.

Dana was grateful to have another woman in the male-oriented environment, even if she could be a little territorial and judgmental. At this moment, Dana wasn't sure if Shelly's anger was directed at the detective or at Dana's cooking skills, so she concentrated on her work. She could ignore

Shelly's mood as long as the older woman kept her supplied with baked cookies and muffins.

The station house was on the main road through town, situated in a newer building with white vinyl siding that matched the town hall next door. The inner walls and front desk were white, which was probably intended to make the cramped interior seem larger, but the effect was that of a cross between a doctor's office and a prison.

All the furniture was cheap, but sturdy enough to do the job, including the desk she shared with Xavier, which was metal with a fake wood top. Two cells stood at the rear of the station. The lack of space meant there wasn't enough room to partition them off, so they were clearly visible from the front desk, which for some reason made her uneasy.

Ramirez swallowed his mouthful of cookie and brushed some non-existent crumbs from his lips. The action drew Dana's attention to his hands. He had the most perfectly manicured nails she had ever seen on a police officer. In fact, he was impeccably groomed, which was a little off-putting. His short dark hair was flawless. The same could be said for his pressed white shirt, which had to be hard to maintain, especially if he had to chase a suspect. "The ME has given us an estimated time of death. He thinks North died between five and midnight yesterday evening,"

Dana straightened away from her computer. "Did you question the protesters at the gate? They might've seen someone or…"

Ramirez raised an eyebrow "Or what?"

"If the killer was a local, they would know about the back roads," Dana explained.

Ramirez took his notebook out of his pocket. "What back roads?"

"There's a maze of trails that lead into the forest. Some of them pass the base of the mountain."

Booley left his small cubicle office and joined the detective at her desk. "He was shot with the handgun."

It was a statement not a question, but Ramirez answered him anyway. "We'll have to wait for the ME's report, but I don't think that's what killed him."

Booley's face flushed. "What do you mean?"

"Not enough blood," Dana answered and then cursed herself. Booley wasn't the type of boss who appreciated his underlings having more experience than him.

"That's right." Ramirez smiled at her. "You'd make a good detective."

She went back to typing on the computer and tried to ignore them, which was impossible considering they were camped at her desk.

"So what killed him?" Booley demanded.

Ramirez stood and made his way past the front counter, headed for the door. "I don't know. The ME's hoping to get back to me in a couple of days. I'll let you know as soon as it comes in." He reached the exit, stopped, and turned to stare directly at the chief. "I'll have one of my people come by and collect exclusion prints from you, the mayor, and his wife. Don't give them a hard time."

Booley nodded. "I won't."

Dana suspected the detective wanted to say more. She would have if she'd been handed a willfully contaminated crime scene.

"Did you know the gun didn't kill him?" Booley challenged the moment Ramirez was gone.

Dana shrugged. "It occurred to me, but you can never draw conclusions. You have to let the techs do their thing and then work with what they find."

Booley paced to his office at the front of the building. His hand jerked to the doorknob and then dropped to his side. He stood there for a moment as if thinking, but then entered, slamming the door after him.

Dana relaxed into her chair. She'd heard about this position from friends of her parents who still lived in town. She had taken a demotion and a pay cut to secure the job. Her grandmother's house had sat empty since her death a year ago. It was the perfect opportunity for a fresh start and a new beginning for her son, Logan. The police chief hadn't wanted to hire a woman, especially one who was a trained detective. It was the town council who had insisted on her appointment.

Booley wrenched open his door and marched back to her. Color had risen high on his cheeks. "Why didn't you say something sooner?"

"What? About the bullet holes?" What did the circumstances of Ben's homicide matter? The man was dead, and the facts were the facts.

"Booley?" Victoria Anderson, a retired schoolteacher and member of the town council, stood at the front desk with Joe Freeman by her side.

Mrs. Anderson's short, white, wavy hair coupled with her horn-rimmed glasses and stern expression reinforced her authority as a retired schoolteacher. She was both feared and respected. Dana had seen grown men bow to her wishes because they'd learned to fear her as small children and they were still scared of her today.

Joe, on the other hand, had a slow, easy smile. It was rumored he'd only left Montana once, and that was a trip to New York City. To mark that life-altering trip, he always wore a Yankees baseball cap. It was threadbare with age, but he refused to go anywhere without it. He was the town postmaster. Recent cutbacks meant the post office was only open part-time. Joe seemed to take the slower pace in stride. He claimed working fewer hours suited his advanced years.

Dana was grateful for the interruption. She seemed to spend all her time holding her temper when what she wanted to do was let fly and tell Booley to shut up. The man was a nightmare of clichés. He was a rude, chauvinistic, and a poorly trained policeman who showed no interest in upgrading his skills. Rumor was that he'd tried to hire his family for positions within the police department, but the town council had stopped him.

Booley stared at Victoria and Joe, then smiled and strode toward the counter. The way he walked reminded Dana of a snake slithering along the ground. "What can I do for you?"

"I'm going to be putting up posters for the community fair around town, and I don't want you quoting regulations about posters on lampposts," Victoria said.

"Well, don't paste them to the lampposts, or I'll give you a ticket."

The mayor, Paul Harris, entered the building while Booley dealt with Victoria and Joe. He nodded to her and then proceeded to Booley's office as if he owned the place.

Good. Harris was probably here to talk about everything that had happened this morning, which meant the chief would be tied up for a while.

She'd thought being a small-town cop would be a good match for her, but after two months, she had her doubts. Not just about her boss and the integrity of the Hopefalls Police Department, but also about her ability to do the job. She was damaged, a shadow of her former self, and she didn't know if she would ever be whole again.

Dana continued typing, hoping to complete her report soon so she could go back on patrol and escape Booley.

She had just finished when Logan slammed through the door and ran around the reception desk.

She stood and met her son at the counter. "What happened? Why aren't you in school?"

"Mom, we were charged by a bear. Tim sprayed it so we could get away." A slim, dark-haired man followed Logan into the station. She was five feet eleven inches, and the man was at least a head taller than her. She estimated him to be at least six-foot-six.

He moved in the fluid, muscular way of an athlete and had the hard-eyed look of a fighter. His build was deceptive. He seemed thin, but that was just because he was so tall. The well-toned pectoral muscles of his shoulders along with his biceps told her he worked out regularly and was fit and strong. She'd wrestled a lot of drunks in her time on the force and knew how to size a man up. In her estimation, it would take three or four policemen to take him down.

"Thanks for saving…" She couldn't finish her sentence. Staring into his hazel – green eyes was like being punched in the gut. He was handsome in a rugged way. The weathered skin around his mouth and eyes was etched with deep lines. His hair had grayed at the temples, making him appear distinguished. Everything about him seemed masculine. It was as if he oozed testosterone.

Booley emerged from his office and approached the stranger. "Officer Hayden, I'd like you to meet Tim Morgan."

The air whooshed out of her lungs. This was the man who'd killed Aunt Alice. How could he be so devastatingly handsome, so attractive? The man who was responsible for shattering her family should be an ogre, someone who looked as ugly on the outside as he was on the inside.

Morgan blinked. His face was slightly red as if he had a mild case of sunburn, and the whites of his eyes were pink. His hands were fisted at his sides, but otherwise he showed no reaction to Booley's introduction.

"I'm here to inform you there's a grizzly with cubs in the area of Wind Valley and Molly's Mountain." Morgan stood to attention and stared straight ahead while he made his announcement. The contained way he held himself was unnerving. His physical power was obvious, but she sensed he was a man of determination and control, which was unexpected, considering his past.

"Is that right?" Booley said as he moved to stand next to Morgan.

Morgan didn't acknowledge Booley and didn't react. He didn't even blink.

"Timothy Morgan, I'm arresting you for the murder of Ben North." Booley grabbed Tim's hand and wrenched it behind his back.

Morgan spun around so he was facing the chief, his hands no longer in the chief's grasp. "Ben's dead?"

Booley's fist connected with Morgan's face. "You killed him over that fancy Colt revolver he purchased with Jack."

The force of the jab knocked Morgan off balance so he fell against the front desk.

"Don't pretend you don't know. I'd bet my last dollar you had something to do with it." Booley punched Morgan's face again.

Morgan grunted as he absorbed the blow but didn't try to defend himself.

Xavier entered the building and took in the scene. He pulled his gun. "Do not resist arrest."

Xavier's words and the fact he'd drawn his weapon propelled Dana in to action. She pushed Logan behind her. "Everyone stop," she shouted, making sure she put power behind her words. Booley had overreacted. They had no reason to arrest Morgan. No probable cause, no arrest warrant, nothing. They needed to question him, certainly, but the chief had no reason to use force.

Morgan straightened, squaring his shoulders. His rage-filled eyes glittered as he allowed Booley to cuff him.

Dana stepped forward. "Mr. Morgan, we are assisting the Granite City-Elkhead County Police Department with their investigation in to the homicide of Ben North, and we need to question you about your movements yesterday."

She'd always been honest and liked to think she was fair. It was that impartiality that made her such a good detective. From what she could gather, Morgan had saved her son from a bear, and the least she could do was prevent him from being beaten. But if he had killed North, she would make sure he was prosecuted to the full extent of the law.

Morgan's red-rimmed eyes blinked. He tilted his head to one side. "Question me or beat the crap out of me?" He turned to glare at Booley and then slanted his gaze back to her. "And why the hell would I kill Ben? I haven't seen him in years."

"Have you had any contact with him?" Booley asked. The chief seemed to have lost all control when it came to

Morgan and had decided to question him here in the open where anyone could walk in off the street.

Dana stood with her hands on her hips. "Sir, I think you should interview him in private, and I don't want anyone to touch him."

Booley was used to laying down the law in his own way, but this was different. She wanted everything done by the book so charges would stick. "We're not talking about vandalism, graffiti, or a traffic stop. This is a homicide investigation. There is no way I'm going to let a murderer escape justice by claiming we infringed on his rights. I don't want some lawyer saying we didn't adhere to the proper procedure."

Morgan scowled at her and then snarled, "Give me my phone call. I want a lawyer."

Chapter Six

Tim sat in the police cell, gingerly feeling the tender skin around his left eye. It was already starting to swell and was possibly changing color. Between the bruise and the burn from the bear spray, he probably looked like he'd gone ten rounds in a boxing ring.

The attractive policewoman with short, wavy blond hair passed an icepack through the bars. "This will help the swelling."

He reached for the pack, careful not to get too close. "Thanks. How's Logan doing?"

She'd just returned from dropping her son off at school, but hadn't been gone long, five minutes at the most.

"Fine." She avoided eye contact and returned to her computer, subconsciously tugging at her short, fair bangs, as if she were trying to make them longer. It was an odd cut. The hair on top of her head was short and then longer at the back. It was as if the stylist had cut the top and then been too scared to continue with the rest. It reminded him of the mullet hairstyle from the eighties.

She was tall, fit, and magnificent. Her name badge read Officer Dana Hayden. Judging by her age, he would guess her to be Alice Hayden's niece. Alice had an older brother. Tim couldn't remember his name, but he'd moved away after his sister's death. This woman had a child, so maybe Hayden was her married name. But then again, she did look familiar. There had been a Hayden girl in school who was a couple of years younger than him. She'd been tall and ungainly, not trim and statuesque like the woman before him. It was hard to believe Logan was her son. She must've had him when she was a kid herself. Either that or she just looked young for her age.

Surprisingly, she was the only reason Booley hadn't beat the crap out of him. She admitted she wanted to build a solid case against him, but what that case could consist of he had no idea. Any evidence would be manufactured. The people of Hopefalls believed in Booley, but Tim hadn't liked him since that awful night nineteen years ago.

The police chief stood at the door to his office. "Ramirez will be here any minute. Do we know anything about Morgan's Lawyer?"

Officer Hayden shook her head as she concentrated on typing.

Booley shrugged and returned to his office, leaving Tim in peace.

Normally, Tim would've called Finn Callaghan for help. As an FBI agent and his best friend, he knew he could count on Finn to back him up. But they'd had lunch yesterday, and Finn had mentioned plans to fly to the FBI headquarters in Salt Lake City today. So he'd called David Quinn, one of his oldest allies. He'd met David when he'd run away from home at fifteen. They'd lived on the streets of Granite City together and had watched each other's backs. It had just been the four of them: Tim, David, David's twin sister, Sinclair, and Michael. They'd all joined the army at the same time and had completed their basic training at Fort Leonard Wood where they'd met Finn. The five of them had remained close for the last sixteen years.

A smartly-dressed woman carrying a briefcase strolled into the police station.

Officer Hayden met her at the reception desk.

"My name is Sophia Reed. I will be representing Timothy Morgan." Ms. Reed's soft brown hair escaped her bun and red lipstick smudged her teeth.

Booley stepped out of his office. "I'm Chief Booley. I'll be handling the case."

Officer Hayden gasped and then covered her action with a cough. She turned on her heel and marched to her desk.

Once seated, she started typing, each keystroke hard and deliberate.

Booley stood too close to Ms. Reed, invading her personal space. She stepped back.

Tim wasn't an expert in reading body language like his friend, Finn, but even he knew the lawyer was setting boundaries.

Booley didn't seem offended by her actions. Instead, he bent his head, his lips moving. Tim couldn't make out what they were saying. He heard his name, but the legal speak might as well be a foreign dialect for all he understood.

David Quinn and Marie Wilson filed into the police station. David had met Marie after she'd invented a new type of solar panel. Marshall Portman, a prominent Granite City businessman, had planned her death and set David up to take the fall. As ex-special forces, David had thwarted Portman's plan when he'd saved Marie and fallen hopelessly in love with her.

David's gazed locked on Tim, who stood in the middle of his cell. "What the hell happened to you?"

"Bumped into a momma grizzly with cubs." He pointed to his face. "This was caused by blowback from discharging bear spray." He decided not to tell his friend that the police chief had assaulted him. David had played the part of protector when they were on the street. Tim didn't want him to step back into that role. Picking a fight with Booley would not do them any good.

David arched his eyebrows. "I always thought you'd have to bail me out, not the other way around."

Tim grunted. It was the closest he could get to a laugh. "Welcome to the toxic town of Hopefalls, a place where reality and good judgment have ceased to exist."

Booley pummeled the countertop with his fist. "Hopefalls is the place where you will finally be brought to justice."

Tim forced himself not to flinch at the policeman's outburst.

David looked like he was ready to beat the snot out of the police chief, but Marie grabbed his arm, and his friend visibly relaxed. Small, pretty Marie, who was surprisingly strong-willed, had tamed him when nothing else would.

"We're here to support Tim," Marie announced. "We're paying for his lawyer and will post bail if that becomes necessary. Have charges been laid?"

Sophia Reed cleared her throat. "Dr. Wilson, if you don't mind, that's my line." She walked around the reception desk to the cell. "Mr. Morgan, Dr. Wilson has hired me to represent you in this legal matter. Do you agree to this arrangement?"

He would've liked to hire and pay for his own lawyer, but given the state of his finances, that wasn't possible. He could go with a public defender, but then he ran the risk of getting an attorney who didn't want to fight for him. And if he went to jail, his dad would probably end up living on the street. He nodded to Ms. Reed. He'd swallow his pride and accept help for his father's sake, if nothing else.

The front door slammed against the wall as Detective Ramirez entered the small, packed police station. Tim breathed a sigh of relief. He remembered the detective from the hospital after David had been shot in the leg. Ramirez had been tenacious in his questioning but had proved himself to be trustworthy and incorruptible.

Ramirez recognized David straight away and shook his hand. "Mr. Quinn, how's the leg?"

Officer Hayden, who had quietly sat at her desk watching everyone arrive, put on her sunglasses and grabbed her keys. "Time for me to go on patrol."

He watched her leave, unable to tear his eyes from her toned, muscled body. He didn't know why, but he'd always been drawn to strong, powerful women in uniform. She didn't use unnecessary movements, but strode with determination for the door, everything about her screaming discipline and restraint. Man, if she hadn't been a Hopefalls cop he might have asked her out for a coffee. There was no way he would do that now. Not only was she one of Booley's flunkies, she was also Alice Hayden's niece and believed he was responsible for her aunt's death.

But her timing was interesting. She'd remained at the police station until Detective Ramirez had arrived, making Tim wonder if she had stayed to protect him from Booley. Maybe that was wishful thinking on his part. She wouldn't go out of her way to safeguard him. Perhaps she just disliked Detective Ramirez.

A man in a sharp gray suit, white dress shirt, and navy blue tie emerged from Booley's office. He walked across the room and took the chair Officer Hayden had vacated. Tim hadn't seen him enter the police station and had no idea who he was.

Miss Reed ignored everyone else in the room and addressed Booley. "I want to talk to my client. In private."

"You can use my office." Booley pulled his handcuffs from his belt and marched toward Tim.

"Those won't be necessary," Miss Reed countered.

"I think they are. He resisted arrest." Booley unlocked the cell, but blocked Tim's exit.

"No, I didn't." Tim held his hands up in a show of surrender, hoping Booley would get the message. "Until three years ago, I was a staff sergeant in the 75th Ranger Regiment. I'm trained in hand-to-hand combat. If I'd resisted, you would have been on the floor bleeding. You punched me when I turned to you in shock." He nodded to the handcuffs in Booley's hand. "Those cuffs won't stop me if I want to escape." That was a bit of an exaggeration. He had no idea how to get out of cuffs, but he was fast and lethal enough he could take care of an out-of-shape, old man like Booley. He wasn't so sure about Ramirez.

Booley stared at the man in the gray suit as if asking for guidance.

Detective Ramirez pointed to Gray Suit. "Who are you?"

"I'm Paul Harris, the mayor of Hopefalls."

"You're one of the idiots who stomped all over my crime scene."

The mayor flushed. "I did not. My wife found the body."

"Don't you mean Ben?" Ramirez pointed at Mayor Harris. "And aren't you the brains behind the plan to force North from his land? Which is reason enough to consider you a suspect."

"You can't talk to me like that. I'm the mayor."

"I don't care who you are. If you've broken the law, I will arrest you. Leave now. I will question you and your wife later." Ramirez walked to the cell, elbowing Booley out of the way. "This is my investigation, and I will not tolerate interference from the Hopefalls Police Department or its mayor. I've a mind to move this interview to Granite City."

David nodded in silent agreement.

Sophia Reed pointed at the Hopefalls Police Chief. "You told me this was your investigation." Then she rounded on Ramirez. "In the interests of my client, I suggest you question him here so he can leave. We will also be suing the Town of Hopefalls for wrongful arrest and damages caused by Chief Booley's assault."

Booley shrugged, not seeming to care, pulled a cigarette from his pants pocket, and lit it.

Ramirez stepped into the cell. "I want your word as a Ranger that you won't try to escape or attack anyone."

"You have my word," Tim answered, shocked that he had to give it. He hadn't even been questioned yet.

Ramirez stepped aside, allowing Tim to cross the threshold.

Sophia Reed walked to meet him. She shook his hand and then reached into her jacket pocket, pulled out a business card, and passed it to him. "These are my numbers. You can reach me twenty-four hours a day, seven days a week." She turned, heading toward Booley's office. "Come this way."

Tim followed, praying that Ms. Reed could work some legal magic so he didn't end up in jail.

Chapter Seven

Dana pulled into the parking lot just in time to see Detective Ramirez shaking Timothy Morgan's hand on the front steps of the police station. Morgan's lawyer stood next to him, smiling.

Damn it. She slammed the door of her car. He wasn't in custody. Dana opened the trunk and moved her crime scene materials around, pretending to organize her stuff as the trio chatted.

Alice had died at the tender age of twenty-two because Tim Morgan had played a childish prank and stolen a stop sign. She had been on her way to meet her boyfriend on Wind Ridge, which was a popular spot for young couples. On the way up, she drove through a junction that should have been marked and had died when her car was T-boned by a logging truck.

Everyone suspected Morgan had committed the crime, but he ran away before charges could be filed. She doubted a charge of murder would stick. Murder generally required intent, and even to her, the theft of a stop sign was a prank. The charge would probably be manslaughter, and there was no statute of limitations for manslaughter in Montana.

"I've got your numbers. I'll call you if I have any further questions." Ramirez walked to his unmarked police-issue Ford sedan.

"Aren't you going to tell me not to leave town?" Morgan called as he made his way down the steps accompanied by his lawyer.

"You are not under arrest, so he has no right to tell you where you can or can't go," Ms. Reed answered as she escorted her client to a newer black Ford truck. "That only works in cop shows."

Morgan unlocked the truck door. "Interesting."

Dana threw her Kevlar vest on the ground at her feet. The rat-bastard was getting away again. Using more force than needed, she banged the trunk shut.

As a little girl, she would climb onto her aunt's lap with a storybook in hand, never afraid she would be turned away. If Aunt Alice didn't have time, she would tickle Dana until she laughed and then kiss her on the head. They were cherished memories, filled with laughter and happiness. All that had been stolen by Morgan's irresponsible behavior.

Morgan looked in her direction, smiled, nodded, mouthed the words "thank you," and then climbed in his truck and drove away. What the hell was that? Why had he thanked her? She hadn't done anything to affect his release. All she'd done was stop her boss from beating the crap out of him, but that had nothing to do with Morgan. That was all about her. She refused to disparage her own character because of him.

And that perfect smile. Why had he smiled at her? Was he rubbing his release in her face? She opened the trunk and slammed it again, just because it made her feel better.

She needed a timeout, a chance to get her feelings under control. Maybe if she could discuss the facts of the case with Ramirez, she would feel better about Morgan walking away, but he had left as well. She opened the trunk again, slowly this time, threw the vest inside, and then leant against the car, waiting to calm down. She didn't want to be grateful to him, and she most definitely didn't want to be attracted to him. Her focus should remain clear—get justice for Aunt Alice.

Never mind that Tim Morgan was appealing. He wasn't good looking exactly; his eyes were a little too narrow and his hair was graying prematurely, and yet he affected her on a gut level that was hard to pinpoint and even harder to reconcile with everything she knew about him.

Emotionally, she was too close. If she were still a detective in Spokane, there would be no way she would be allowed to investigate. She needed to keep that in mind. Booley tended to lead with his emotions, which was fine in theory. But there were rules in place for a reason, even if they stunk.

Booley met her as she entered the station. His nostrils flared, like a bull ready to charge. "He doesn't have an alibi for the time of death. You should've let me beat a confession out of him."

Shelly gasped. She must've returned while Dana was on patrol. The older woman froze in front of the filing cabinet, a manila folder in her hand. She didn't move. She just stared at Booley, saying nothing.

Dana drew in a long, slow breath, controlling her reaction. She hated to see a suspect, especially one that had caused her so much pain, walk away, but she had to be true to herself. "Stopping you wasn't about him. It was about me." She sat at her desk.

"I don't understand." Booley crossed his arms as he lounged against the front counter.

Dana stared at Booley. From her first day at the police academy, she'd been taught a good police officer should try to be trustworthy, honest, take responsibility for her own actions, and be a team player. She aspired to these ideals and worked each day to be the best cop she could be, no matter what the circumstances. She had a feeling these rules of conduct were a foreign concept to him. "I've always been a straight arrow. I don't break the rules. I don't cheat and I don't lie. I do what I believe is right. Letting you beat on him wouldn't be right. Plus, my son was here watching."

"Not that either of you have asked, but I agree with Dana. We're a small-town force, and the people of Hopefalls need to be able to trust us." Xavier stood at the coffee machine. Dana hadn't noticed him until now. She'd been single-mindedly focused on Morgan and then Booley. That kind of distraction could prove deadly. She needed to get her act together before she went out on patrol.

She turned to Xavier as he sipped his coffee. "What are you doing here? Your shift doesn't start for another two hours."

He smiled, revealing his perfect teeth, white against his dark complexion. As a recent graduate of the Montana Law Enforcement Academy, he was still enthusiastic and hadn't been worn down by the rigors of the job. "I was here earlier, remember? The chief called me in early and filled me in on everything that happened. This is the most excitement this town has seen in a long time."

Booley rubbed the back of his neck. "Well damn, I've never mistreated a suspect in my life, but Morgan just rubs me the wrong way. And what about all the crap he was spouting?"

"What crap?" Xavier took another sip of his coffee.

"Said he was a Ranger and he could take me even if he was handcuffed."

"I don't think he was lying about that." Xavier stepped away from the counter. "A girlfriend of mine works at the Montana Department of Military Affairs so I asked her to run a check on Morgan."

"And?" Dana liked his resourcefulness. It was no surprise he had a girlfriend who could help him. In the last two months, Dana had learned he was a man who had a lot of girlfriends, none of whom were exclusive.

"Like he said, he was a staff sergeant in the 75th Ranger Regiment. Served four tours in Afghanistan. He received the Medal of Honor for saving a village and a whole bunch of United Nations observers. He got shot in the process."

"A Medal of Honor." Booley stared at Xavier. "Timothy Morgan really was a Ranger?"

"It seems so." The young officer emptied his cup in the sink.

"His mother was very proud of him," Shelly added. She wouldn't look at them. She obviously knew more about

Morgan than Booley. The older woman glanced at the wall clock and then stuffed another beige file folder into a drawer, her movements hurried.

"The kid who stole a stop sign and killed my aunt grew up, became a Ranger, and received the Medal of Honor?" Dana couldn't believe her ears. All these years she'd imagined him to be some kind of criminal.

Xavier nodded. "According to Arlene. She's sending me everything that's not marked classified."

"Damn." Booley pursed his lips. "You know sometimes these soldiers can't adjust to civilian life. Who knows? Maybe he had a psychotic break and killed Ben." He walked to his office. "Dana, are you busy tomorrow?"

"Yes, sir, it's Saturday. I'm working."

"Xavier and I will do your shift. You're on special duty."

"What am I doing?" The hairs lifted on the back of her neck, reminding her Booley's moral compass was skewed.

"Your assignment is to follow Morgan. I want him watched everywhere he goes."

"Won't he recognize me? I don't exactly blend, and there's not much traffic in Hopefalls or out at his ranch." Technically, the police were allowed to tail a suspect out of their jurisdiction, but their powers were limited.

The chief smiled. "Not if you do your job properly."

"But I can't be on him twenty-four hours a day." She wanted to say she had a son but didn't. Booley wasn't the type of boss who appreciated officers who had family obligations.

"Once he beds down for the night, call me. I'll come and take over. I can nap in my car."

Shelly grabbed her purse from the bottom drawer of the filing cabinet. "I'll look in on Logan tomorrow."

"Thanks, Shelly."

"It's no problem. He's a sweetheart. He told me he wants to learn to bake. Maybe I'll teach him." Shelly had two grown sons who were twins. Both of them lived in Granite City. One was a carpenter and the other an accountant. Dana had heard from the locals they were hellions in their teens. Shelly rode roughshod over them, forcing them to stay in school, which meant she probably had a degree in how to deal with difficult teenage boys.

"I appreciate that." Words weren't enough to describe just how grateful she was to have someone as balanced as Shelly to keep an eye on Logan. He was fifteen and liked to be independent, but he had gotten into trouble in Spokane, and part of living in a small town was that it afforded her the ability to check on him at a moment's notice.

Shelly left without another word. The events of the day had been upsetting. Ben North, who'd been a fixture of the community, had died an unnatural death, and Timothy Morgan was suspected of the murder.

Dana remembered Tim from school. He'd been a heartthrob then, tall, athletic, and devilishly handsome. He'd been easy-going, charming, and popular. All the girls had wanted to be with him. It was rumored he'd slept with many of them. She was years younger, and he hadn't spared her a glance, so she shouldn't be surprised he didn't recognize her. Although, when it came to her appearance, she hadn't changed much. She was still long and big-boned. Her features were striking rather than pretty, her nose a little too long and her mouth overly wide. And her hair... She groaned. She didn't consider herself particularly vain. She didn't paint her nails or wear much make up, and up until recently, she had always been neat and well-styled in a minimalist sort of way. Unfortunately, she was currently sporting the worst haircut in living memory, which included the time when she was three years old and had cut it herself.

She'd decided to chop off her long thick hair because she didn't have time to style it. The washing, drying, and straightening took time she didn't have. After putting in twelve-hour shifts, all she wanted to do was get home and touch base with Logan. Zoe Harris had recommended Jezebel's in Granite City. She had ranted and raved about how great they were. Unfortunately, they hadn't lived up to their promise.

Now, every time she looked in the mirror, she didn't see her normal, confident self. She saw a mess. The woman reflected back at her was lost, doubtful, and unsure, although those feelings had nothing to do with her hair or her physical appearance. They were caused by a completely different nightmare.

"Are you with me?" Booley snapped.

Dana came to with a start. She'd been gazing into space, lost in her own thoughts. "When do you want this to start?"

She wasn't sure how she felt about this assignment. She wanted Timothy Morgan brought to justice for the pain he'd caused her family, but she was too close to the case and didn't know if she could trust herself. And then there was the way he looked at her. It was as if he were studying an alien creature. It made her self-conscious, and she didn't want to find herself under his microscope.

"I heard him tell his lawyer he was leaving at six in the morning." Booley braced his shoulder against the doorjamb, obviously happy with himself.

Dana glanced at Xavier, who stood motionless, staring at the chief. She turned to face Booley. "Did you listen in on his conversation with his lawyer?" She couldn't believe the chief had violated Morgan's attorney-client privilege.

"Relax, I only heard enough to know he doesn't have an alibi for the time of the murder. Besides, how much secrecy can he expect in a police station? I'm ordering you to track him to see where he goes and what he does. He's shady. He got away with killing once, and I don't want him to get away with it again."

Dana didn't know what to react to first, the fact the chief had listened in on a conversation between Morgan and his lawyer, or her new assignment, one where she would be harassing a suspect.

"He plans to stop at the diner first thing in the morning and pay his respects to Frank Bryant's widow, Eva. You can catch up with him there."

"What about Detective Ramirez and the Granite City-Elkhead County Police Department? Won't we be stepping on his toes?" Xavier asked.

Booley shrugged. "I don't see how. We're allowed to pursue a suspect out of our jurisdiction." He pointed to Dana. "You can do that, can't you?"

She nodded. She didn't like this. It was all wrong. The chief's total disregard for Morgan's rights rubbed her the wrong way. Plus, it was all too personal. She wanted nothing more than to see Morgan charged in Aunt Alice's homicide, but at what cost? Yes, she had a score to settle with him, but she wanted evidence or a confession. Now, there was a thought. Nineteen years had passed since Aunt Alice's death, and in Dana's experience, everyone talked—eventually.

She made eye contact with Xavier and raised her eyebrows, silently asking his opinion. They had only worked together a short while, and despite his lack of experience, he was a solid, straightforward officer. She had come to rely on him, especially since Booley was known to disappear for hours at a time.

If she was on special assignment, then Xavier would have to work a double shift and the chief would just do his regular duties—if that. He nodded, letting her know he would be okay.

"What was that look about?" Booley asked. "Are you two in cahoots about something?"

Xavier moved to the reception desk and faced the chief. "Sir, I wanted to get your opinion on the video from the ATM."

The young officer could certainly think on his feet. He'd been scouring security camera videos, hoping to get a lead on the vandalism that had occurred throughout Hopefalls. They couldn't very well tell the chief to his face he was lazy, and they couldn't trust him to cover their backs. Looping him into the investigation was a great way of distracting him and keeping the peace.

"The one at Crawley's?" Booley's question was moot. The only bank machine in town was outside Crawley's general store.

"I've been going through the photos to see if the security camera took a picture of the person who plastered it with glue. Also, if you get a chance, can you call the lab in Granite City and see if they have the results from the sample I sent them?" Xavier was on a roll.

The chief's eyes narrowed. "What sample?"

"Remember when someone set fire to the mayor's shed?"

Booley nodded.

"I had the State Fire Marshall isolate some of the propellant, and then I sent it off to the lab for analysis."

"Good thinking. This criminal has got to be stopped. Did I sign off on that lab work?"

Xavier nodded. "You did."

Dana suppressed a smile. Xavier had probably stuffed the paper under Booley's nose while he was on the phone, and the chief had signed without looking.

"Do you think the vandalism is connected to Ben's murder?" Dana needed to consider all the possibilities. Booley wanted it to be Morgan so badly he was sending her to follow him, but what if they were wrong?

The chief walked to his desk, leaving his office door open. "Why do you ask?"

Dana shrugged. "We're the police. We're supposed to ask. Ben North was fighting for his land against Third Estate Mining. They are a multimillion-dollar corporation. They could've killed him to get his property."

"Third Estate didn't kill him. The mayor made it plain that everything's tied up until they find Ben's heir. Then there's probate and death duties and all that crap. This has delayed Third Estate's timeline."

"But it hasn't stopped it?"

"No, not from what the mayor said. Why?"

"There were a lot of people camped at Ben's gate, who are both for and against. Temper's get frayed and emotions run high. Things happen."

"I thought you wanted it to be Morgan, given that he got away with murdering your aunt."

Dana tensed. Booley was trying to manipulate her emotions. "It doesn't matter what I want. The facts of the case should lead the investigation, not personal bias. Besides, the charge would be manslaughter, not murder. The accident was a prank that went horribly wrong."

"How would you know? You weren't there." Booley placed his feet on his desk and stretched back in his chair.

Xavier stood against the front counter, his eyes wide, unmoving.

"I've read the file. Morgan was upset about blowing his knee. He'd lost his chance of getting a football scholarship. He claimed he went up on to Wind Ridge to think."

"Then he stole the sign." Booley crossed his arms, getting comfortable.

"He never admitted to that. Even if he had, there's nothing to suggest he stole the sign with intent to kill," Dana reasoned.

Booley sat up straight, placed his feet on the floor and stared at her through the open door. "You're awfully forgiving for someone who lost a family member."

"No, I'm not. I'm going to get justice for my family—not revenge. I will get him on Aunt Alice's death, but I have to be realistic. The charge will probably be manslaughter unless I can prove intent."

Booley straightened, put his feet on his desk again, crossing them at the ankles. Then he shifted his white cowboy hat so it covered his eyes. "Go and get some rest. You've got a long day ahead of you tomorrow."

Dana released a breath. She'd been dismissed. She had her orders and was expected to obey them without question. Tomorrow she would get up at the crack of dawn and follow

Timothy Morgan. And when he admitted his guilt, she would be there to document it.

Chapter Eight

Supervisory Special Agent Finn Callaghan walked at a slow pace as he entered the six-story concrete slab building that housed the FBI field office in Salt Lake City. Ex-Army CID Special Agent Michael Papin and Special Agent Kennedy Morris accompanied him. They were early for their four o'clock meeting. The hour and a half flight from Granite City, Montana had been smooth with no delays. But there was a lot of walking even when traveling through a small airport. Michael limped along, helped by a cane, not saying a word. He'd refused a wheelchair. Finn could see the tension in his friend's face. Michael's jaw was clenched, and he winced with every step as beads of perspiration dripped from his black hair.

They had come to Salt Lake City at the insistence of Finn's superiors. Michael, a computer genius, had gone undercover, without authorization from his superiors at Army CID, when Granite City businessman, Marshall Portman, had accused their friend, David Quinn, of kidnapping. He'd used an alias created for use with his work in the cyber crimes division. Spider was a world-famous hacker who could access any satellite, computer, or street cam. In the end, the situation with David had been resolved, but not before Portman had hit Michael with his car. The left side of his pelvis and his left shoulder had sustained multiple fractures. He was two months into a long-term recovery. It would take three months for his bones to knit; his soft tissue damage would probably take longer.

They made their way through security and rode the elevator up to the fifth floor. The doors pinged open to find Special Agent in Charge Martin Deluca waiting for them. "Special Agent Callaghan."

Finn shook his superior's hand.

Deluca, a short, fit man in his early forties, was known for his tireless energy and flashes of intuition that had helped keep an investigation on track on more than one occasion.

In a glance, he seemed to take in Michael's condition. He dispensed with the pleasantries and shuffled them into an office. Finn held the door for his friend as Kennedy grabbed an armchair from the back of the room and dragged it to Deluca's desk.

She waved to Michael. "Sit here."

Michael nodded and then slumped into the chair, winced, and then readjusted his position. "Thanks."

Deluca sat behind the desk. "I wanted to talk to you about the Granite City corruption case."

Finn and Kennedy made themselves comfortable in the vinyl-cushioned guest chairs and waited for Deluca to continue.

"I understand you believe Marshall Portman was connected to an organization called the Syndicate."

Michael nodded. "I heard Portman refer to them."

"Can you tell me the context and circumstances?"

Michael tried to straighten, grimaced, and then slumped back in his seat. "Portman was looking over my shoulder watching me work. He wanted me to track down Dr. Marie Wilson."

Deluca's gaze centered on Michael. "Yes, I understand he wanted to destroy her solar panel."

"That's right. Brad Harper came in—"

"Who was Harper?"

Finn forced himself to stay silent. Deluca knew damn well who Harper was. He'd read the file and was well acquainted with the case.

"A hired gun," Michael answered as he reached into the pocket of his cargo pants and pulled out a bottle of ibuprofen.

"Hired by whom?"

"The Syndicate." Michael popped two capsules into his mouth and swallowed them without water.

"What makes you think that?"

Michael eased back into his chair, his eyes alert despite his condition. "Portman was angry with Harper, and he said something about him being the Syndicate's pick for the job, not his. There was also an email from Lucy Portman to her husband that mentioned the Syndicate. Do you have that?"

"No." Deluca's face was blank, giving away nothing.

"No? How can you not have it? I went undercover, got hit by a car, and you've lost the evidence I collected."

Deluca sighed. "Sometime in the last month, someone went to the evidence locker in this building and stole the data files."

"What about the backup copies?" Finn wasn't the most computer savvy agent, but even he understood that digital files existed. Michael had emailed copies to Finn and had also transferred the files onto a flash drive. The drive was sealed and held as incorruptible evidence that could be used in court. The material he had sent to Finn was useless as proof because they had not been secured, and any lawyer worth his retainer could claim corruption of evidence because they could have been doctored.

Deluca shook his head. "Gone. We don't have anything we can use in court."

"You're shitting me," Michael snapped.

"What about Harper? Will he testify about the Syndicate?" Finn said, hoping they had a way to save the case. Harper had been charged with attempted murder but had, as far as Finn knew, refused to name his employers.

"He died in custody two weeks ago. Mr. Papin, you are the only proof that the Syndicate exists."

"Let me get this straight. The two other people, Harper and Portman, who could confirm the existence of the Syndicate, are both dead, and the evidence I collected is useless," Michael stated baldly.

His frank assessment of the facts sent chills down Finn's spine. "What about the corruption of the Granite City-Elkhead Police Department? Where does that trail lead?"

Deluca shook his head. "It leads to Marshall Portman."

"And he's dead." Kennedy put a hand to her mouth.

Deluca leant back in his chair, his eyes narrowed. "Yes, but we might have something there."

"How? I thought he died of a heart attack." Michael adjusted his position, shifting his weight to his right side. It seemed awkward but was probably more comfortable than having constant pressure on his broken pelvis.

"We managed to get his body flown back to the US from the Cayman Islands. There was a minute needle mark in his arm. He tested positive for suxamethonium chloride, otherwise known as SUX, a chemical that mimics a heart attack. It is almost impossible to detect unless you specifically look for it. Marshall Portman was murdered."

Finn sucked in a breath. That made sense. If the Syndicate were real, they wouldn't want to take the chance that Marshall Portman would betray them.

"My money would be on the wife. We know Lucy was involved in her husband's activities, and she has taken over Public Domain Energy," Kennedy said.

Michael cleared his throat. "So you're saying the Syndicate managed to murder a man in custody, they have someone in the FBI who has access to evidence, and we suspect Lucy Portman is part of the Syndicate?"

Deluca nodded.

"What part of that statement don't you agree with?" Finn asked Michael.

Michael turned to him, his lips pressed in a thin line. "I agree with all of it, but we are suggesting that a group of rich, powerful businessmen have people in place to override the system which, in theory, means they can control the Department of Justice."

"What are you getting at?" Deluca asked.

Michael shifted in his seat. "Who knows about this meeting?"

Deluca shrugged. "My assistant. It's in my calendar."

Michael gave a long slow blink. "Mark this meeting as cancelled. If anyone asks, I was sick."

Deluca tilted his head. "Do you really think they know?"

"Yes, they will come after me. The only reason I'm still alive is because I used my hacker legend, Spider. That afforded me a certain amount of anonymity. But this meeting has brought me out into the open."

"But we're in the FBI headquarters, it's a secure building, and our computers work on an independent system."

"It doesn't matter because they have someone on the inside."

Deluca's face flushed as he loosened his tie. "Damn."

Finn had heard enough. He turned toward Michael. "You need to hide. You're in no condition to protect yourself."

Kennedy stood and paced to the back of the small office. "Finn and I will continue to investigate. We can incorporate the Syndicate into the Granite City public corruption investigation so there's no paperwork. Perhaps if they think we're not looking into them, they'll leave you alone."

Deluca squared his shoulders. "How can I help?"

Finn rubbed his jaw. "Surveillance on Lucy Portman. She's our best lead. We know she was involved in her husband's business affairs, and Marshall was involved with the Syndicate. Maybe she'll lead us right to them."

"Do you have men you can trust with this?" Kennedy asked.

Finn stilled, holding his breath. For Kennedy to remind their superior to use only trusted men was impertinent, and most SACs wouldn't tolerate such brazen insolence, but Deluca was made from a different mold. Finn had worked with him for five years and knew him to be a man who had put his life on the line, working undercover to bring down one of the biggest cartels in the country. He would see it for what it was—a need for assurance.

"Already done. I've men in place. If anyone asks, they're on leave so our mole won't be able to track them." He stared at Michael. "Now, Mr. Papin, the only remaining question is, what shall we do with you?"

Finn answered. "Don't worry, I have a friend who can hide him so he'll be completely under the radar."

"I need to know how to get in touch in case anything happens to you or Agent Morris," Deluca said.

Finn looked to Michael for approval.

Using his cane, Michael levered himself to his feet. "You need to remember this information. Don't write it down anywhere."

"You have my word."

Michael limped toward the door. "Go to the town of Hopefalls in Northwestern Montana. Look for a man by the name of Timothy Morgan. He's an ex-Ranger who owns a ranch west of town."

"Timothy Morgan in Hopefalls, Montana—got it."

Chapter Nine

Dana parked in the carport at the side of the house and entered through the kitchen. She'd had the fifty-year-old bungalow inspected before she'd moved in. Everything was in working order, although the inside was an assault on the senses. Avocado green carpet covered the main floor, and dark wood paneling obscured the interior walls. She kept promising herself she would spend one of her days off redecorating, but so far it hadn't happened, mainly because she couldn't decide on colors or style. Plus, she had no idea how to paint a wall or pull up a carpet. Those things had never interested her.

Her son came out of his bedroom as she entered the house. "Mom?"

"Hi."

He'd just finished showering. His still-wet, blue hair was a shade darker than its normal vibrant hue. His brow wrinkled. "Is Tim under arrest?"

Dana walked to the kitchen and opened the fridge. "No." She buried her lingering disappointment. They didn't have enough for an arrest warrant, and there was no way she would manipulate or manufacture evidence.

Logan followed and sat at the small white kitchen table. "There's chicken casserole left over from yesterday."

She lifted the lid on a plastic container and sniffed, inhaling the scent of mushroom, onion, and herbs. It smelled good, but she craved a big plate of fries. Nothing soothed her like a pile of grease and salt.

"Do you think he killed that North guy?" He rubbed the hem of his T-shirt, something he only did when he was nervous or uncomfortable.

She placed the leftover casserole in the microwave. "I don't know."

"Your boss, Booley, thinks he did it."

"It isn't his case. A detective from the Granite City-Elkhead County Police Department is the lead."

Logan headed for his room. "That's good. Booley shouldn't have hit him. He wasn't resisting arrest." He raised his voice so she could still hear him. "He was just surprised."

She strolled to his room and propped her shoulder against the doorjamb, watching him as he sharpened a pencil. The shavings fell neatly into his wastebasket. Her son broke stereotypes. He didn't like junk food, and his room was always tidy. His penchant for neatness was a pain in the butt because he was constantly nagging her to clean up her mess. It was a role reversal, one that fueled her hope he would grow into a responsible adult.

She loved him with all her heart and soul, but knew he wasn't perfect. He had gotten in with a bad group of kids in Spokane and had been arrested for shoplifting. The cop who caught him was a friend who had investigated thoroughly. At first, she hadn't wanted to hear the details of Logan's activities, but in the end, she couldn't hide from the truth. Logan had been stealing to buy marijuana. Pot use in Washington State was only legal for persons over the age of twenty-one, not fifteen year olds who were skipping school. And the fact he'd been stealing to support his drug habit was a warning she couldn't ignore. She'd seen it all before when she had dated his father in high school. Oliver had been thoroughly disreputable and self-involved. It wasn't until he dumped her after she became pregnant that she had seen through the handsome face and fake charm.

The move to Hopefalls had been hard on Logan, but she firmly believed his life would have been a lot harder if they'd stayed in Spokane. Maybe things would have been better for him if he'd had a father, but she couldn't change her past no more than she could decide his future.

A pad of paper was open on the bed. He was working on a charcoal sketch of a bear. There was another drawing lying on the floor. It was of Morgan, his arm outstretched with a can of pepper spray in his hand.

"Tough day." She nodded to the pictures, hoping he would talk about what happened without her having to prod him.

"Yeah." He sat on the bed, not looking at her.

She stepped closer. "Do you want to talk about it?" Damn, she sounded desperate.

"I screwed up." He picked up the sketch of the bear.

"Why'd you skip school?" She tried to control the accusation in her voice. Next year he would be in grade eleven. She wanted him to graduate and have a future that didn't involve drugs and stealing.

"Tim told me not to run. He said the bear would chase us…"

"And?" She allowed him to change the subject. Maybe it was wrong to use police interrogation techniques on her son, but if she wanted to understand him, she had to let him talk. Later she would circle back to her original question.

"It did. I was down the hill. He was still up there, facing the bear. I was a coward." His head drooped forward so his long blue hair covered his face. She didn't need to be a cop to know her son was ashamed of his behavior.

She sat on the bed next to him and wrapped an arm around his shoulders. "I think you're being a bit hard on yourself."

"Tim called me a bastard."

"He what?" She ground her teeth as she tried to control her rage. The man who had torn her family apart had the nerve to judge her son. If he were in the room now, she would break his handsome face.

"I suppose, technically, I am, but that wasn't what he meant. He was angry because I ran."

"Where were you going when you started running?"

"To his ATV at the bottom of the mountain. He gave me the keys."

She wasn't sure what to make of that. Why had he given the keys to someone who was little more than a child? Then another question occurred to her. "What mountain? Where were you?"

"I was on Molly's Mountain. I wanted to see what all the fuss was about. All the kids in school were arguing about it, and I have no idea what's going on, so I went out to take a look."

"Is that why you skipped school?"

He nodded.

"Why didn't you ask me? I'm a cop. I could've given you an overview and asked Ben if we could take a tour."

"I wanted to see for myself and make up my own mind."

She inhaled, reminding herself that becoming independent was a natural part of growing up. "So what did you decide?"

"I don't like the idea of some mining company coming in and forcing Ben off his land."

"Yeah, they're using a law called Eminent Domain. They own the mineral rights to whatever's beneath Molly's Mountain."

"How can they own what's beneath the land if it belongs to Ben?"

The microwave dinged. Her food was warm, but she ignored it. "Back when Montana was being settled, the government sometimes severed the surface estate from the mineral rights, which means, even though you own the land, someone else might own what's beneath it."

"So what has emin-eminent—?"

"Eminent Domain is a law that says the government can take your land to build roads, schools, and for economic development. But they have to give you fair compensation for it. They can't just take it and give you nothing."

"So basically the government is trying to buy Ben's land, but he doesn't want to sell."

"In this case, Third Estate Mining is working on behalf of the government, and yes, you're right, Ben doesn't want to sell. He says the surface and mineral rights were never severed, and he owns what's above and what's beneath the ground."

"And that's why people are camped out at the entrance to his property?"

"Yes, some of them support Ben. They think forcing him off his land is a criminal act and should be stopped. Others want the work a mine will bring. Hopefalls could do with some good paying jobs. It'll keep the town alive and stop people from leaving."

"What do you think?"

She stood and headed for the door. "I think I'm a cop who's not allowed to take sides." It was an evasive answer, and she knew it. "But I want you to stay away from the protesters. People can get pretty worked up over stuff like this. Sooner or later, someone's going to get hurt, and I don't want it to be you."

"Someone already did get hurt. Do you think the mining company had Ben killed?"

She stopped at the entrance to his room. "Why would you say that?" Booley had been so fixated on Timothy Morgan, he couldn't see anyone else, but even her fifteen year old could consider other suspects.

Logan stood. His pale blue gaze, so like his father's, held hers. "I don't think it was Tim. He could've walked away and let the bear eat me. No one would've known, but he didn't."

She strode to the kitchen to retrieve her dinner. "We don't know anything about him, let alone if he's capable of murder. Besides, I don't think you have to worry. By the look of it, he has rich friends and a high-priced lawyer." She pictured Detective Ramirez shaking hands with the scarred man. Quinn, yes, that was his name. The detective knew him. Come to think of it, the couple looked familiar. She'd seen them somewhere before. The way the detective greeted them suggested they weren't criminals, but Quinn seemed too dangerous to be a civilian.

Logan paced after her. "Do you think Tim killed Aunt Alice?" She sensed his tension and uncertainty.

"I don't know." She collapsed into a chair at the kitchen table. The past and present seemed to have collided into one big mess. She didn't know what had happened on that mountain road west of Hopefalls. All she knew was that her aunt had died, and the person responsible had never been brought to justice.

Logan grabbed a glass of water and headed for his room.

"I don't want you to skip school again. Do you understand?"

He stopped at his bedroom door and gave her a mock salute. "Yes ma'am."

She rested the casserole dish on a pile of papers and then bit into a mouthful of chicken without tasting it. Her son would do whatever he pleased. It wasn't like when he was small and she could punish him by taking away a toy or giving him a timeout. He was older now. In a few short years, he would be a man. She needed to find a way to reach him, and getting angry wasn't going to achieve that. "I want you to graduate high school, have options, and not flunk out," she shouted, not knowing if he could hear her or if he had his ear buds in and music playing.

"There's no point. I'm not good at anything. I can't even do shop," he shouted back.

"You're good at art," she said, grasping at the one thing she knew he loved.

"There's no money in art, and Grandpa said it's not a real job." She cursed under her breath. Her father had put the idea in Logan's mind that art wasn't for real men. He wanted Logan to follow in his footsteps and become a firefighter. Her father's negative attitude had done a number on her son and was another reason why moving to Hopefalls was a well-needed change.

She left her food in the kitchen, walked to his bedroom, and stood at the door. "You know your grandfather can be wrong. I got pregnant with you when I was your age. I missed a lot of school and graduated a year late. I would rather you didn't have to go through that."

He grinned. "Don't worry, Mom, I won't get pregnant."

"Smartass, and if you do get a girl pregnant, you're going to support her."

His brow crinkled as he considered his answer. "Not like my dad."

Dana suspected his father's abandonment had hurt Logan in ways he couldn't explain. Her ex hadn't just dumped her as a pregnant teen. He'd left his child, too.

Her voice softened. "You're a better man than he ever was. Don't forget that."

"I won't." He gave her a small smile.

She returned to the kitchen table, grabbed her dish of chicken, and made her way to the shabby living room. If she kept the avocado green carpet and dull-brown, overstuffed furniture another twenty years, they might come back into fashion. That would save her a lot of work.

She picked up the remote for the small flat-screen TV but didn't turn it on. A face flashed in her mind—Alex Rowe. She remembered his body slumped in a heap on the ground, blood pooling from a wound to his chest. As far as her superiors in the Spokane Police Department were concerned, her actions had been justified, but his face was the last thing she saw every night as she drifted off to sleep.

Logan's shoplifting and her "incident" had happened in the same month. She hadn't just moved to Hopefalls for her son's well-being. She'd come here to put some distance between herself and the memories that had altered her perception of who she was. Gone was the confident, able policewoman who could analyze situations and act decisively to protect the public. She hoped that being in a small town where she wouldn't be required to draw her weapon would help her conquer her uncertainties about her reactions and decisions because, if she couldn't overcome her doubts, she couldn't be a cop anymore.

She switched on the TV and turned up the volume. Leaving it on, she rose slowly, crept to the kitchen, and placed the dish of chicken on the table. Then she peeked around the wall that separated the kitchen from the hallway. Logan had closed the door to his room and probably had his ear buds in, but just in case he could hear, she tiptoed to the linen closet in the hall. Very carefully, so as not to make a sound, she extracted a bag of chips from under a pile of towels. Then she snuck into her room. She popped open the bag. The smell of potato, fat, and salt made her sigh. Logan didn't approve of her junk food habit, but sometimes a woman just needed to cut loose and have a bag of chips.

Her move to Hopefalls wasn't working out the way she'd planned. She'd wanted a better life for herself and her son, but what constituted a better life? Logan was unhappy here and she went to work every day unsure of her abilities. The problem lay with her. She was off-center. Her doubts about herself leached into every part of her life, and she didn't know how to overcome them. There were times when she felt so alone. She'd become an expert at putting on a brave face and carrying on, but there were moments when she wished she had someone to talk to, someone she could count on.

She hoped for a future where her world had balance, and not only in her work, but in her personal life as well. She'd planned to start dating once Logan finished high school and moved out. She was still in her early thirties. There was time for her to have more children. She pushed the thought aside. Her last boyfriend had told her she was the most unfeminine woman he had ever met. The trouble was she couldn't argue the point with him. She hated cooking and housework, and she never wore dresses. She liked working out and investigating crimes. She used to enjoy going to the firing range and had worked hard to ensure she was an accurate shot and could hit center mass every time. Those weren't desirable qualities in a woman. She stuffed a few more chips into her mouth. She didn't need a man. She needed to get her act together. Once she was no longer haunted by the past, she could look to the future.

She finished her chips and lay on the bed. Maybe she'd get lucky and wake up tomorrow with amnesia. Then she could forget about homicide, manslaughter, her fears, her son's truancy, and the incredibly attractive Tim Morgan who was suspected of murder.

Chapter Ten

Tim's stomach tightened as he turned onto the Hopefalls Highway. Leaving the ranch always filled him with a sense of loss, but today it was gut-wrenching. Yesterday had been a kick in the teeth. All his years of proving his worth and becoming an upstanding human being had gone down the drain. In the eyes of the residents of Hopefalls, he was still a fifteen-year-old boy who had gone up to Wind Ridge to think. He hadn't stolen the stop sign, but that didn't matter. Booley had latched on to him like a pit bull and wouldn't let go. Then Tim had made the worst mistake of his life. He ran away, and that had made him appear guilty.

He hadn't slept well. His dreams had been filled with Officer Dana Hayden. He had been slammed with an almost euphoric high at their immediate physical attraction. All that had been lost the minute she had heard his name. He'd seen shock in her startled gray eyes, which then turned to suspicion as she pushed Logan behind her, shielding her son from his presence.

He reached the gate that marked the long drive up to Ben's cabin. There was only one tent left. It wasn't surprising. The pro-jobs group were mostly locals who could go home at night, and the environmentalists, who normally camped out, had probably scattered with the announcement of Ben's death. The news there was a bear in the area had given any stragglers the final push they needed to leave.

He stopped as a muscular, bearded man in a wool cap held up a sign that read *Save the wilderness*. What was left of the campground was a mess. Garbage was strewn everywhere. A small camp stove sat on a table next to the tent. There were large rubber containers lined up neatly next to the table and two red jerry cans sat on the ground between the table and the tent.

Tim rolled down the window. He smelt pancakes and maple syrup. "Hi, I'm Tim. I own the spread next to Ben's."

The man nodded. "Ethan Moore."

"Have you heard there's a grizzly bear with cubs in the area? I encountered her yesterday. It was pretty scary."

Ethan scowled. "Are you trying to scare me off?"

"No, but you seem to be doing everything you can to attract a bear. Your food should be cooked and stored at least a hundred yards away from your tent." He pointed to the jerry cans. "Any strong smells, even gasoline, will bring her here."

"That's a pile of shit," Ethan spat. "The smell of gas will scare her away. I was going to pour it around the tent."

"Don't do that." Was he trying to get eaten alive? Tim sighed, reigning in his reaction. Ethan was already confrontational. Tim didn't want to fight with him. All he wanted to do was warn him. Then he could leave with a clear conscience. "When I go into the mountains, I have to cache my food and gas at least twelve feet above the ground so they don't get it."

Ethan cocked his head to the side. "The food I can see, but there's no way a bear will eat gas."

"They don't eat it. They're attracted to the smell. If you don't believe me, look it up on the Internet and then get yourself some bear spray."

"I have a rifle." That comment seemed wrong, but Tim couldn't figure out why. He dismissed it. He hadn't stopped to assess some random protester's character.

"Statistics show that you have a better chance of survival with spray. If you use your rifle for defense, you need to kill her with the first shot. You'd have to be a marksman with ice water in your veins to do that."

"You're making this up to scare me." Ethan smiled, but his eyes remained cold and emotionless.

"No, if it's any consolation, I hope you win. My property won't be worth as much if there's a mine next door." He rolled up the window and put his truck in gear, aware that Ethan was watching him as he drove away.

There was something about the activist that made Tim's hair stand on end. It was like the itchy feeling he got in combat the moment before they hit an IED.

No, he was just being paranoid. He was shaken up because Booley had rattled his cage. He had to get a grip. Ramirez was in charge, and the detective had told him there was nothing to suggest he would be arrested.

Did one of the protesters kill Ben? He shook away the thought. It wasn't his job to play detective, and he'd always been lousy with puzzles.

The small town of Hopefalls seemed to spring up out of the forest. There were only two main roads in town. The Hopefalls Highway, which ran from the Cabinet Mountains and the Kootenai National Forest in the west through Hopefalls to Granite City. And the secondary road that ran north to south. They intersected at a four-way stop in the center of town.

Evergreens lined the streets and popped up between the police station, the town hall, the post office, Crawley's general store, and the diner. This wasn't like the tree-lined streets of suburban America. It seemed as if the town had been hacked out of the forest. Even the northbound road up to the exclusive part of town known as The Heights seemed untamed. As if the wilderness had only loaned the land to the citizens of Hopefalls.

Tim turned his gaze toward The Heights. Although he'd never been up there, he'd heard it was a newer development that boasted sprawling mansions that sat on acres of land. It was said that each residence had a panoramic view of the mountains. From what he could tell, it wasn't a subdivision for the locals, who were generally of modest means, although it was rumored the mayor's home was located in The Heights.

This would be the first time he'd stopped in town since his mother's funeral. On that occasion, he'd worn his dress uniform. Luckily, Booley had been away and the residents had left him alone. He wasn't sure if that was out of respect for his parents or the regiment.

He parked in front of the Hope Junction Diner. Frank and Eva Bryant were his childhood friends. They hadn't stayed close, but he'd heard through Mrs. Anderson that Frank had recently passed away from pancreatic cancer. He had only lasted three months from the date of diagnosis. Tim hadn't attended Frank's funeral. Booley was Eva's uncle, and she had enough on her plate without him starting any trouble.

The diner had seen better days. Red paint peeled off the doorframe and windows. The black and white tiled floor was cracked, and the red vinyl seats were frayed and had been repaired with electrical tape. A few locals sat in the booths. Tim recognized the faces but couldn't remember their names. They eyed him with blatant suspicion, which wasn't a surprise.

Eva stood behind the counter. She seemed to be the only person working. He remembered her at fourteen. She had been young and pretty with a figure that left all the boys panting, but she'd only had eyes for Frank. Confident, happy-go-lucky Frank who wanted nothing more than to stay in Hopefalls and make a life with the girl he loved.

Eva's hips had grown wider in recent years, her light brown hair was tied in a ponytail at the nape of her neck, and fine lines etched her eyes and mouth, but for all that, she was still a very attractive woman.

"Good morning." Tim smiled. "Can I have a coffee to go?"

Eva's light brown eyes lit up. "Tim." She stepped around the counter and threw her arms around him.

He returned the hug. "I wanted to tell you I was sorry to hear about Frank."

She nodded as she led him to a booth by the window. "Me, too."

He sat with his back to the door. "I couldn't make it to the funeral."

"I understand." She grabbed a crumpled tissue from her pocket and dabbed her eyes.

Tim gave her a minute to collect herself. He was uncomfortable being in the presence of such heartache, but at the same time he understood. In Afghanistan, he'd lost friends, comrades, and a lover. Besides, this wasn't about him.

"You got a busy day ahead?" Eva tried to smile as her lips trembled.

"Yeah, I took yesterday off and have to make up the time. You hear about Ben?" He might as well get the inevitable gossip over with. "Your uncle thinks I did it."

"Why?"

"Does he need a reason? I'm sure if a stranger died in Mongolia, Booley would find a way to blame me."

She sniffed and dabbed at her eyes again. "Uncle Levi's always been good to me."

He wasn't sure if she was sniffing because she'd been crying or because she, too, disapproved of him. "Ah, well he's not my uncle, is he?"

****

Dana spun her truck into the diner parking lot. Her eyes were gritty, and her head throbbed. She hadn't slept last night. The idea of shadowing Morgan made her uneasy. It wasn't that she considered herself to be in danger… No, she couldn't think like that. She had to be on alert. This was a man who was responsible for at least one woman's death. And he had admitted, in front of witnesses, he was dangerous.

She'd lain awake, wondering if this assignment crossed the line from trailing to harassment. But what if he had killed Ben North? She was duty bound to investigate. She would tail him today, see what she could learn, and reassess tonight.

She climbed out of her rusted, forest green Chevy truck. First thing on the agenda was coffee. There was nothing suspicious about a cop grabbing a cup at the local diner.

She slammed through the door and strode to the counter. The diner was a long rectangle with the counter and door at one end. Booths lined both sides, which meant every seat was near a window. A wide isle stretched down the middle, giving patrons and wait staff lots of room to maneuver. Eva Bryant sat in a booth next to the door, her eyes red-rimmed, probably from crying. She bent forward, revealing her ample cleavage. Tim Morgan sat opposite. Dana could only see the back of his head and was unable to gauge his reaction to Eva's display.

Dana stiffened. She didn't like the idea of Eva and Morgan being involved. It wasn't right. Eva was a widow who had recently lost her husband. She was hurting. Morgan on the other hand was a devastatingly handsome man who probably had his pick of women. It wasn't surprising that a snake like him would horn in on Eva. Dana watched the couple while she waited to be served. All was quiet in the diner, making it impossible not to overhear them.

"You know I've always been attracted to you," Eva purred.

Morgan inched back, distancing himself. "Don't."

"Why not? We're two unattached adults." Eva's swollen eyes hindered her attempt at seduction. She was trying to be sexy, but her runny mascara coupled with her pinched, tired appearance made her seem sad, lonely, and desperate. Dana couldn't help but pity her. Eva was heartbroken. Unfortunately, there was no cure for grief.

"Because you're hurting, and Frank was a friend. I can't do that to him or you."

Maybe Morgan had some scruples after all.

"I'm tired of being sad and lonely. I want to forget, just for a little while. Can't you do that for me?" Eva was pleading with Morgan to have sex with her.

Dana couldn't say why she was so shocked. Timothy Morgan was the quintessential bad boy wrapped in a very fine exterior. From personal experience, she knew his type drew women by the dozen. She had her own string of failed, impossible relationships, mainly because she was only attracted to sexy men like Timothy Morgan.

Morgan crossed his arms. "I understand, but it can't be me. Although I do know someone who can help you."

Dana gasped. He was pimping Eva out.

Eva sat straighter in the booth. "Who would that be?"

"I'll tell you tomorrow. I'll pick you up here at noon."

From her spot at the counter, Dana could only see the back of his head and the left side of his face, but she could tell he was smiling. The slimy jerk.

"Sounds like a date, honey," Eva purred.

Dana tried not to gag, but the thought of Morgan introducing Eva to one of his sleazy friends turned her stomach.

He stood, grabbed his coffee cup from his table and threw some money down. There was no sign of surprise at her presence. He must've known she was standing there, listening. "Hello, Officer Hayden. You're up early."

He squeezed past her as if he had no choice but to get too close and invade her personal space when, in actuality, there was plenty of room. Butterflies danced in her stomach, and she had an overwhelming urge to inhale his scent. Damn it. Of all the men in the world, why did she have to be attracted to him? She had enough doubt about her abilities. She didn't need him added to the mix.

He smiled down at her. His gaze started at her hiking boots and slowly rolled up her body, taking in her jeans, cotton T-shirt, and old leather jacket.

"I could say the same of you." She glared at him, hoping to convey some of the hostility she felt and none of the attraction.

"I have to get an early start." He stepped back and then shoved open the door.

"Do you have a long way to go?" She doubted he would reveal his plans, but it was worth a shot.

He stopped, one hand on the door, and turned toward her. "I'm not leaving Montana if that's what you're asking."

"I wasn't."

He wasn't going to tell her, not that it mattered. She would trail after him. She just couldn't act as a policewoman once she was out of her jurisdiction. She made herself meet his gaze, not wanting to back down. His eyes shone gold in the morning light. She'd never seen eyes that color before. She didn't want to stare but couldn't stop herself. He looked at her with an intensity that threatened to burn her insides. It was impossible for her to turn away. Once again, those traitorous butterflies danced in her stomach. No, this couldn't be happening. She refused to be attracted to the man who had done so much damage to herself and her family.

"Like what you see?" He tilted his head to the side. A dark lick of hair fell over his forehead.

She stepped back, resisting the urge to brush his hair back in place. "And what is it I see?"

"Yesterday, I was the son of a ranch owner and an innocent man." His golden eyes were hard and cold.

She straightened. She was a cop not a teenage girl. She wouldn't moon over a man, especially when that man was a suspect in a murder investigation. "And today?"

"Today, I'm a feed salesman and still an innocent man."

"The jails are full of men who claim to be innocent."

"Of that, I have no doubt." He walked out, allowing the door to slam in his wake.

"Damn." There was no time for coffee. She ran out of the diner. Morgan was just pulling out of the parking lot as she climbed into her truck.

She put her phone on speaker, threw it on the passenger seat, and hit Xavier's number. "Hi. It's me," she said when he answered. Gravel spewed from her tires, and she gunned the engine, following Morgan's black truck.

"Hey, Dana." He sounded tired, not surprising given he was on call twenty-four hours a day until Ben's death was solved.

"Did Ramirez find out any more about Tim Morgan?"

"Yes, he emailed me the information this morning." The sound of finger's tapping on a keyboard echoed down the line. "Morgan's father has Alzheimer's. He's in Shady Pines Care Facility. It's expensive."

"Who pays?"

"Timothy Morgan."

"How can he afford that?"

"He can't. He has a separate account set up to deal with Jack's expenses, and he has power of attorney over his father's estate. Ramirez spoke to Morgan's personal banker. It seems two years ago he sold off all the livestock and equipment from the ranch to pay for Jack's care, but all the money is gone."

"So maybe he wanted to sell that fancy six shooter that shot Ben. Do we know how much it's worth?" Dana pictured Ben's body lying flat on the floor, the gun by his side.

"I'm not sure. I did a quick Internet search. If it's a limited edition, like everyone says, then it could be worth as much as ten thousand dollars. We'd have to get an expert to look at it to know for sure."

"I suppose the exact amount doesn't matter." There was something off about the body and the gun, but without access to the reports from the crime scene technicians it was hard to make a reliable determination.

"What do you mean?"

Dana realized she was gaining speed and eased up on the gas. She didn't want to get too close. "It's what Morgan thinks, not the real amount that matters. If he thought it was worth a fortune, then he might kill for it."

"I get what you mean. If he thought it was worth nothing, then why bother? Besides, the gun could have nothing to do with it. The banker seemed to think Morgan was going to sell the ranch. It's worth millions."

She passed the red brick post office. Trees lined the front parking lot, which was empty. She pulled her mind back to the case. She'd driven past the gate to Wind Valley Ranch as a child and knew the land stretched for miles. "Not if there's a mine right next door."

"Depends on what type of mine goes in. And maybe the company that owns Ben's mineral rights also owns the rights to whatever is beneath Morgan's land. If that's the case, then he'd want the deal to go through," Xavier reasoned.

"But if he just wants to sell the ranch, then he could've killed Ben to delay the court case."

"I never thought of that."

"So what we have is a man desperate for money, who could've killed for the gun, or because he wants to sell his land to a mining company, or because he just wants to sell his ranch and needs to delay Ben's case."

She cleared the town. The road now curved through the wilderness. The forest was so dense it was impossible to see anything beyond the evergreen trees that lined the road.

"So you're saying he has motive to spare," Xavier said.

Dana smiled. "Your words, not mine, but yes. Although there is one thing that bothers me, why did he leave the gun there? If he was prepared to kill for it, he would've taken it with him. Did Ramirez say anything about the medical examiner's report?"

Xavier tapped his keyboard. "Nothing yet."

"It's probably too early." Dana kept Morgan in her sights. Her cell connection would soon drop out, and there was nothing on this road for an hour, just the evergreen forest and the occasional lake that ran parallel to the highway.

"Are you looking for anything in particular?" Xavier's voice crackled down the line.

"I want to know the cause of death and what the white powder was on Ben's face. It's the only thing that doesn't fit.

Look, I'm going to lose you. I'm on the Hopefalls Highway heading east towards Granite City. I'll call when I reach civilization.

"Sounds—" The line went dead.

Dana pressed the disconnect button on her phone. One of the reasons she'd relocated to Hopefalls was its isolation. Never had she imagined she would be following a dangerous suspect on a lonely stretch of road carved out of the wilderness. She shuddered. Someone like Morgan could dump her body out here, and she would never be found.

No, she was a cop. She was trained and resourceful. He would not intimidate her, and he would be brought to justice.

Chapter Eleven

Tim pulled his black Ford onto the shoulder, waiting for the old green Chevy to catch up. The pretty cop had been stalking him since Hopefalls. Every now and then, when the sun hit her head, he got a glimpse of short, wavy blond hair. He thumped the steering wheel. Damn it all. He had enough going on without the Hopefalls PD hounding him. He wasn't sure how to react to Dana Hayden. She was obviously suspicious of him, not surprising given his past. And he knew she had been listening to him at the diner. He'd seen her reflection in the window as she stood at the counter, hanging on his every word. She looked different out of uniform. Her tight-fitting jeans accentuated her shape.

He got out of his truck and stood in the middle of the road. There was no way he would put up with this shit. She rounded the bend and slammed on her brakes. He held his breath, hoping the beat-up old truck wouldn't hit him.

She was out of the truck the moment it stopped. Weapon aimed at his chest, she marched toward him, her hand trembling. "What the hell are you doing?"

He raised his arms in a show of surrender. "Why are you following me?"

"What makes you think I'm following you?" She gave a slight nod as if agreeing with him while her words said the opposite. Finn had once told him that a suspect's body language said more than their words. In Officer Hayden's case, it seemed to be true. Something in her gaze told him she didn't want to shoot him. She had the look of a cornered animal. She was anxious, but not scared...exactly. This was something else. Her breathing seemed labored, coming in small gasps as if she were having a panic attack.

"How's Logan? He had quite a scare yesterday." He tried to change the subject to one that was less likely to get him shot.

"I'm not going to discuss my son with a suspect, even if you did save him from a bear."

"You're welcome, by the way. You know, normal people would thank the man who saved their child from a horrible death. They wouldn't point a gun at him."

"Do you have a weapon?" Beads of sweat appeared on her forehead.

"I have a Beretta 92 A1 locked in the glove compartment of my truck." He smiled, trying to reassure her.

She glanced at his waist. "Not on your person?"

He shook his head "I have a concealed carry permit for the gun and for my Ka-Bar, although I hardly ever hide the knife. It's on my belt." He turned to the side so the sheath and hilt were clearly visible.

"Why do you carry a knife? Most people would be happy with just a handgun. Having both is overkill."

He shrugged. "It's a handy tool. Very useful when I'm working at the ranch."

"And when you're not there?" She still hadn't lowered her weapon, but she seemed more centered, in control.

"It stops trouble before it begins. When people see a big-ass knife on your belt, they think twice about messing with you. You don't get the same reaction with a gun. Any idiot can pull a trigger, but not everyone is trained to fight with a knife. Besides, it's way too easy to kill someone with a gun. But I'm guessing you know that."

She flinched as if she'd been slapped. She'd killed someone. "Are you?"

"Am I what?"

"Trained to fight with a knife?" She took a step forward. She was way too close for his liking.

"I was a Ranger, remember? We're trained in hand-to-hand combat."

"Give me one good reason to believe you didn't kill Ben."

He sighed. "Because I have no motive."

"Actually, I can think of three reasons." Her hands shook, causing the SIG Sauer to wobble.

"Three? How the hell could I have three?"

She ignored his question. "You've been guilty for a long time. Now it's catching up with you." And that was her real motive for harassing him. She couldn't convict him of killing her aunt, so she would follow him hoping to charge him with another murder.

"Lady, you've completely lost touch with reality. In fact, you couldn't tell the difference between the truth and your own crazy fiction if it walked up and kicked you in the shins." He stepped forward and snatched her SIG out of her hands. His left hand held her at arm's length. Using his right hand, he pushed the button to release the magazine from the handgun. It clattered to the ground. He straightened his trigger finger so he wouldn't shoot himself and then slid the handgun down his side, catching the notch for the sight on his belt. The action racked the cartridge, ejecting the bullet loaded in the barrel, rendering the weapon useless. Then he shoved it at her.

She clasped it, her mouth hanging open.

"Shooting me is something we'll both regret." He stalked back to his truck, praying she wouldn't put the SIG back together and shoot him before he had time to drive away.

Chapter Twelve

The wind blew across the flat prairie fields of north central Montana. Dana's stomach rumbled as she watched Morgan make his way across the dusty, gravel parking lot, heading back to his truck. He hadn't stopped for lunch so neither had she. It was now late afternoon, and she could feel a headache forming behind her eyes.

She'd called in her report to Booley, letting him know Morgan was aware of her presence. The police chief wasn't fazed. He seemed to enjoy hearing about their confrontation. Of course, she left out the part where he'd disabled her weapon with one hand. And she would never mention her panic attack. Once again, she questioned her fitness for the job. What if the circumstances called for her to shoot a suspect? Would she be able to? Most cops went their whole careers without killing anyone. Unfortunately, she wasn't one of those cops. And it wasn't as if she could discuss her concerns with Booley. He was just waiting for an excuse to fire her.

The chief's biting laughter still echoed through her mind. Why he should find it funny that Morgan had caught her tailing him was beyond her. The fact the suspect had made her so easily should have troubled him. She was out here alone with a man they believed had murdered his neighbor. Booley should've recalled her for her own safety, if nothing else.

Morgan had visited four retailers as a representative for Tillman's Organic Feed. She made a mental note to check them out. They could be a legitimate company, but she doubted it. He'd worked from west to east, finishing in an out-of-the-way store situated in the center of the state where the forested foothills gave way to the prairies.

She'd watched him while he talked to the store owners who made up his client list. To them he was charming, professional, and gracious. He even helped one elderly man unload a large delivery of feed, hoisting the oversized bags as if they weighed nothing.

It would be easy to believe he was a handsome, amiable businessman if she didn't know better. In their clash this morning, he'd been hard, uncompromising, his cold eyes glittering with barely contained rage. That was the real Timothy Morgan.

Dana approached him as he walked across the parking lot, raising her hands away from her sides so he knew she wouldn't go for her weapon.

The idea behind her trailing him was to unnerve him, force him to make a mistake, but it didn't seem to be working. If anything, the opposite was true. She was the one who was unsettled. The confrontation on the Hopefalls Highway had brought up memories she would rather leave buried. He obviously had no intention of hurting her since he could easily have killed her after he'd snatched her gun. It was time to try a different approach. Besides, sometimes you had to use a little sugar to get what you wanted.

"That was a neat trick with the gun. Where'd you learn that?" She stopped in front of the driver's door so he couldn't get in his truck without forcing her out of the way.

He didn't face her. Instead, he turned to face the store and slanted his gaze in her direction. "I told you I was a Ranger."

"So, Morgan, how long have you been a salesman for Tillman's?" She rested against the door, getting comfortable.

"You can call me Mr. Morgan, Timothy, or Tim, not Morgan. And I've worked for them for three years." He marched to the passenger side, reached through the open window, grabbed his black cowboy hat, and put it on.

"Do you like it?" Her gaze met his as he walked back to join her. His eyes, shaded by the brim of his hat, now looked green instead of gold. A quiver of awareness scattered down her spine as her body reacted to him. It was a warning. Her attraction to him was inappropriate, and yet she couldn't seem to control it.

"What's not to like? It's a comfortable hat." The lines around his mouth deepened as he grinned.

He'd been deliberately obtuse just to goad her. "I meant the job." She squinted against the bright afternoon sun, her head throbbing. She needed food and drink. That was why she was responding to him physically. It had nothing to do with him and everything to do with dehydration.

"I get to drive through Montana, which I love. I talk to people about their store or farm. I sell a good product, and most of my customers are happy." He seemed comfortable with this line of questioning.

"And you claim to make a living doing this?" She allowed her skepticism to show. His job could easily be a front for a drug operation.

"I do okay. I'll never get rich, but I've built a decent customer base. It was slow at first. Organic eggs and chicken is a growing market. It's something people want on their supermarket shelves." He stood next to her so they were shoulder to shoulder. "Okay, your turn. How long have you been a police officer?"

She allowed him to change the subject, lulling him into the idea they were having a simple conversation.

"Twelve years, including six years as a detective in Spokane." She hooked her thumbs onto her belt. She wanted him to know he wasn't dealing with some country bumpkin with no experience.

"A detective?" His voice had risen.

"Yep." She'd shocked him. Good.

"What the hell are you doing working for an idiot like Booley? Everyone knows he's only ever worked in Hopefalls."

"Logan needed a change and my grandmother left me a house in town. The rent-free accommodation more than made up for the drop in salary." Too late she snapped her mouth shut. She'd revealed her situation without thinking, blurting out the words. What was wrong with her? She'd never let her guard down with a suspect—ever.

"Does Booley know?"

"About what?"

He pointed to the SIG Sauer at her side. "Your little problem."

She had overreacted this morning and given herself away. She glanced at him and then shifted her gaze to the endless prairie. He'd obviously guessed she'd experienced some kind of trauma. He could have Googled her while she was following or maybe it was just instinct. "I don't have a problem."

"Have it your way. I noticed you didn't argue about Booley being an idiot."

She breathed a sigh of relief at the shift in conversation and tried to think of something to say to defend the chief, but nothing came to mind. She couldn't even say she got along with him because she didn't. Booley was part of the deal she made to ensure her son had a future where he didn't end up in jail. Plus, there was no way she could work in a city. She had hoped the slower pace of a small town would help with her panic attacks, but after this morning, she wasn't so sure.

Morgan's phone buzzed. He looked at the screen. "A friend of mine is back in town so I'm heading to dinner." He tapped out a text and then reached around her to open the door to his truck. He faced her, crowding her personal space. His scent, a combination of hay, earth, and sweat, surrounded her. His breath warmed her neck. She held still, resisting the urge to reach up and kiss him.

What was she thinking? This man was the enemy. The way he'd position himself was a tactic: use his larger size and proximity to intimidate her. It wouldn't work. She wouldn't allow it. She stood her ground and tilted her face, meaning to stare him down. Her pulse jumped when she caught a glimpse of his mouth. "It's too early for dinner." She was grateful that she managed to get the words out without stuttering.

His gaze was hard and unrelenting. "Good, 'cause you're not invited."

He stepped to the side and tugged open the door, which propelled her forward and out of his way.

She turned to face him, her determination returning. "Who are you going to meet?"

"I told you, a friend." He climbed into the driver's seat.

"Where are you going?"

He shrugged, yanking the door closed. "I'm not giving you directions. You decided to stalk me. Now you have to keep up."

Chapter Thirteen

Dana trailed Morgan to Granite City. Given their last conversation, she'd expected him to drive like a maniac and try to lose her, but he was surprisingly steady and deliberate.

Granite City was small compared to other cities in the United States with only fifty thousand residents, but it was a good size for Montana. She and Logan had explored it after their move to Hopefalls.

She parked her beat-up Chevy next to Morgan's shiny black Ford. He stood at the rear of her vehicle waiting for her. His hands were empty and hanging loose by his sides. She didn't know if he was relaxed, or if he was purposely keeping his hands where she would see them. After this morning, it could be either scenario.

She joined him as he walked across the lot to the square. "Tell me where we're going?"

He grinned. "The Dumb Luck Café."

"What kind of a place is it?" You could tell a lot about a person by the places they frequented and the company they kept.

"You'll like it. A lot of cops hang out there."

The bistro-style café sat adjacent to the police station, meaning he was probably telling the truth and it was a cop haunt. Tim opened the door for her. It was a gentlemanly gesture and one that was totally unexpected. She nodded a thank you and stepped ahead of him but then came to an abrupt halt because there was a lineup of people waiting to order. There wasn't much space between the door and the cash register.

Heat radiated from Morgan as he crammed in behind her. Quivers of need cascaded down her spine. *Damn.* She tensed. It wasn't that he'd done anything wrong. It was just that her body seemed hyperaware whenever he was near.

It wasn't *his* closeness that made her tingle. It must be that she hadn't had sex in a long time. Yes, that was it. It had been years since her last date. Okay, problem solved. She wasn't responding to Morgan. It was just some errant hormones reminding her of her abstinence.

Morgan tapped her on the shoulder and made a shooing motion with his hand, telling her to take a step. The lineup had cleared, and she hadn't noticed.

If he thought she'd answer to a hand wave, he was sorely mistaken. He could ask her to move forward and be polite about it. She shook her head in reply.

He rolled his eyes and stepped around her.

It was her turn to tap him on the shoulder. "What do you think you're doing butting in line?"

He pinched the bridge of his nose, clearly exasperated. "I was stuck next to the door, and you wouldn't go. You snooze, you lose," he said, resorting to a worn-out cliché.

She folded her arms across her chest. "Maybe if you'd asked instead of giving me a vague hand signal, I might have understood." That was a lie. She'd known exactly what he meant, but she wasn't going to admit it.

Dana decided to let it go. It didn't matter who ordered first.

Wait, maybe it did. She was supposed to be tailing him, which meant he should go first.

He stepped up to the server and ordered a coffee and turkey sandwich from a white-haired woman behind the counter.

Dana took the opportunity to look around the coffee shop. It was surprisingly upmarket with an assortment of high tables with stools, armchairs with coffee tables, and plain tables and chairs. Bold red letters marked the exit at the back of the building, but she didn't think she'd need it. The Dumb Luck Café was clean and nicely decorated with a caseload of fresh baked goods that made her mouth water. And there was a steady stream of customers, many of them in police uniforms.

Morgan made his way to a sectional couch that formed a U-shape in front of an unlit fireplace.

She ordered a mocha coffee, a meatloaf sandwich with potato wedges, and a brownie and then sat on a high stool behind Morgan. She probably could have sat with him, but that would've crossed the line from observing to participating, and she wasn't ready to do that.

Her sandwich was rich, delicious, and instantly appeased the dull pain in her head. She would've preferred thin-cut fries with lots of salt, but they only had wedges, and she would take whatever junk food she could get, especially when Logan wasn't around to tell her off.

A broad-shouldered man wearing a cheap gray suit entered the cafe. Immediately, he made eye contact with Morgan, nodded, and then proceeded to the counter to order his food. His thick black hair was cropped military short, and he had sharp blue eyes that seemed to notice everything. She would bet her next paycheck he was a law enforcement officer.

This was interesting. Morgan was meeting a cop. Was he making some kind of deal? There was no way she would let him negotiate his way out of Aunt Alice's manslaughter charge. Dear God, what was she thinking? This was supposed to be about Ben, but emotionally it was impossible for her to separate the two cases. And that was the problem with this whole set up. She was too involved. She couldn't trust her own judgment. In the past, she'd always been able to think through the variables of a case in a logical manner. She could examine the evidence, talk to witnesses, and do background checks. Here she was lost, and not just because of her personal interest. This case didn't fall under the jurisdiction of the Hopefalls Police so she didn't have access to any of the pertinent details.

Morgan smiled and stood as the officer approached. His jacket opened to reveal a badge—FBI. Morgan was meeting with the FBI. Whatever he was into must be bigger than she imagined.

The pair sat, but before the agent could open his mouth, Morgan looked straight at her. "Do you need us to talk louder so you can take notes?"

The agent turned to stare at her. "What's going on?"

"I'm under surveillance," Morgan announced and then took a sip of his coffee, as if her presence was nothing to be concerned about.

"Why?" The agent narrowed his eyes, assessing her.

"Either Officer Hayden has taken it upon herself, or she's been ordered, to tail me." There was no inflection in his voice—no malice, hate, not even anger, which was surprising given the situation.

The agent took a long drink from his water bottle and then said, "I spoke to David an hour ago. He filled me in on what happened to your neighbor." He turned to face her. "So, were you ordered or did you take it upon yourself?"

"I can't comment on an ongoing investigation." Dana stared at the table, uncomfortable. Although whether she was embarrassed about being so obvious in her task or the job itself she couldn't say. Shadowing Timothy Morgan wasn't panning out the way she expected. She'd known from the beginning he would recognize her, but he didn't seem troubled by her presence. Which meant one of two things— he had nerves of steel or he was innocent with nothing to hide.

The agent patted the empty cushion next to him, signaling for her to sit with them. "Join us. Tim has always had a weakness for policewomen, soldiers, sailors, and strong women in general."

Morgan rolled his eyes. "Officer Dana Hayden, I'd like you to meet Special Agent Finn Callaghan."

Special Agent Callaghan smiled. "Please, call me Finn."

Dana moved to stand next to the empty seat. "Why are you meeting a federal agent? Are you involved in some kind of investigation?" She kept her gaze on Morgan, expecting him to squirm in his seat or show some other sign of guilt, but he smiled, revealing a charming, arrogant, irritating grin.

Agent Callaghan picked up his Rueben sandwich. "This is a social visit. We've been friends for fifteen years since basic training. I can vouch for Tim's good character and would be willing to do so in court if need be."

She sat, a new headache forming behind her eyes. Morgan wasn't meeting some lowlife criminal. He was meeting a friend who just happened to be an FBI agent. What did that say about him? For years, she'd believed he had caused Aunt Alice's death. She'd read the Hopefalls Police Department file when she'd first moved to town but hadn't rechecked the facts or the witness statements. She had accepted Booley's suspicions as fact. But could she believe the assumptions of a man, who just yesterday, had contaminated a crime scene? She was a trained detective. Maybe it was time to reexamine Aunt Alice's case.

Morgan shrugged. "We can pretend she's not here."

Agent Callaghan laughed and then said, "Don't be rude. Besides, it's nice to see you with a woman."

"I'm not with him." The pulse at Dana's temple began to pound.

"So, you heard from David about me?" Morgan changed the subject, playing with a plastic stir stick, rolling it along his fingers. Small scars covered his big knuckles—fighter's hands.

"Yeah, but he was a little fuzzy on the details, and homicide doesn't fall under the FBI's jurisdiction. We can't interfere in an investigation unless we're invited by the local police."

"That won't happen." Dana held her coffee cup to her forehead in an attempt to stop the pain.

Morgan curled his lip in a sneer. "Why, because Booley won't do it? My lawyer pointed out that it's not his case." He turned to Finn. "Detective Ramirez from Granite City-Elkhead County Police Department is investigating."

Agent Callaghan nodded. "He's a good cop. Do you want to talk about it?"

"Not really… As far as I can tell, they think I shot Ben North over a gun. The weapon in question is a limited-edition Colt six-shooter. Apparently, it's worth a lot of money."

"People have been killed for less," the agent admitted.

Morgan's eyes widened as he gave his friend a hard look.

Callaghan shook his head. "Sorry, that was a stupid thing to say. I mean, other people have killed for less." He reached in his pocket, pulled out a bottle of aspirin, and placed it on the table in front of her.

"I know, but why would I? I'm talking to a realtor about selling the ranch. Even if I drop the price to make it competitive, the property will still sell for millions."

"Are you sure there's no other way?" Callaghan asked. "You love that place,"

Morgan shook his head. "Doesn't matter. Technically it's not my land. It's Dad's. Everything will go toward his care."

"I wish there was some way I could help." Callaghan patted Morgan's upper arm in a male show of sympathy.

Morgan shrugged. "It's probably for the best. These accusations about Ben's death have put an end to the idea of ever settling there. I would be happy if I never set foot in Hopefalls again."

Dana pictured the Morgan place, situated between Molly's Mountain and the Kootenai National Forest. It was vast and stretched for miles. She hadn't driven past the gate to Wind Valley Ranch since her return to Hopefalls, but she remembered it from before Aunt Alice's death. The Morgans had been rich. They'd employed people from the town. It was mostly seasonal work, but still, they had authority and clout. All that was now gone.

The conversation turned to cooking. An FBI agent wouldn't lie about them being friends since basic training. It seemed that Timothy Morgan wasn't the man she imagined him to be. She hadn't seen anything today to suggest he was a criminal. That trick with the gun was impressive. If she hadn't been on the receiving end, she would've found it entertaining.

She took a sip of her mocha. It was smooth and rich with the perfect amount of foam. She hated that her body reacted to Morgan. Even now sitting in this coffee shop with a pounding headache, she felt the live wire of sexual excitement skittering through her veins.

"Why are you frowning at me?" Morgan's question brought her back to the conversation.

Her face heated. There was no way she would admit she'd been thinking about his physique. "I need to go to the restroom."

"Don't worry, I'll keep an eye on him." Callaghan winked. "You have my word as a federal agent. He won't get away."

As she made her way to the washrooms at the back of the coffee shop, she realized that at no time was she worried about Timothy Morgan skipping out on her.

****

Tim watched Dana's perfectly round butt as she walked away. She had the most eye-catching behind he'd ever seen. Enjoying her shape was easy. She was his type—tall with the perfect amount of muscle. The big surprise was that he liked her. She was doing her time as a cop in Hopefalls to make a better life for her son. He could respect that. He also liked that she had more experience than Booley. Maybe she would investigate properly and get to the truth.

What a stupid idea. She was a Hopefalls cop and Alice Hayden's niece. Objectivity was too much to hope for.

The anxiety she displayed when she'd held her weapon on him told him there was something else, something in her past. She'd probably shot someone in the line of duty and was having trouble coming to terms with it. That was something in which he could relate.

Maybe he should cut her some slack. Working for Booley had to be hard, and she was obviously uncomfortable with this duty. He could create a stink and report her to Ramirez.

He was almost certain the detective would want to know the Hopefalls Police were investigating his case. No. He'd give her the benefit of the doubt, and if she proved to be Booley's flunky, he'd deal with it. Until then, he'd enjoy the view.

"I wouldn't if I were you," Finn said

"Wouldn't what?"

"Make a move on Miss Hopefall's PD."

He stretched back in his chair and smiled. "She'd probably shoot me."

Finn tapped the table with his index finger. "Listen, while she's in the bathroom, I need to talk to you about Michael."

He sat up. "What's wrong?"

Finn's humor from a moment ago was gone. "He needs a place to lay low while he recovers. I was wondering if he could stay in that cabin."

He lowered his tone to match Finn's. "What cabin?"

"The one you put David and Marie in when they were in hiding."

Tim shook his head. "That's not possible. It belonged to Thomas George, a friend of my father's, who passed away last year. His daughter owns it now. It was only safe then because of the blizzard. I figured no one would drive into the mountains in those conditions. Even if I could put him there, I don't think it's a good idea to leave him alone in an off-the-grid house with no running water and no electricity. He can't haul water or build a fire. How the hell would he survive?" He wanted to help, but what Finn was suggesting was not practical. "What's going on?"

Finn rocked back in his chair and then hunched forward again. "I can't go into details, but the FBI are compromised. I believe Michael's in danger. I think the only thing protecting him is the fake identity he used when he went undercover to expose Portman."

"So this has something to do with David's case?"

"Not directly."

He waited for Finn to elaborate, but he didn't. "Michael's in bad shape. He needs a place to hide."

Tim blew out a long breath. Damn. Their friend must really be in trouble if this was his only option. He pointed toward the washrooms at the back of the coffee shop. "I'm being watched by the police. I can't go anywhere without someone finding out. He's welcome to stay with me until we can figure out something else."

"At the ranch? I don't think that's a good idea." Finn pressed his lips into a thin line. "There's only one road into your place. He'll be seen going in."

Tim grabbed a napkin. "There's a back road. It's the old track that used to lead to the Kootenai Forest. State engineers changed the course of the road to one that wouldn't flood. It runs parallel to the Hopefalls Highway. You drive through Hopefalls and turn left at the stop sign instead of going straight. Then take the next right. It turns into a dirt track a few miles out. Drive past the base of Molly's Mountain until you reach the creek. Then turn north. To get across the stream you'll have to cross the bridge on the highway, but at least no one will see you going through town. He drew a rough map, showing how the trail ran past Molly's Mountain and into Wind Valley.

There was an old saying—trouble always comes in threes. First, he was suspected of killing Ben and had the police stalking him, and now Michael was in trouble, which must be serious or Finn wouldn't have asked for help. How could someone have access to the FBI? He pushed aside the question. The workings of law enforcement had always eluded him. And he had no interest in figuring out their problems. He had enough trouble coping with his own. Still, this was a lot of shit to deal with at one time. But Michael was more than a friend, he was family. He'd gone out on a limb to help David, and Tim had no doubt he would have done the same for him.

"Thanks. This is not ideal, but it should work for a few days until I can figure something out." Finn tucked the map into his pocket just as Dana joined them at the table.

"So, what did you talk about while I was gone?" She seemed more alert, brighter now that she'd eaten.

Tim switched the subject away from Michael. "We were wondering if you had a husband or a boyfriend."

Her gray eyes widened as her face flushed. "That's none of your business."

He was surprised he was able to throw her off balance so easily. Not that he'd planned to make her uncomfortable. His initial intent was to take the conversation away from Michael, but her reaction was fascinating. It was thoroughly enjoyable to watch her squirm. Maybe he should make a habit of asking her personal questions and see how she responded. He smiled. He was going to have a lot of fun with Officer Dana Hayden.

Chapter Fourteen

The early evening sun crested the western mountains and cast long shadows across the city square. Dana walked with Morgan back to the lot where they'd parked their trucks. Neither of them spoke. It had been a long, tiring day. The futility of this assignment sucked at her self-esteem, pulling her down, making her wonder why she had agreed to do this in the first place.

She needed to clear her mind, think, and identify her problem. Today was the first time she'd drawn her weapon since arriving in Hopefalls. She'd been hesitant, nervous, anxious, and an utter failure. Morgan had been hostile, standing in the middle of the road, and forcing her to stop was an aggressive act. But did she really feel threatened? That was a question she couldn't answer. As a Spokane policewoman she was trained to perceive every encounter as a potential threat, to always be on her guard. But she wanted something different. She wanted to be part of a community where she knew and understood the problems that faced the residents. She wanted to get to know the citizens in her care.

Morgan fished his truck keys from his pocket as they neared their vehicles. He seemed open and frank, but she knew from personal experience that some people were competent liars. Logan's father, Oliver, would look her in the eye and smile while he lied to her and then steal her wallet and all her money. She had to question whether Morgan was more of the same. Was he a liar and a snake? Or a hard-working salesman who wanted nothing more than to be left in peace to care for his sick father?

"I can see why you like your job. All you have to do is drive around and chat to people," she said, breaking the silence.

He shrugged, smiling, but it didn't reach his eyes. "Today it was just stores, which I can do on Saturdays, but I try not to because it's their busiest day."

"What about tomorrow? Are you staying home?" She knew he wasn't. He'd made a date with Eva but wondered if he would tell her as much.

"I have to do some work around the ranch in the morning."

"And in the afternoon?"

"I have to pick up Eva and drop her off somewhere, and then I'm going to visit my dad."

"Where are you taking her?" It didn't matter if they went for an innocent cup of coffee. Booley would have a fit. And if she was being honest, she didn't like the idea of him—a handsome, sexy, charming man—spending time with a susceptible, grieving widow. "You know she's delicate right now. It wouldn't be right to take advantage of her."

He bent down so his lips were close to her ear. Her breathing hitched when his breath warmed her neck. A low thud of anticipation started deep in her core. Her breasts seemed to swell, rubbing against her bra. She didn't move. She couldn't.

"If you think I'm that bad an influence, then you should come with us. Meet me at the diner at noon." He pulled back and stared at her as if daring her to join them. Then without another word, he climbed into his truck and slammed the door, effectively ending their conversation.

She tugged her jacket tight over her chest, not allowing herself to look down. She suspected this attraction was one-sided, which meant he had the upper hand.

She headed to her vehicle and followed him out of the parking lot. She needed to push her desire and her emotional involvement aside and sort through her observations. There was nothing she'd seen today to suggest he was involved in any kind of suspicious activity. In fact, all the available evidence suggested the opposite, but then, it had only been one day. For nineteen years, she'd believed he was the boogeyman and wasn't sure about letting go of her preconceived notions. Leaving him unguarded for the whole morning was out of the question. Tomorrow, bright and early, she would drive to Wind Valley Ranch and see what he was up to.

****

She was tired and a little cranky by the time she reached the outskirts of Hopefalls. Ben had been murdered. Someone had…had what? She was almost certain the shots to his chest hadn't killed him. Which meant someone had shot his corpse. So what was Ben's cause of death?

She was supposed to handover to Booley and give him a report of the day's activities but didn't have the patience to deal with his attitude. She called Xavier instead. "Can you tell Booley we're nearly at Hopefalls? He can wait at the entrance to Wind Valley Ranch."

There was a low murmur in the background and the sound of a door slamming shut.

"He just left," Xavier announced. "I hear Morgan made you straight away?"

She could hear the laughter in her colleague's voice. "Yeah." She'd allowed her personal interest in the case to override her common sense. She'd known from the start it was idiotic to shadow Morgan on a quiet country road. She should have refused this assignment, talked to Detective Ramirez, and worked in conjunction with the Granite City-Elkhead County Police Department.

"Don't be too hard on yourself. I did more checking into Morgan. Not only was he a Ranger, he also lived on the street for a few years. He probably has well-honed survival instincts."

"He was homeless?" She knew from her days as a beat cop in Spokane that street kids had a hard life. Most children, boys and girls, were forced into prostitution in order to feed themselves. It was a place where predators thrived, turning innocents into criminals, or worse, slaves.

"Where else would a fifteen-year-old runaway go?" Xavier reasoned. "He lived rough in Granite City and was taken in by Marshall House. He got his GED there."

Her heart sank. "All because he played a teenage prank and stole a street sign." Aunt Alice's death had hurt her family in innumerable ways, but now she had a fifteen-year-old son of her own, one who'd gotten into trouble with the police. She had a better understanding of how the teenage mind worked. There seemed to be an inherent lack of awareness, as if they had no idea of the consequences of their actions.

"Yeah." Xavier lowered his voice. "I'm not from around here so maybe I don't get how things are done, but why does Booley have such a hate-on for this guy? You, I can understand. Alice Hayden was your aunt, but with Booley it seems personal, or am I imagining it?"

Dana took a deep breath. "I don't know, but you're right, this does seem more personal than it should. For the record, I don't hate him. It would be easier if I did."

"Starting to like him, huh? It's understandable. He's forbidden fruit."

"You have got to be joking—"

"And he's handsome and charming."

"Xavier?"

"You're right. Girls hate that," he joked.

Even though Xavier was teasing, his words rang true, and she couldn't deny her attraction so she settled for her tried-and-tested backup answer, guaranteed to end every argument. "Shut up."

Xavier gave a deep-throated chuckle.

Dana thought about the information Xavier had supplied. "It's like I said before—if Morgan wanted the gun, then why leave it with the dead body? I mean, we're talking about an ex-Ranger who used to be a street kid. His survival instincts have to be sharp. If he wanted the gun, he would've taken it with him."

She hung up to concentrate on following Morgan's vehicle. They drove through Hopefalls to the long dirt road that marked the entrance to Wind Valley Ranch.

Booley sat in his truck, waiting. She waved at her boss, did a U-turn, and carried on driving, heading toward home. If he wanted to talk to her, he'd call.

It had been an unsettling day. It wasn't her first as a cop and probably wouldn't be her last. When Logan was little, she would go home after a bad day, cuddle up with him, and watch cartoons. Being close to her son had grounded her in a way nothing else could. It helped her make sense of the world and her place in it.

How was she going to deal with Morgan? He hadn't said anything, but he knew she had a problem. From what she'd witnessed today, she didn't think he would use that knowledge to coerce her, although her thinking could be clouded by her sexual attraction. Xavier was right. Timothy Morgan was forbidden fruit.

He was also a complicated man. In one moment, he was charming and relaxed, and in the next he gave her that cold, hard stare. Of course, his mood changes could have something to do with her tailing him. What a joke. She hadn't shadowed him. She'd spent time with him and enjoyed it.

He was a suspect in a murder investigation. That was her assumption, but it wasn't necessarily correct. Ramirez had released Morgan, which meant one of two things. He was either a suspect and they didn't have enough evidence to hold him, or he wasn't a suspect and this whole endeavor was a waste of time. That was something she really should check. In any case, she needed to get a grip on her emotions. She would tail him again tomorrow, and she would be observant and professional. Despite her pep talk, her heart did a little flip at the thought of seeing him again.

Chapter Fifteen

Tim held the kitchen door open, allowing Michael to limp through. A cool spring breeze freshened the stale air of the house, waking Tim. He'd tossed and turned all night. Every time he drifted off, he dreamt of Dana. Her long legs were wrapped around his waist as he thrust into her. Then he would picture her suspicious gray eyes and wake in a cold sweat. He'd never had any woman tie him in knots the way she did. If things were different, he might have asked her out to see if there was more than sexual attraction. But under the circumstances, that would never happen. He ignored his semi-erect penis and his visions of the long-legged policewoman who had caused his discomfort, concentrating instead on his injured friend.

Finn had wasted no time delivering Michael to Wind Valley. His friend had been sitting on the couch when Tim arrived home last night. Michael had insisted on sleeping in the bunkhouse. A couple of years ago, that would've been fine, but now the place was filthy, vermin-ridden, and structurally unsound.

Michael's hair had grown since the last time Tim had seen him. That was two months ago when he'd been lying in a hospital bed. His injuries were so severe that even sitting made his face twist in agony. Now he was disheveled, unshaven, and smelled like stale sweat. He held his cane in his right hand as he maneuvered to the kitchen table. Exhaustion showed in his pale face, and a fog of pain shadowed his eyes.

"Your pelvis is broken on your left side, isn't it?" Tim grabbed a frying pan from the cupboard.

Michael slowly sat and winced as his butt touched the seat. "In three places, why?"

"Wouldn't it be easier to hold the cane on the left so you have support on your injured side?" He lay bacon in the pan and turned up the heat on the stove.

Michael shook his head. "I broke my left collar bone. My shoulder hurts like a bitch. It can't take the strain of supporting my weight."

Damn. He'd forgotten about the broken shoulder. "Who's been looking after you since you were injured?" Tim propped himself up against the sink, his hands in his pockets, trying to keep his voice level. Michael wouldn't appreciate an overt show of sympathy.

"My mom came down from Canada. She went back a couple of weeks ago. Actually, I was doing really well until yesterday—"

"You overdid it on the flight?"

"Yep." The clipped answer meant Michael didn't want to talk about it.

Tim pushed. "Normally, I don't ask, but this sounds…" He had no idea how it sounded. The events of two months ago, when Marshall Portman had tried to kill David, had shaken them all. But this seemed to be more than a corrupt businessman.

Michael eyed him as if trying to decide how much to say. Finally, he sighed. "It's big. For your own safety, I can't go into details.

"What happened with David is still ongoing, isn't it?"

Michael nodded.

Tim put a hand to his mouth as he considered the ramifications. Being in trouble wasn't new. In fact, it was all too familiar. But it was made worse because Michael was incapacitated. He had to be able to protect himself despite his broken bones.

"Got any coffee?" Michael said, changing the subject.

Tim poured him a cup. "I'm making eggs, bacon, and toast. You want some?"

"Sounds good. I'm starving."

Tim turned the bacon and then set another pan on the stove and cracked four eggs into it. "Then you can take a shower."

"That bad, huh?"

"Yes." Talking about everyday things helped ground him. He felt as if his world had become a tangled mess, and he needed a chance to sort through the problems and catch up.

"Do you have a chair you can put in the shower stall in the bunkhouse?"

Tim could've slapped his head. Michael needed the cane to stand up. He had to use his good arm to support the cane, which meant he was essentially immobilized unless he was seated. "You need to stay in the main house. It's cleaner, more comfortable, and I'll be able to keep an eye on you."

"It's only a matter of time before these guys find me. They have access to the FBI's files. It's known we're friends. Plus, Finn said you have your own legal worries at the moment."

Tim refused to talk about Ben's death, the residents of Hopefalls, or Dana Hayden and her belief that he was capable of murder. "You can see the dust plume from the road for twenty minutes before anyone reaches the house."

Michael shook his head. "This place is not a good idea. If someone does come, they can search the house and find nothing. That'll give me time to get away and you can deny I was ever here."

"I'd kill them before I'd let them take you. And in the shape you're in, you wouldn't get far."

"I forgot how scrappy you are."

Tim smiled and scratched his cheek. "How could you forget? We were in enough fights together back in the day." Meaning when they'd been homeless on the streets of Granite City. Their time living rough, watching each other's backs, had cemented their bond.

They lapsed into silence as Tim laid the cooked bacon on a paper towel to drain the excess grease, placed the eggs on two plates, and then brought them to the table.

"Don't you have a tent or something? I could sleep up in the mountains." Michael took a bite of the crispy bacon.

"No, and even if I did have one, I wouldn't let you camp out. Two days ago, I ran into a grizzly with cubs. You're in no condition to save yourself against a human, let alone a bear."

"You wouldn't let me? I'm a grown man. You don't get to 'let' me do anything."

"Then you need to start acting like a grown man. You set yourself back going to Salt Lake City with Finn. You're hurt, and you're in trouble. One of us will find a place for you to hide. In the meantime, concentrate on getting better. You need to be able to hold a weapon so you can protect yourself. That has to be your priority. After breakfast, I'll put a chair in the shower and move your stuff into this house. Then we'll go through the gun cabinet and pick a weapon for you."

Michael's gaze held his for a few moments. Then his dark, perceptive eyes grew tired. He didn't have the energy to argue.

"Give yourself a couple of days to get your strength. Then if you want to take off, I won't stop you." Tim finished his breakfast and placed his plate in the dishwasher. A brown-gray plume caught his eye. He grabbed the binoculars that sat on the kitchen counter near the window and trained them on the newcomer. "Damn."

"Who is it?"

"A policewoman from Hopefalls."

"What do you think she wants?"

"I told her I'd meet her at the diner at noon. She's over an hour early."

"Do you think she's come to arrest you?"

"No, Wind Valley Ranch is out of her jurisdiction. But if there's a problem, can you call David and ask him to send his fancy lawyer?"

"You got it."

"It's better if she doesn't see you. I'll keep her outside."

"If you seem like you want to get rid of her, she'll be suspicious. Relax and have a coffee with her."

"Okay, I will. The road is slow going. We have about twenty minutes before she reaches the house, so I'll get you setup." He grabbed his key ring and worked a small key free. "Here's the key to the gun cabinet. Take a look and see if one catches your eye. Do you need anything else?"

"Just the password for your Wi-Fi."

"I don't have Internet or cell service."

"What?" Michael's eyes widened.

Tim shrugged. "I used to have satellite TV and Internet, but I had to cancel them."

"You have a smartphone." He pointed to the device that lay on the table.

"Yeah, but it only works in town. There are no towers out here. There's a landline." An old yellow phone sat on the kitchen wall near the door. Next to the phone, there was a base station radio and a walkie-talkie he'd been meaning to sell. It was an older model but had a range of thirty-five miles. He really needed to get his act together and put an ad online. He dismissed the thought and focused on Michael, taking in the dark circles under his eyes and the protective way he curled to one side in his seat. His friend was in pain. "Will you be okay out here on your own?"

"Sure. I was going to look some stuff up on the computer, but I guess I'll just shower and practice my shooting." Meaning he'd been planning to do some cyber investigating.

Tim headed for the door. He wanted to fetch Michael's belongings from the bunkhouse before Dana got any closer.

"Finn said you like her." Michael's words stopped him as he reached for the handle.

Then he turned the knob and kept on walking, without comment. It didn't matter that her pale gray eyes and long toned body had haunted his dreams. His attraction to Dana Hayden would never amount to anything.

****

Dana steered her old Chevy along the pothole-ridden, bumpy dirt track that led to Wind Valley Ranch. She'd called Booley this morning and given her report. He'd been predictably rude, saying he should have sent Xavier instead of her. He seemed to think Officer Robinson would have succeeded in finding proof of Tim's guilt where she'd failed. She'd ended the conversation as quickly as possible since the strain of holding her tongue had made her clench her teeth, and now her jaw hurt.

Once Logan was done with high school, he would move on to some kind of post-secondary education and she could get another job, one where she didn't work for a woman-hating jerk. Maybe she should think about getting out of police work. Her gut twisted at the thought. The trouble was she loved her job; being a policewoman was part of her identity. But a police officer who couldn't fire her weapon was useless. Perhaps she could get a desk job somewhere or teach self-defense courses to women. She liked that idea. There were a lot of women who had no idea how to make themselves safe. That was worthwhile work, but it wasn't the same as being a cop.

She and Logan had shared a Denver omelet for breakfast. She didn't consider herself much of a cook, but she made spectacular omelets. Logan was planning on spending the day painting the walls of his bedroom white. Then he was going to cover them with a mural. She didn't care what his room looked like. Her son was occupied and interested so, as far as she was concerned, it was a win-win situation. Later, he was going over to Shelly's again to do more baking, which seemed like a strange thing for a teen to be into, but who was she to judge?

Sooner or later, Logan had to be responsible for his own life. Learning to make good decisions was part of being an adult. At least that was what the Spokane Police Department therapist had said in their sessions after Logan's arrest. She needed to be able to trust her son, and he needed a chance to earn that trust.

She pushed away her worries about Logan and focused on the bumpy driveway. It was a glorious spring morning. Sun slanted from the east. The long shadow cast by Molly's Mountain fell across the land. Open fields that occupied the central part of the valley were covered in dry hay, which gave the ground a yellow glow. The hay was from last year. All the other ranchers and farmers in the area were plowing their fields, making way for a new crop, but on the Morgan's ranch, last year's harvest had decayed in the field without being reaped.

The homestead came into view. It was a collection of six buildings surrounded by a circle of trees. Three of the structures were log cabins, the largest of which had a wraparound porch. Her breath caught at the view of the rustic house engulfed by the wild valley with the snowcapped mountains in the distance.

She reached the house, climbed out of the truck, and was hit with the scent of pine, dirt, and hay. When she inhaled, her talk with Booley and her concerns about Logan drifted away with the mountain breeze.

Tim opened the door, carrying two steaming coffees. "Beautiful, isn't it?"

She nodded, accepting the mug from him. "Do you have any milk or cream?" Contrary to how television portrays cops, she seldom drank her coffee black. She didn't take sugar either, just a double helping of cream.

He shook his head, still looking at the scenery. "Sorry, I used all the milk to treat the burns I got from the bear spray, and I didn't have time yesterday to pick up more. I had this pretty policewoman stalking me all day."

"That's terrible. Maybe you should give me her name so I can investigate." Suddenly conscious of her appearance, she tugged at her too-short bangs and tucked the longer pieces behind her ears.

He gave a deep, melodic chuckle that made her all too aware that he was so close they were almost touching, and yet she didn't pull away. This was the first time she'd heard him laugh. He smiled all the time, but somehow that didn't quite seem real. It was a façade he presented to the world.

"It must be hard for you to give this up." She followed his gaze to the mountain range in the west, not wanting to look at his disheveled hair or the dark stubble on his chin. Or think about the fact that she was trailing the man who'd faced down a bear in order to save her son.

He was silent for a long moment, so long she wondered if he would just turn and head back into the house. But he grabbed her hand and tugged her toward the porch. She could've easily pulled away but didn't. They walked along the wraparound deck until they reached two wooden Adirondack chairs and a coffee table. The furniture looked like it needed a coat of varnish. In fact, the whole place was in need of painting. She imagined the upkeep on a property this size was a round-the-clock job. And a man who worked full time to pay for his father's care wouldn't be able to maintain it. Tim sat in one of the chairs.

"How does your dad feel about you selling the place?" She dropped down into the seat next to him.

"He doesn't even know it's happening. He doesn't understand. I was in Afghanistan when he first got ill. I didn't know. He was fine when I attended Mom's funeral. Then I went back overseas for ten months. Mrs. Anderson, my second-grade teacher, got in touch to tell me Dad was sick and I had to come back and check on him."

They were facing the valley now with Molly's Mountain to her left. The yellow fields and a wide swath of forest stretched between the two properties, the distance so great it would be impossible for Tim to see or hear the perpetrator who had killed Ben. "What happened when you got back?"

"Dad didn't recognize me." Tim's feet were bare, and like the rest of him, they were long, slim, and well-shaped.

A hum of appreciation lodged in her throat. *Good God.* She was ogling his feet. She turned her gaze back to the view and concentrated on their conversation. "So, in less than a year, your father's health deteriorated?"

He nodded. "Getting Dad the care he needs, and paying for that care, have become my top priorities. I always had mixed feelings about living here. I love the land but hate Hopefalls. I sold the cattle and equipment, put the money in savings, and used some of it to pay for a caregiver to come in while I was at work."

"And then?"

"Angela, that was Dad's nurse, called to say she'd quit. Dad had wandered off. People with Alzheimer's do that. Anyway, when she tried to get him to come back to the house, he hit her."

Dana put a hand to her mouth. "He hit her?"

"I feel so guilty about putting Dad in the care home, but I have to work, and I couldn't look after him twenty-four hours a day."

"You put him in the best one you could find. That's all anyone can ask." She placed her hand over his, and then realized what she was doing and pulled it away.

The heartache of the man sitting next to her was palpable. Alzheimer's was a cruel disease that robbed its victims of not only their ability to reason, but also took the essence of who they were. They no longer recognized people they'd known their whole lives.

Tim didn't look at her. He was lost in his own thoughts. "Shady Pines is a good place. The grounds are spacious and beautiful, and the staff are excellent. They can give him the care he needs."

"But it's expensive." She was stating a fact. The cost of his father's care was the reason behind his alleged motive for killing Ben.

Tim nodded. "The money from the sale of the assets is almost gone."

"And now you have to sell the ranch?"

He turned and stared at Molly's Mountain, his eyes squinting against the bright morning light. "You know, when I was a kid, Dad and I used to sit out here on cold, dark evenings. He'd tell me stories about the Wild Bunch, Kid

Curry, Butch Cassidy and the Sundance Kid, and how they used the valley as a hideout. Legend has it they buried their gold here but were killed before they could come back to collect it. Dad said on a windy night you could still hear them thundering down the valley. I don't know that any of it's true, but it's fun to think about.

"You must miss him."

"Yeah, and my mom. All I ever wanted to be was a rancher like my Dad. I was born here, and I figured I'd live here until I died. When I was on the street, I used to walk to the edge of the city, stare at the mountains, and imagine I was standing on this spot."

Her stomach knotted at the thought of him at fifteen, homesick and alone in Granite City. His poor mother, she must've been so worried. Dana pictured Logan lost and starving, begging for food. A lump formed in her throat. One way or another, Tim Morgan had paid for his crime in fear, hunger, and hardship. "Why did you join up? Why didn't you come back here?"

He stood and walked to the railing. "How could I when everyone in Hopefalls thinks I caused Alice's death? This"— he swept his free hand in a wide arc—"is temporary. It can never be a real home." Once again, he'd been careful in his choice of words and hadn't admitted to causing the accident.

"It was a long time ago." Just two days before, she'd painstakingly preserved the evidence and protected the scene of Ben North's homicide, hoping he wouldn't escape justice again. And here she was all but forgiving him.

"People have long memories. My friends were joining up, and it was a chance for me to prove myself. To shake the idea that I was a worthless kid who got into trouble and begged for food. I needed to be one of the good guys, and the army offered me a way to regain my self-respect." He threw the dregs of his coffee over the railing and then took her cup. "Shall we go?"

She sat in her truck as he carried the empty mugs into the kitchen. She enjoyed watching him move and appreciated his long legs, his firm, tight butt and long hard body. She salivated at the thought of feeling his arms wrapped around her, encircling her in his warmth. She sighed, turning away to stare at the overgrown fields.

Her attraction to Tim was dangerous. She shouldn't let her guard down...but she already had. She no longer thought of him as Morgan, but as Tim. And she couldn't imagine him as a lowlife. There was nothing in his record or his life to suggest he was anything other than what he said— a hard-working ex-Ranger who was caring for his sick father. Somehow a barrier had been broken, one she had erected to protect herself from him. She couldn't say he had demolished it. He hadn't done anything other than be himself. It was her. She simply couldn't stay mad at a man who seemed decent and honest. Of course, liking Tim wasn't the problem. It was her physical attraction to him. How the hell was she going to keep him at arm's length when she couldn't stop wondering how he would taste when she kissed him?

Chapter Sixteen

Dana parked in front of the diner and rolled down her window as Tim got out of his truck and strode to her door.

She gave a low whistle, pointed in Eva's direction, and then turned to Tim. "She's dressed to kill."

Eva sat on the steps of the diner, waiting. She'd straightened her long sandy-colored hair. Her eyes were circled in black eyeliner and her lips were painted a garish shade of red. She wore a skintight, low-cut, see-through blouse, which revealed a lacy black pushup bra. Hookers showed less cleavage. Her too-tight blue jeans were tucked into a pair of tan cowboy boots. It was hard to believe she'd lost her husband just a few months ago.

Tim frowned. "It would be really helpful if you would ride with me. I tried to tell her she's not my type. I should have been firmer."

"I thought you were introducing her to one of your friends for a bit of fun."

Tim shook his head, his eyes widening. "I did not say that."

She nodded. "That's the impression I got."

"Damn it all to hell." He scrubbed a hand over his face. "I screwed up. You distracted me, and I screwed up. Promise me you won't leave me alone with her."

So she had got to him. He just hadn't messed up in the way she'd expected. Dana smiled. "Are you scared?"

"Of course, I'm scared. She's Booley's niece."

"Where are you taking her?"

"I thought it might help her to chat with a friend of mine—a priest."

"Are you trying to tell me that your circle of friends consists of an FBI agent and a priest?"

He smiled, and her stomach did a little flip.

"Am I ruining your preconceived ideas?" Tim waggled his eyebrows.

Dana laughed and then stifled her reaction when she spotted Zoe Harris and Mrs. Anderson walking toward them. Personally, she didn't mind Zoe. The mayor's wife was always pleasant and had baked cookies to welcome her when she'd first arrived. Mrs. Anderson was another story. The retired schoolteacher never smiled at her. The most she ever got in greeting was a mere nod of the head. That coupled with Victoria's stern expression gave Dana the feeling she'd been judged and found wanting.

Tim was halfway across the lot, heading towards Eva, when Victoria accosted him. "Timothy Morgan, what do you think you're doing? Luring Eva like this."

Dana had no idea how the women knew about Eva's meeting with Tim, but it was obvious they didn't approve.

Zoe Harris stood next to Mrs. Anderson, nodding. She had a little dog tethered to her wrist that yapped as Victoria talked, as if it, too, were telling Tim off.

He stepped back, his movements stiff and controlled. "I'm not—"

"Levi's going to skin you alive." Victoria spun around, and Zoe followed. The dog flew off the ground and then landed, unfazed, as they walked across the parking lot in the direction of the police station.

"Wait." Dana jumped out of her truck and ran to catch up with them, ready to reassure the older women.

Eva strode toward the group, joining them in the middle of the empty lot. "This is none of your business."

Dana moved between Zoe, Victoria, and Eva. She opened her leather jacket to reveal her badge and gun. All three women knew who she was, but flashing her badge was a display of power and a reminder she could take action if things got ugly. "Don't worry, I won't be leaving Mr. Morgan's side. Nothing untoward will happen."

Eva gasped. "You're not coming."

Tim joined them, standing beside Dana. He gave Eva a slight nod. "I think she should."

"We'll take my truck," Dana announced, taking control of the situation.

Eva slipped her arm through Tim's and then leaned close so her red lips almost kissed his cheek. "But I thought we were going to have some fun—you said you had a friend."

Dana resisted the urge to shove the widow away from him, which was a ridiculous reaction. Her job was to tail him and report her observations. Not that the chief had asked her for a detailed report. He just wanted the facts and had even tuned out when she'd mentioned Tim's close friend, the FBI agent, which reinforced her suspicion that Booley had his own agenda.

Tim stiffened, but didn't push Eva away. Instead, he escorted her to Dana's truck, opened the passenger door, and shifted the front seat so Eva could climb in the back.

Dana waved goodbye to Zoe and Victoria who stood in the middle of the parking lot, watching them. Once again, there was something about Victoria that made Dana squirm. Maybe Mrs. Anderson thought Dana was indecent because she was a single mother who had never been married.

Dana shrugged it off. She couldn't change the mistakes she'd made as a teenager, and wouldn't, even if she could. One of those mistakes had resulted in Logan, and he was worth all the condemnation the town busybody could throw her way.

Zoe Harris on the other hand, always smiled and greeted Dana as if she were a friend. The mayor's wife looked as if she'd stepped off a magazine cover. Her short fair hair was perfectly straightened, and her complexion and make-up were flawless.

Dana drove out of the parking lot, spewing gravel in her wake. Tim's jaw was clamped tight, and every muscle seemed tense, ready to strike. He was right. He didn't have a future in Hopefalls. He couldn't even be in the same vehicle with a woman without someone thinking the worst. A glance in the rearview mirror showed Eva undoing the top button of her blouse, revealing even more of her ample bosom. She was a real man-eater. Then Dana remembered her promise. Tim didn't want to be left alone with her. Victoria and Zoe had it wrong. Eva didn't need protecting from Tim. He needed to be protected from her.

****

The drive to Granite City was long and silent. She'd inserted her favorite country CD into the player. She would've preferred a playlist from her phone, but her truck was too old for Bluetooth. The music had cycled through the songs twice before they reached the city. Tim directed her through the streets until they came to a small building near downtown. A sign on the front lawn read St. Mark's Church.

"We're here," Tim announced. He jumped out and slid the seat forward so Eva could climb out.

They entered the church by a side door, which led to an annex. Long tables stood at one end of the room, and stacks of chairs lined the walls. There were no windows, but skylights in the ceiling made the church hall sunny and bright.

He faced Eva, taking her hands in his. "Sex won't help you get over Frank. Trust me, I know. When my fiancée died, it took me a long time to come to terms with the fact that playing musical beds wasn't helping. You live in a small town. If you go down that path, it will be bad for you in the long run."

Tim had a dead fiancée. That was another unexpected revelation. She hadn't considered his previous relationships, mainly because she didn't want to think about them.

"This isn't what I want," Eva spat. "I want a good fuck. What the hell is the point of being a bad boy if you don't fuck?"

He dropped her hands and stepped back, wincing as if he'd been struck. Pain shone in his eyes. "I'm sorry you feel that way."

A balding, middle-aged man wearing a priest's collar entered the room. He adjusted his coke-bottle glasses and then held out his hand. "Tim, it's so good to see you."

"You too, Father Meade." Tim smiled at the priest, seeming to shake off his pain from a moment ago, or maybe he was just masking it. "I'd like you to meet one of my oldest friends, Eva Bryant. Eva recently lost her husband."

He didn't introduce Dana, and she didn't care. She was too busy witnessing the scene and absorbing the information. Eva had clearly hurt Tim with her words. He'd believed she was a friend, possibly the only friend he had in Hopefalls.

Dana didn't know Eva well. The diner had been closed after Frank's death and had only opened a few weeks ago. They'd said hello to each other on a few occasions but had never talked. All the town gossip suggested she was an upstanding woman who was a pillar of the community. Dana wasn't so sure about that. Her opinion of Eva had nosedived in the last few hours. She understood the widow was hurting and could also see how having a lover could be a short-term comfort. But Eva was totally selfish in her quest and didn't seem to care that her actions could harm Tim in immeasurable ways. Maybe her grief had blinded her to the very real chance that Booley would kill him.

Dana found the whole thing distasteful and wanted to get away from Eva as fast as possible. She would've walked out, but she'd made a promise to Tim, so she had to stay. Besides, this way she could report back to her boss and assure him she had played chaperone.

"Father holds a bereavement meeting here every Sunday afternoon," Tim explained.

Father Meade stepped forward and took Eva's hand. "I find Sundays are hard for those who have recently lost a loved one. So I hold a non-denominational meeting mid-afternoon. Nothing formal, we just chat while we drink coffee."

Eva stared at the priest without saying a word, but she didn't pull her hand out of his grasp.

"Eva, give it a chance," Tim ordered, his voice sounding military in tone.

"Come and help me set up. We can talk while we work." Father Meade guided Eva to the stacks of chairs.

"Let's go." Tim grabbed Dana's elbow as he beat a retreat out of the church.

Dana's phone pinged as she reached her truck. It was Booley. She sucked in a calming breath and then answered, "Hello, sir."

"I want my niece returned to Hopefalls—now."

"She's in a bereavement meeting at St. Mark's church in Granite City. I left her in the company of a priest."

"She's what?"

"We just dropped her off."

"What do you mean we?"

"Didn't Mrs. Harris and Mrs. Anderson tell you? I'm driving. I thought it would be best for all concerned if I took control. I accompanied Mr. Morgan so you could be certain your niece was in good hands, and the counseling might help."

Booley didn't reply.

"She's fine, and I'll pick her up once the session is done."

"Make sure you do." He hung up without saying goodbye.

Chapter Seventeen

Finn Callaghan sat in his ergonomic swivel chair. Whenever possible, he spent his Sunday afternoons catching up on paperwork. As a rule, FBI agents had to be ready to go twenty-four hours a day, seven days a week, but Sundays were generally quiet.

Unable to concentrate, he slid the form he'd been working on across his desk. Stashing Michael at Tim's had been a bad idea. Even a rudimentary investigation would turn up Tim's name as an associate.

Finn stared at his phone. Maybe he should call Ramirez and ask for the details of the case. No, that wasn't a good idea. The detective wouldn't appreciate the interference, and Finn had no doubt if Tim was a suspect, sooner or later Ramirez would question him.

But Michael…he was another matter. He was injured and vulnerable.

Finn picked up his phone and called Sinclair. Sinclair Quinn was David's twin sister. Gifted with languages, she had served in the army before becoming an investigator for the non-profit organization, Child Seekers International. The charity had safe houses all over the globe. Maybe she could help.

"Hello," she answered on the first ring.

"Sinclair, this is Finn."

"What's wrong?"

"I call and something has to be wrong?"

"Yes."

He hesitated for a moment. She was right. He only ever contacted her when there was trouble. Maybe he needed to take more time out for his personal relationships, especially his friends. He decided to get to the point. "Michael needs your help."

"I'm in Russia."

Fuck. "Any idea when you'll be back in the country?"

"It's hard to say." She was being deliberately vague. It could be that she was in the company of a human trafficker, or maybe someone was listening in on her calls.

"Michael was wondering if you still had that holiday cottage?" As codes went, it wasn't great, but then being cryptic wasn't his forte. If he'd known beforehand, he might have come up with something better.

She was quiet for a moment. He pictured her twirling her long strawberry-blond hair as she thought about his request. "Not a problem. Give me a few days." The line went dead. He wasn't sure if she'd lost her cell signal or if she'd hung up.

Finn threw his phone on the desk. She'd been abrupt, but she'd understood. Good. Hopefully, Michael would be safe at Tim's until Sinclair could move him to a secure location.

Getting back to work, he switched on his computer and opened the file containing the surveillance photos of Lucy Portman. Deluca had wasted no time in assigning agents to the case. Lucy sat at a table in the Big Sky Steak House. It was a five-star restaurant in Granite City and served a delicious, award-winning menu.

One picture showed Lucy Portman sitting at her table, sipping her water. Beside her sat a classically handsome man with neatly trimmed, graying hair. His coloring, coupled with the deep contours that lined his face, suggested he was in his late-forties. He wore an expensively tailored suit that must have cost a small fortune.

Lucy now owned her husband's power company, Public Domain Energy. She had also inherited a commodities brokerage, Holstein Brothers, from her father. She was a powerful woman. Was her companion equally powerful?

Another photo captured Lucy's hand under the table, touching the stranger intimately. Obviously, this was not a platonic relationship.

In the third image, the couple were joined by Lance Ackerman. In his sixties, with a large waistline, Ackerman was famous for ruling his empire with his bullish personality and hardline tactics. His firm, Ackerman Enterprises, was a Fortune 500 company with interests in newspapers, electronics, and social media outlets.

Finn was convinced Lucy Portman was part of the Syndicate. Was Lance Ackerman also a member? This meeting could be anything: friends getting together to share a meal, a legitimate business dinner, or two members of the Syndicate planning Michael's death. It was impossible to know without listening in, and there was no way they had enough evidence for that kind of monitoring.

He needed to know the identity of the third man. He could just be an escort, a paid lover, but would Lucy bring a gigolo to a business meeting?

Kennedy strode into their shared office. They'd moved to the federal building around the corner from the police station a month ago and had decided sharing an office enhanced their working style rather than hindered it.

"What are you doing here?" She threw her windbreaker over the back of her chair.

"Catching up." He didn't need to elaborate. She knew what he meant.

His cell phone played the annoying jazz ringtone he'd been meaning to change. Finn accepted the call from Detective Ramirez, preventing the melody from grinding on his nerves.

"I need to talk to you about your friend, Tim Morgan."

Finn grimaced. There were times when he hated being right. "My place or yours?" The location of the interview could set the tone of the conversation. If Ramirez chose the police station, then he was probably about to charge Tim, but if he decided to come to the federal Building, there was a good chance the detective was just working through the variables.

"Your office is fine. I can be there in five minutes."

On the other hand, he might just want to go for a walk and stretch his legs, and meeting Finn here was a good way to do that.

Ramirez strolled in, minutes later, looking as confident as ever. The corruption of the Granite City–Elkhead County Police Department at the hands of Marshall Portman didn't seem to bother him at all, but Finn knew morale within the department was at an all-time low.

"What can I do for you?" Finn pointed to the cheap, hard plastic guest chair that was situated on the other side of his desk.

"I need to ask you about Timothy Morgan's movements on the day of Ben North's homicide, which was last Thursday."

"I can only account for his whereabouts between twelve and one. We had lunch together."

"Where was this?"

"At the Dumb Luck Café on the Square." Finn always went to the Dumb Luck for lunch. Not only did they serve good food, but they also had the best coffee in Granite City.

"Did you have to wait for him?"

Finn shook his head. "No, he was there when I arrived."

"And he left with you."

"No, he had his laptop out. He said he had some work to do. I assumed he was going to use the free Wi-Fi. His ranch is too remote to get a signal."

"Do you know what time he left?"

"No, but Peggy might." Peggy was the owner of the Dumb Luck who'd purchased the coffee shop with the insurance money when her husband was killed in a freak fishing accident.

"If she doesn't know," Finn continued, "ask if she still has last Thursday on file." Peggy's security cameras covered the interior of the coffee shop and the sidewalk outside.

"Sounds good. I'll probably pull the surveillance anyway so there's no question of bias."

"Is there anything you can share?"

"I don't think there's any harm in telling you…the medical examiner changed the time of death. The color of lividity suggested the body had been exposed to freezing. On further investigation, the ME discovered the temperature on Molly's Mountain dropped to below freezing Thursday night—"

"Which delayed decomp?"

"Correct. The new time of death is between eleven a.m. and two p.m. on Thursday."

"So Tim's in the clear." Finn breathed a sigh of relief.

"Not necessarily. He could have raced back and killed North within our timeframe." The detective shifted his chair closer to the desk.

Finn's gut cramped. "Is there anything else in the ME's report?"

"The gunshots didn't kill Ben North. That much was obvious at the scene. He died of a heart attack, which was induced by poisoning. The ME thinks it was an accident. Ben didn't ingest the poison, and there are no needle marks on the body, but his face was covered in a white powdery substance." Ramirez placed his elbows on Finn's desk. Dark circles shadowed his eyes. He looked like he hadn't slept in a month. "It will take a few days for the lab to give us a name, but presumptive tests indicate it belongs to the nightshade family."

"Do you think it was self-induced?" Kennedy asked. "Perhaps he mistook the powder for cocaine."

"Anything's possible. We'll know more once we know what kind of poison was used." He crossed his arms on the desk, used them like a pillow, resting his head on them. Closing his eyes, he said, "Coffee isn't keeping me awake anymore."

"You need sleep. Go home," Finn ordered.

"I will." Ramirez opened his eyes and stared at Finn's computer screen. Finn turned the monitor away but not before the detective glimpsed the photo of Lucy, Ackerman, and the mysterious third man. "I know that guy."

"Yeah, he's Lance Ackerman."

Ramirez sat up straight. "No, the other one."

Finn glanced at Kennedy who was halfway out of her seat, ready to cross the room. "Who is he?" she demanded.

"He's the mayor of Hopefalls. His name is…" He put a hand to his mouth. "I shook his hand. His name is…" He snapped his fingers. "Harris. That's it."

Finn tilted his head to the side. "Does the mayor have any connection to Ben North's homicide?"

"Umm. He was at North's place when the police arrived. According to Officer Hayden, who secured the scene, Chief Booley, Mayor Harris, and his wife, Zoe Harris, were stomping all over the evidence when she arrived."

"Seriously?" Kennedy joined Finn.

"He's also behind the push to put a mine on Ben's land," Ramirez added.

"What can you tell us about this mine?" Kennedy asked.

"I don't have all the details, but it seems that Third Estate Mining has filed condemnation proceedings for Ben's land. They were forcing Ben off his property, using the Eminent Domain Law."

"Which is all perfectly legal." Finn hated when a large corporation forced a little guy off his land. But his job was to uphold and enforce the law. He didn't have to like it.

"According to the district attorney—yes, but Ben's lawyer was fighting it. He said the rights were never separated, and Ben owns the land and everything beneath it."

"Where does the mayor fit in?" Finn drummed his fingers on his desk.

"Ben was in some news articles. You can imagine the headlines. 'Government makes Vietnam War vet homeless.' Not to mention the environmental impact. When it comes to the mayor, I haven't figured out his angle. Being mayor of a small town like Hopefalls can't pay much, although he doesn't need the income. He made his money working as a landman."

Finn rubbed his jaw. "A what?"

"A landman. They work for the oil and gas companies to secure mineral rights from property owners. His official line is he's trying to save the town."

"Unofficially?" Finn stood and extended his arms over his head, working the kinks out of his neck. Did the Harris's link to Lucy Portman mean Ben North's death was connected to the Syndicate? There was something about Harris's former occupation that made him suspicious, but he couldn't put his finger on what. He needed more information.

Ramirez shrugged. "I haven't figured that out yet."

"Do you think Ben could've stopped them?" Finn paced behind his desk.

Ramirez shook his head. "The district attorney said there has never been a case in Montana where the Eminent Domain process has been stopped."

"You're saying there's no way Ben could win?" Kennedy perched on the edge of Finn's desk.

"No, but he could make them pay through the nose for it," Ramirez said.

Finn stopped and stared at Ramirez. "The publicity and hype wouldn't have helped?"

"There are, or were, protesters at the entrance to Molly's Mountain—that's Ben's property. One side wanted the jobs. The other wanted to keep the pristine wilderness." Ramirez's eyes brightened. His fatigue from a moment ago seemed to have disappeared.

"Let me guess, the mayor wants the jobs because the town dies without work," Kennedy stated.

"Makes sense. The question is, did he kill to bring jobs to the area and ensure his reelection as mayor? Although, I still think there has to be more to it," Finn added. "Do you know who owns Third Estate Mining?"

Ramirez stood, and walked to the center of the room, seemingly reenergized. "I'm looking into—"

"I think there's another question that needs answering," Kennedy interrupted.

Ramirez's gaze took in her compact swimmer's body, and then his eyes met hers. "What's that?"

"What are Ben's financials like?" Kennedy asked.

"I can't find any. He didn't have a bank account."

"Did you find a hoard of cash when you searched his house?"

Ramirez shook his head. "No, nothing."

"How much land did he have?"

"Two hundred acres, Molly's Mountain is huge. Why? Do you think he hid his money on his land?"

"I don't know, but lawyers are expensive. I think we need to know where Ben got his money and how he paid his bills. I mean, he must've had some form of income."

Ramirez ran a hand through his short-gelled hair. "Shit."

"We can talk to his lawyer if you want," Finn offered.

"I don't want you interfering in my investigation. Your friend is a suspect."

"Is he your main suspect?"

Ramirez groaned. "No, to be honest I haven't narrowed it down."

"So you have the mayor and—

"That idiot police chief from Hopefalls." Ramirez wrinkled his nose as if he'd smelt something bad.

"Booley? What's he like?"

"He's a joke. The guy has no clue how to conduct an investigation. He doesn't want to do the work. He just wants to charge the nearest suspect without caring whether or not they're guilty. We were lucky Officer Hayden is trained and knew how to protect the scene. Why'd you ask?"

"Curiosity, I've heard stories over the years." This particular police chief had altered the direction of Tim's life.

"I have another question," Kennedy cut in. "What do they want to mine?"

"I don't know. Does it matter?" Ramirez rubbed the back of his neck.

"For your case, I doubt it, but maybe it's something the FBI should know. And I wonder if this Eminent Domain case has something to do with these three." She pointed to the photo of Lucy Portman, Lance Ackerman, and the mayor of Hopefalls.

"Why are they under investigation?" Ramirez opened the door, obviously eager to leave before his case got even more complicated."

"We're collecting evidence in the PDE public corruption case," Kennedy lied.

"How is there a link between Ben North's homicide and Marshall Portman and Public Domain Energy corrupting the Granite City- Elkhead County Police Department?" Ramirez asked.

That was a good question. One for which Finn didn't have an answer.

"We need to ascertain whether Lucy was involved in her husband's activities," Kennedy said, avoiding a direct answer.

Ramirez sighed. His burst of energy from a moment ago was gone. "I don't think there's anything there but have at it. I assume you'll share any information pertinent to my case."

"Of course." Finn nodded. "Text me the details for Ben's lawyer and then go get some rest. We'll visit him tomorrow and call you once we're done."

Kennedy locked their office door the moment the detective left. "You were sloppy. Ramirez should never have seen your screen."

Finn slumped into his chair. "Luckily, it worked in our favor."

"This time." She sat on his desk next to his swivel chair, facing him, invading his personal space. "Do you think the Syndicate is behind Ben North's death?"

Finn shrugged. "We don't have any evidence to suggest that." Meaning all they had was supposition and conjecture.

A cold vice twisted in his gut, his instinct told him the Syndicate was interested in Hopefalls and Molly's Mountain. He had driven Michael through the small, sleepy town yesterday on the way to Wind Valley Ranch. Damn, his friends were in the heart of the storm.

Chapter Eighteen

From the outside, Shady Pines Care Facility seemed more like a luxurious hotel than a nursing home. Wide gates opened to a long tree-lined driveway. The main building was of log construction with small cabins scattered about the property. Ponderosa pines were peppered between the buildings, giving the property a relaxed, woodsy feel.

"This seems like a nice place," Dana said as they walked through the sliding glass doors into the air-conditioned interior.

"It's pricey, but Dad deserves the best. He always loved being surrounded by the wide open spaces of Wind Valley Ranch, and I wanted him to be able to look out of his window and see trees, even if it isn't the wilderness."

Tim stepped up to the reception desk and greeted the guard as he signed in, "Hey, Randy, how's it going?"

"Hi Tim, your dad's having a good day." The guard, a round man in his early forties, smiled back. There was no suspicion or hint that Tim was anything other than a caring son visiting his sick father. Even the priest had been pleased to see him, but then again, he was a man of God. He was supposed to be gracious and forgiving to everyone—even sinfully sexy, tempting men like Tim.

He led the way down a long corridor. The walls were painted light beige and decorated with beautiful, framed Montana landscapes. The facility wasn't as sterile as a hospital, but it was still antiseptic.

They reached the end of the hall, turned left, and were greeted by a nurse as she wheeled a cart of fruit cups along the corridor. "Hi, Tim."

"Randy said Dad's having a good day."

The nurse's gaze roamed his body, taking in his long form, his shoulders, and his flat stomach. Finally, she settled on his face and smiled. "He had a tough morning, but once we got him to do his exercises, he was much better." The nurse placed her hand on his arm, leaving it there.

Dana suppressed the urge to shove her away.

"The exercise is helping?" Tim stared down the hallway, not seeming to notice her touch or the admiration in her gaze.

"He's definitely more lucid afterward." She checked her clipboard. "I was about to give him a snack. Do you want to do it?"

Tim smiled and picked up a fruit cup and spoon. Without saying goodbye, he took off, striding down the hall. Dana ran to keep up and almost crashed into him when he stopped suddenly at the end of the hall. He inhaled, seeming to collect himself, and then entered without knocking.

"Hi, Dad." He made himself comfortable in a chair next to his father's bed.

"Who are you?" Jack Morgan frowned and then stared, unseeing, into the distance. He sat, propped up by the adjustable bed. His skin hung loose on his thin frame. Even reclined, she could tell he was tall like his son. Once upon a time, he'd been a handsome, vibrant man, but now he was a white-haired, vacant shell with rheumy eyes.

Dana stood by the open door, not wanting to intrude on a private moment between father and son. The room was homier than she expected. A large armchair and a small coffee table sat in front of a bay window that looked out over the grounds. An oak chest of drawers was positioned against the far wall, and a matching nightstand stood next to the head of the bed. The bed was the type used in a hospital with handrails on both sides. It was covered with a beautiful hand-stitched quilt, which was decorated in sunflowers surrounded by a periwinkle blue border. Family photos covered the walls. At first glance, they seemed random, but on closer inspection, all of them showed Tim at various stages of childhood and then as an adult. There was even one of him in his dress uniform. He had fewer wrinkles around his eyes and the creases around his mouth weren't as deep, but other than that, he hadn't changed much.

Dana focused on one of him as a teen wearing a cowboy hat as he sat astride a horse. He had a wide smile. His eyes were light with laughter. It must've been taken before Aunt Alice died, when he was like every other teenage boy.

Tim grabbed the over-bed tray and rolled it until it stopped at Jack's chest. "It's me, Tim."

"You're not my son. He's run away. I told him I'd get a good lawyer, but he ran." A sob erupted from the old man's throat.

"That was years ago, Dad. I came back before mom died. I joined the army and became a Ranger." Tim pointed to the photo on the wall and then opened the fruit cup.

Jack's eyes focused on his son. He grabbed Tim's hand. "Your Mom was so proud of you. She told everyone you were serving your country."

The fact that Jack had suddenly remembered him didn't seem to faze Tim. "Hey Dad, do you remember that gun you and Ben bought years ago? It was a Colt six-shooter."

"Damn it, I gave Ben that revolver. Has that old coot accused me of stealing it? He's gone senile. That's what it is."

"Did you give it to him before Mom died?"

"Your Mom died? That's sad, but I suppose it happens. My mother died in 1974 after...after..." He faded, his lucid moment gone. He seemed lost in his distorted, traitorous mind.

"Would you like some fruit salad?" Tim scooped a piece of peach onto the spoon and put it in his father's mouth.

Jack swallowed and then said, "Who are you? You're not my regular nurse. She's pretty. I want the pretty nurse back."

Tim smiled and stood. "I'll send her in to clean up." He seemed to know how to handle his father.

"You do that."

"Bye, Dad." He kissed Jack's head. "I love you. I'll be in tomorrow."

"My son's a good boy. He didn't do anything wrong. That Booley is just protecting his own," Jack shouted as Tim exited the room.

"What did he mean by that?" Dana asked as they climbed into her truck.

"By what?" He sounded tired and weary as he fastened his seatbelt.

"That comment about Booley?"

"I don't know." He turned to stare out of the passenger window. "My father's sick. On a good day, he recognizes me. I don't worry about the other stuff. I care about whether he's eating, that he's safe, and getting the right treatment."

Dana turned the key in the ignition and then sucked in a deep breath, repressing the urge to question him. "Where to?"

"Back to St. Mark's."

She headed toward the church. It had been an emotionally charged day. Zoe Harris and Mrs. Anderson had accused Tim of mistreating a grieving widow. The widow in question, Eva, wanted to use him as a sex toy and was very put out when he'd refused. His father was sick and hardly recognized him. On top of that, she had been trailing him for the last two days because the police chief of Hopefalls believed he was guilty of murder. It was a lot for him to deal with.

Her own opinion had gone through a dramatic change since she started shadowing him. She simply couldn't imagine him committing cold-blooded murder. But then again, she had no clue as to the actual cause of Ben's death. Maybe he'd died of natural causes, and someone had shot the dead body. Shooting someone who was already dead required an awful lot of hate. If that were the case, then she needed to discover who hated Ben.

"Are Eva and Booley close?"

Tim shrugged. "I've no idea."

"What about when you were kids?"

"When I was a kid, all I thought about was football. I figured I'd go to school on a scholarship. I imagined people would cheer when I played, and girls would line up to have sex with me." He smiled, but it didn't reach his eyes. "It's shallow, but that's how a teenage boy thinks."

He continued to stare out the window. "I thought I was the best thing in a pair of sneakers. Then I blew my knee in the state championship and had to deal with the fact that I wasn't as shit-hot as I thought, and my future had changed."

She remembered the photo of him in his father's room, obviously taken before that awful night. He'd been a good-looking boy; his confidence had shone through his smile. He must've thought the world was his for the taking, and then everything had fallen apart.

She shook away the sadness she suddenly felt for the future he'd lost. "So what happened?"

"I took Dad's truck and drove up to the ridge to think. I decided even without being a football star, life could still be good. I'd just stay on the ranch and work with Dad. I was wrong about that, too." His voice was flat, emotionless.

He hadn't mentioned stealing the stop sign and causing Aunt Alice's death. She let it slide. If only because he would deny it, and she wasn't in the mood to fight with him.

"Tell me about your fiancée. What was her name?" She'd wanted to ask since the moment he'd mentioned her at the church.

"There's nothing much to tell. Her name was Caroline. We were in Afghanistan together. She was killed by an IED. Now it's your turn. Are you divorced, separated, or what?"

She stored that bit of information and allowed him to change the subject. "No, I've never been married."

"What about Logan's father?"

"I got pregnant in high school."

"Seriously, I can't picture you as a pregnant teen, but I guess it makes sense. You're pretty young to have a teenage son."

"Logan's father, Oliver, was the tempting bad boy, and I was the good girl." She made light of it, but at the time, sex with the school troublemaker had been an irresistible thrill ride. He'd dumped her the moment she discovered she was pregnant, leaving her embarrassed and humiliated.

"So how did it happen?"

Her mouth fell open at his question, and it was a moment before she recovered enough to answer. "Do you mean how did I get pregnant? I'm not going to draw you a diagram. It happened in the usual way. There were no miracles or test tubes involved."

He laughed, the sound warming her insides. Once again, she was struck by how different he was from her preconceived notion. Then an idea hit her, like a fist slamming into her chest. She had to concentrate on her breathing so she didn't pass out while driving. She'd been chasing an illusion—the fictional persona of Timothy Morgan the criminal. It was a story kept alive by people like Booley. No one in Hopefalls knew who he was because he had limited his contact with the town since his return three years ago. Maybe it was time she put all her assumptions aside and got to know the real man.

Chapter Nineteen

Dana drove a little slower than the speed limit on the way to pick up Eva. She wasn't in any rush to deal with the widow's unpleasantness. Although, to be fair, Eva had been blindsided. At no time had Tim mentioned his plan to take her for counseling. That was something he really should have told her, but then again, she might not have listened. She was so set on having sex with someone—anyone. As a cop, Dana had seen the seedier side of life and knew there were a lot of men who would think nothing of exploiting a grieving woman. Tim had proved himself a gentleman.

"Are you taking your time?" he asked, smiling.

"That obvious, huh? I understand why you wanted me around."

"It got uglier than I thought it would. I hadn't seen her since before Frank died. When I stopped at the diner, I thought I was visiting an old friend and paying my respects."

"And you had no idea she had the hots for you?"

His green eyes slanted to her. "God, no."

"She was pretty upset with you."

"I hope that was just the grief talking, and once some time has passed, she'll understand."

Dana parked at the sidewalk in front of the church. Eva wasn't outside. They found Father Meade in the meeting room, stacking chairs.

"Did Eva already leave?" Tim asked.

The priest shook his head. "She left before the meeting got started. You can't make people accept help."

"Any idea where she went?"

"There's a bar two blocks over. I'd start there."

They walked the two blocks in silence until they saw a sign over a large oak door that read *Moose Call Saloon*. The smell of stale beer hit them before they opened the doors.

The interior was just one small windowless room with a dark wooden bar that ran along one wall. The floor was covered in a carpet so filthy it stuck to the soles of their shoes as they walked.

Eva sat at the end of the bar flirting with a large, sweaty man. He wore a light gray suit, white shirt, and red tie. Eva unfastened the man's tie and tugged it slowly, seductively from his neck. Then she knocked back a shooter of amber-colored liquor.

Tim tapped her on the shoulder. "It's time to go."

"I'm not leaving," she said over her shoulder and then turned back to the man in the suit.

"I promised your uncle I'd get you home safe," Dana added.

Eva glanced at her. "Look at you, miss shit-hot police woman. You think you're so cool because he"—she nodded her head toward Tim—"looks at you like he'd like to eat you."

Dana didn't react to Eva's words. She wanted to believe Tim was as attracted to her as she was to him, but that was something she would explore later.

Tim moved the shot glass out of her reach. "I think you've had enough to drink."

"No, I haven't had nearly enough," Eva slurred.

Tim pinched the bridge of his nose and then said. "Frank's only been dead—"

"Why the hell should you care how long he's been dead?"

"He was my friend."

"Friend? He was a lying, cheating asshole. That's what he was. Do you know what he did? Do you?" She slid off her stool and poked Tim in the chest. "He stole that stop sign up on the ridge and blamed you. Then he persuaded you to run away so you'd look guilty."

Dana gasped. Frank Bryant had killed beautiful, vivacious Aunt Alice, and Tim had suffered for a crime he didn't commit. He'd been wrongly accused. His life and future had been destroyed, and all along he'd been innocent, blameless.

Tim's face paled. His whole body stiffened. "Frank stole the stop sign? Were you with him?"

Eva smirked. "What do you—"

"Were you with him?" Tim roared as he grabbed Eva by the shoulders.

"Yes," she spat and then smiled. She seemed to enjoy hurting him.

Dana touched his shoulder, in part to offer support, and in part to remind him to show restraint. As much as she wanted to arrest Eva for manslaughter, protecting Tim from his own reaction was her top priority. She didn't want him to do something stupid and end up in jail.

He glanced at her. His face was rigid, except for his jaw, which twitched. High spots of color appeared on his cheeks. It seemed to take a supreme effort for him to release his grip on Eva. He fisted his hands by his side. His muscles coiled so tight he trembled, probably from the effort to suppress his response.

"You ruined my life," he hissed through clenched teeth.

Dana tugged his elbow, trying to pull him away.

Instead, he stepped closer, forcing Eva to back up until she was pinned against the bar. "I lived on the street. I was hungry." The muscle in his jaw twitched again.

Dana didn't like this. It would be easy for the situation to spin out of control. She yanked his arm again. "Eva has admitted she was involved in manslaughter. Let me deal with it."

Eva gasped. She finally seemed to realize she'd confessed her guilt in front of a witness, who was also a cop.

He glared at Eva for what seemed like an hour but was probably only a minute. Finally, he stepped back, his movements forced, contained. He turned, not making eye contact with Dana and marched out of the bar.

****

Tim was stunned. Frank and Eva had killed Alice Hayden, lied about it, and then used him as a scapegoat. And worse, Frank had pretended to be his friend and kept in touch.

He didn't know how he found his way to Dana's truck. Maybe she guided him.

She was quiet on the road back to Hopefalls, which was just as well because he was too angry to talk. It was lucky Frank was already dead because Tim would have beaten the crap out of him if he were alive.

There was some relief mixed in with all the anger. Frank and Eva had caused Alice Hayden's death. "Tell me you heard that?"

Dana frowned. "Heard what?"

His breathing hitched in a moment of panic. "You heard Eva say—"

"She and Frank stole the stop sign. I told you in the bar I heard it. Eva's a nasty piece of work. I can only think she and Frank must've been well suited for each other."

"So I have a witness?"

"I told you that, too." She smiled and placed her hand over his. "You have a witness."

They pulled up next to his truck at the diner. It was early evening. The sun, sinking behind the mountains to the west, cast gold and pink rays across the sky.

Tim opened the door before she came to a complete stop. He wanted to call Finn and get some advice on how to deal with this. But more importantly, he needed some time alone to absorb this news, away from Dana's astute gaze.

She scrambled to follow him. Tim climbed into his Ford as she caught up. She placed her body between the truck and the door so he couldn't close it. "Let me deal with this. I'll start legal proceedings against Eva."

"Eva is Booley's niece. She will never be charged."

"Tell me something, how did Booley get involved with this case in the first place? The ridge is the other side of your land in Elkhead County."

"What are you saying?"

"It comes under the jurisdiction of the Granite City-Elkhead County Police Department. Booley should never have been involved in the investigation."

He stood, pressing her against the open door. "You really are something." He bent his head and pressed his mouth to hers.

She opened her soft lips with a sigh.

That was his undoing. He'd kissed her on impulse. His attraction to her had gnawed at the back of his mind since yesterday, but she was off limits, a cop, and Alice Hayden's niece. Now he was free, free of the insinuation of guilt and the repercussions that went with it. He could indulge. He wrapped his arms around her slim, toned body, drawing her closer. Her small breasts touched his chest. He plunged his tongue into her mouth, feeling, probing, tasting, deepening their kiss.

She responded, wrapping a leg around his hips so his erection was pressed against the apex of her thighs.

A frisson of pleasure coursed through him. He reached under her shirt to caress the bare skin of her back. She groaned into his mouth.

He wanted her, wanted her naked beneath him while he moved within her warm moist flesh.

She tensed, going rigid, and wrenched herself away.

His arms fell to his side. "Sorry, I didn't mean to—" Didn't mean to what? He'd meant to kiss her. She was smart, sexy-as-hell, and direct, plus he loved the way she subconsciously tugged at her hair.

"No, it's not that." She glanced around, biting her lip, seeming self-conscious. "I-I don't want to get carried away…here." She pointed to the ground.

They were in the diner parking lot, acting like a couple of teenagers. There would be a right time and place for them, but this wasn't it. He rubbed a hand over the stubble on his chin. "Point taken."

She smiled. "Tim Morgan, you sure know how to show a woman an interesting time."

He climbed in, tugged his seatbelt across his chest, snapping it in place, and then started his truck. "*Interesting* is a good word for it."

She didn't step out of the way so he could close the door. Instead, she moved closer, her hand stroking his knee. "I need you to promise me something."

"What?" He liked that she continued to touch him. It meant he hadn't overstepped.

"Go straight home and don't return to Hopefalls until you hear from me." Her gray eyes were serious, intent.

"Why?"

"I need to confront Booley. After that, I'm going to present my case to the mayor. I also want to get some advice from Montana's Attorney General's Office." She ran her fingers through her hair, making the shorter strands stand on end.

He wasn't sure if it was a sign of frustration or if she was thinking.

She headed to the driver's side of her truck, raising her voice so he could still hear her. "I need to get this out in the open. And I want to do it tonight before Eva has a chance to convince everyone we're lying."

He sat in his truck, watching her drive down the block to the Hopefalls Police Station. After being labeled a killer for so long, it was hard to believe the facts would come out and everything would change. Even if Eva recanted her story and they could never prove the truth, it was good to know that for a brief moment, Dana believed in him.

Chapter Twenty

Dana pulled up to the police station. She planned to talk with Xavier and apprise him of the situation. Then she would call the Attorney General's office. It was Sunday evening and doubted anyone would be available, but she would leave a message, start the paperwork, and send an email.

Her phone rang. Xavier's number appeared on the screen. She answered on the first ring. Without waiting for him to talk, she said, "You'll never believe what happened."

"Y-you need to get to the town hall." Xavier's voice shook.

Dana was instantly alert. "Why, what's going on?"

"Booley has called an emergency town meeting. He and the mayor have been working themselves into a lather all day. He wants to arrest Tim Morgan. I don't mind arresting a guilty man and bringing him to justice, but I don't think that's what Booley has in mind."

"Come on, Xavier, when was the last time you heard of a lynch mob?" There had to be some kind of mistake. Booley hated Tim but executing him in an act of mob violence was extreme.

"I grew up in New York. I've seen things like this get out of control. I need you to back me up." The young officer's voice was clipped and urgent.

"I'm next door." She climbed out of her truck. "And on my way." She clicked off the phone and started running. Thank God, Tim had gone home. With any luck, she could diffuse the situation before things got out of hand.

Xavier stood at the door, his hand on his gun, fear in his young eyes. The town hall was a simple affair, just one large room. A plain white podium stood at the far end opposite the door. The rest of the space was filled with stackable chairs. Now most of the seats were scattered and turned on their sides. The room was packed, the noise of angry voices deafening.

Mrs. Anderson stood nose to nose with Booley, both of them screaming at the top of their lungs. Zoe Harris shrieked at a tall, slim man in a knit hat who looked familiar. He could be one of the protesters. Joe Freeman, the postmaster, stood with his arms crossed, scowling at Booley. And Paul Harris, the mayor, stood on the podium, watching the proceedings. Not once did he bang his gavel to ask for silence.

Shelly approached Dana. "Stop this."

Dana didn't try to yell over the noise. Instead she dragged a chair to the center of the room and stood on it, waiting for everyone to quiet down.

Finally, they all stopped to stare at her.

"What the hell is going on here?" She spoke to the room, but stared directly at Booley, waiting for him to answer.

He cleared his throat. "A group of us are going to drive to Wind Valley Ranch. It's time we dealt with Tim Morgan."

"You'll do no such thing," Mrs. Anderson snapped.

The room erupted again.

"Enough," Dana roared. One of the advantages of being big and strong was that she was also loud.

She waited until everyone was still, and then she said, "Booley, if you try to do this, I will arrest you and make sure you are charged to the full extent of the law. I will also charge anyone who aids you."

"It's time he got his comeuppance. I'd have thought you'd want to join us, considering he killed your aunt."

A hum of agreement resonated around the room.

"What about Eva? Are you going to arrest her?" The question came out of the blue, but Dana wanted to blindside him and see how much he knew.

"She hasn't done anything..." Booley looked at the ground and then back at Dana. "Zoe said he took her—"

"I told you he took her to grief counseling at St. Mark's church. You can check with Father Meade if you don't believe me." She made sure her words were clear so everyone could hear.

"Oh." Booley's face reddened.

"He left her there and went to see his father, Jack."

Booley grunted at the mention of Jack's name.

"He's a good son," Mrs. Anderson announced with a nod.

Dana jumped down from the chair and strode over to the police chief. They were about the same height. She straightened her spine and squared her shoulders, making herself as tall and imposing as possible. It was time to confront him about what really happened nineteen years ago. "Are you going to arrest Eva for manslaughter?"

"What—"

She poked his chest. "Don't tell me you didn't know."

He paled and backed up a step. "I didn't—"

She poked him again, wishing she could drive her fist into his misogynistic, corrupt face. "How could you not know? And the fact you haven't asked what I'm talking about speaks volumes."

He shook his head. "They were just kids. It was meant to be a harmless prank."

Dana gasped. She hadn't thought she would get him to admit his collusion so easily. She seized the opportunity to set the record straight. She turned to the residents, who seemed mesmerized by the exchange. "Today Eva Bryant admitted, in front of me, that on the night of Alice Hayden's death, Frank and Eva Bryant stole a stop sign from Wind Valley Ridge. Then Frank Bryant convinced Tim Morgan the police were about to arrest him and persuaded him to run away. Chief Booley has just admitted, in front of all of you, that he knew Tim Morgan was innocent."

Booley's eyes narrowed into two hate-filled slits. "He was never innocent. He was sleeping with all the girls, leading them astray. We were better off without him."

Dana stepped closer, invading his personal space, forcing him to back up. "There has to be more to it than that. I find it hard to believe you would destroy a family and ruin a kid's life because he slept with a few girls."

Mrs. Anderson came at them from the side, forcing her way into their conflict. "You're right." She pointed to Booley. "He was always besotted with Jack's wife, Georgina, but she was never interested. She loved Jack and that was that."

That explained everything. Booley hadn't just been protecting his niece; he'd used the circumstances to punish the woman who'd rejected him.

Dana strode to Mayor Harris who stood unmoving on the podium. "Are you going to fire Police Chief Levi Booley?"

The mayor blinked. His mouth hung open, seemingly stunned by the turn of events. "I need to look into this matter. Chief Booley has served this community for thirty years. He deserves the benefit of the doubt."

Dana couldn't believe her ears. "Doubt? There is no doubt. He just admitted to a miscarriage of justice." She looked around the room. She estimated there were at least twenty people present. She recognized most of the faces, the mayor's wife, Joe Freeman from the post office, Jeff Spencer who owned the gas station. Then there was Mrs. Anderson, a woman who Dana had obviously misjudged.

She bounced back onto her chair in the middle of the room. "You all heard him. What if Tim Morgan was your son? How would you feel then? I'm calling Montana's Attorney General tomorrow about the chief's conduct. Then I'll call the Granite City-Elkhead County police—"

"Why call them?" Joe Freeman asked.

"Because Aunt Alice died on the ridge, and that's in Elkhead County. This case comes under the jurisdiction of the Granite City-Elkhead County Police Department. Booley should never have been a part of the investigation."

"Good luck with that, missy. It'll be your word against mine," Booley spat.

Dana sucked in a breath. "Until this moment, I was proud to be a police officer. I serve and protect the community. I bring criminals to justice, and when investigating a case, I follow the evidence. I don't frame the innocent. I obey the law. I don't make it up. I don't lie and manipulate public opinion to protect my family. And I most certainly don't whip people into a frenzy. What were you going to do, kill him?"

"I'm still the police chief until the mayor fires me." Booley gave her a cold smile.

"Yes, you are, but I quit. She unclipped her badge, jumped off the chair, and thrust it at Booley. Justice was not just a word to her or an ideological argument. It was at the core of her being. The impartiality, honesty, and fairness her position represented mattered. If her badge didn't stand for that, she didn't want it.

The chief's mouth curved into a sneer. "I want your gun, too."

She pulled her SIG Sauer from her holster and clicked the button that released the magazine, allowing it to slide free of the frame. She racked the slide back to eject the cartridge and then checked the barrel to ensure it was empty. She threw it on the floor at his feet.

Booley didn't bend to pick up the weapon but stared at her instead. Every muscle, every sinew was coiled tight ready to spring. An intelligent woman would back away, but at this moment she was more angry than smart. This man had destroyed a family because a woman had rejected him. He had perverted justice to satisfy his own need for revenge and to protect Eva. She didn't know if he would pay for his crimes, but she could, at least, tell the people of Hopefalls what he'd done. "Do you know what you did to him?"

"Who?"

"Tim Morgan. Do you know where he went when he ran away?"

Booley shrugged as if it were unimportant.

"He lived on the streets of Granite City. He was hungry and cold. Think of how it must've been in winter. When you were tucked up in your bed, he was sleeping in doorways. All because you"—she pointed to Booley—"needed someone to blame."

She heard Mrs. Anderson gasp, but didn't turn to look at her. Instead, Dana continued to glare at the police chief.

Booley said nothing, his face blank.

"And then when most men would have turned to a life of crime, what did he do?" She didn't wait for an answer. "He joined the army and became a Ranger. Despite everything you've done to him, he's still a man of integrity."

From the corner of her eye, she saw Joe Freeman straighten. Hopefalls was a small Montana town, a place where service to one's country still meant something.

"Sounds like you're sweet on him," Zoe Harris said. There was something in her eyes, a malevolence, that made Dana take a step back. This was a side to the mayor's wife she hadn't seen before. Zoe had always seemed meek, a woman who deferred to her husband, but perhaps that was wrong. Maybe Zoe Harris was a force to be reckoned with, a woman who shouldn't be underestimated.

Dana's whole body tensed. She refused to back down. This man had corrupted everything she believed in. "Didn't I just tell you my feelings don't matter? I've always been a cop first. If Tim Morgan killed Ben North, then he will be brought to justice. But it is not right to blame him because it's convenient. The case is in the hands of Detective Ramirez and the Granite City-Elkhead County Police Department. Let them do their job. I don't even know if they have the autopsy results yet. Then there'll be toxicology and any number of other tests to run."

"And fingerprints?" Mrs. Anderson added. "That takes longer in real life than it does on those TV shows."

"Yes, that's right," Dana agreed. But Booley, Paul, and Zoe Harris had contaminated the scene. Could Booley have killed Ben North? Ben's connection to the Morgans went back decades. Maybe Ben knew something about the night Aunt Alice died and had been killed because of it.

Xavier stood next to her. "Let's go."

Shelly joined them at the door.

The three of them walked out amidst murmurs from the crowd.

****

Tim melded into the shadows of the parking lot. He'd been halfway to Wind Valley when Shelly Pearson had called and warned him Booley was on the rampage. He'd stood at the door to the town hall and watched while Dana had gone nose to nose with her boss. And then she'd quit, handing in her badge and gun. He hadn't hidden then. He didn't need to. Everyone was so fixated on the drama unfolding in front of them they hadn't seen him. He understood their fascination.

He was a little overwhelmed by what he'd just seen, and he had no idea what he would say to Dana the next time they talked. She'd resigned because of him. Who would've thought?

He watched her shake hands with her fellow police officer, who turned and headed toward the police station next door. Tim didn't know his name. Then she hugged Shelly, an old friend of his mother's.

Maybe her resignation had less to do with him personally and more to do with the fact that Booley had misused his position. She had quit her job because staying would violate her principles. That was something he understood, and on an emotional level, it made it easier to deal with because he wasn't responsible.

Mrs. Anderson spotted him in the shadows of the tree-lined parking lot. He could never get anything over on her even when he was in second grade. "Shelly warned you to get out of town, not run head-on into danger."

"I was a Ranger. Running into danger is what I'm good at."

She smiled and shook her head. "You always did have more spirit than sense. I'm heading to Granite City tomorrow afternoon. I'll pop in and see Jack while I'm there."

"He'll like that. Thanks for taking the time."

"Oh, it's no problem. There's a group of us who visit Shady Pines on a regular basis."

"Was Ben one of them?" Tim didn't really know why he asked, but it somehow seemed important to know more about his father's friendship with his neighbor.

"I saw him there a few weeks ago. It's funny how people are. Jack and Ben had an on-again, off-again friendship. They could fight like wild dogs, but when push came to shove, they respected each other. I think Ben missed your father."

Tim kissed Mrs. Anderson's wrinkled cheek. "Thanks."

She blushed like a schoolgirl but was smiling as she walked away.

"That's what I get for hiring a whore." Booley pointed at Dana as he stomped down the steps of the town hall.

Dana stood with Shelly in the middle of the lot. She squared her shoulders and turned to face her tormentor.

"Maybe you'll spread your legs for me, too," Booley shouted as he strode toward her.

Tim moved to intercept Booley, but Dana held up her hand, telling him to halt. He stopped six feet from the police chief. "That's enough."

Dana's hands curled into fists. "Tim, stay out of this."

"I see you called in the cavalry," Booley barked as he came to a standstill in front of Dana. "Too weak to fight your own battles, are you?"

Tim said nothing. He was close enough that he could take out Booley if need be, but Dana obviously had a plan and he would let her handle the situation...within reason.

Stragglers from the meeting gathered in the parking lot watching.

Dana shook her head. "Levi, don't do this. I have committed no crime. If you attack me, I will defend myself and you will get hurt. Walk away now."

"You think you're a shit-hot police woman."

"Compared to you, yes I am," Dana said. "Now walk away."

Booley moved fast. He stepped forward and tried to punch Dana.

She blocked his punch with one arm and used her palm to strike him twice in the chin. He stumbled, then regained his balance and pulled his fist back, ready to hit her again. Before he could strike, she used her cupped hands to box his ears. Booley yelped in pain and fell to the side, a small amount of blood leaching from his left ear.

The young police officer came running across the lot. "What the hell happened?"

"Booley attacked me," Dana panted. She was probably out of breath from the adrenalin spike rather than exertion.

"You fucking bitch!" Booley shrieked.

"Mind your language." Tim had seen a lot of street fights in his life. Mostly the participants slugged it out until they ran out of energy and could be broken apart. Dana's blows had been fast and deliberate. With very little effort, she had disabled Booley and had avoided becoming embroiled in a fistfight.

"Arrest him. Charge him with attacking Officer Hayden," Joe Freeman demanded.

The remaining citizens voiced their agreement.

The young officer pulled his cuffs from his belt. "Sounds like a plan." He grabbed one of Booley's hands and twisted it behind his back. Before the police chief had a chance to fight, the officer threw him against a parked car and had both hands cuffed.

The policeman nodded at Dana. "You showed great restraint. If it was me, I'd have broken his nose."

"Thanks, Xavier." Dana smiled at the young officer.

He hauled the still screaming police chief toward the station.

Dana turned to Tim, hands on hips. Everything about her, from her stance to the way she ground her teeth, told him she was angry. "We need to get something straight. When I'm dealing with a degenerate, you will back off and let me handle it."

He tried not to smile at her choice of words. He didn't want to annoy her further, and he had no idea why she was upset. Most people would be happy to know someone had their back. "You expect me to stand back and let you get hurt."

"I expect you to allow me to do my job and not interfere. I can handle myself."

This headstrong, determined, adept woman was the whole package. It was hard to believe that just yesterday he'd thought to tease her and have some fun, but she wasn't a woman to be toyed with. She followed her own moral code and had done what was right. She had given up her career because she stood for more than just a badge. Something inside him had shifted. This wasn't just a physical attraction. He respected her, and that made her special.

She was a police officer, which meant she was highly trained and supremely capable. That was probably why she was mad at him. She didn't need him to undermine her position. "I was raised to believe a real man protected women, but you're not just any woman. You're a cop. It's something I'll have to remember."

She tilted her head to one side and studied him. What she saw he couldn't say. "Apology accepted."

He winked. "You'd make a good Ranger." As words of love went, it wasn't much, but it was the highest compliment he could give. And then he walked away, heading for his truck. He inhaled the cool spring air. Everyone in Hopefalls knew he wasn't responsible for Alice Hayden's death. He was free from the allegations that had haunted him for nineteen years, free of Booley, and most importantly, he was free to pursue Dana Hayden.

Chapter Twenty-One

Ethan Moore sat at the window of Lance Ackerman's fifth-story upscale Granite City hotel room. All he could see was the inky black darkness of the wilderness at night. "Nice view."

Lance Ackerman, his boss, collapsed into the armchair opposite and rested a foot on the coffee table that lay between them. The rolls of his stomach jiggled as he made himself comfortable. "I don't give a shit about the scenery. I came here to close a deal on a coltan mine, and now everything's gone to shit."

The two-bedroom suite was large with a hardwood floor, a full kitchen with granite countertops, and two luxurious bathrooms, but Ethan new from previous experience that Ackerman was used to more opulent surroundings.

As the Syndicate's man, Ethan received a generous allowance. Most of the time, his duties involved payoffs and blackmail, but on occasion, when he was lucky, he got to slice someone.

He fixed his gaze on his boss. "The town hall meeting was a disaster."

Ackerman shifted in his chair. "Really?"

"It seems the police chief has been covering up a crime committed by his niece."

"And this affects me, how?"

"It weakened the mayor's position."

Ackerman's sharp eyes focused on him. "Why?"

Ethan shrugged. "I'm not sure. There were calls to fire the chief, but Harris refused."

"Do you think this policeman has something on him?"

"That would be my guess. It's obvious the cop's a two-bit criminal. Harris should have got rid of him on the spot. The fact he didn't was pretty damning. People are going to ask questions."

Ackerman gave a dismissive wave. "Let them ask. We have a strong position, and it doesn't matter if the whole town's against us. We have the law on our side."

They fell silent. A vein pulsed in Ackerman's temple as he thought through the complexities. He wasn't a man of great intelligence, but he was insightful. He could size up someone's weaknesses, flaws, limitations, and ambitions in an instant, and then use those traits against them. It was his perceptive ability that enabled him to be so successful. "Do you think the cop killed North?"

"I don't know. But I don't think so. I saw the mayor's wife going up Molly's Mountain, and within an hour, the chief and the mayor were riding up there together. But that could all be for show."

"How'd you mean?"

"There's a maze of back roads that run through the property. They could've killed North and then backtracked to the main road to make it appear as if they had come from town."

Ackerman's cell phone buzzed. "This is my private line." He answered on the second ring. Ethan stayed where he was. It wasn't his job to anticipate Ackerman's needs. If his boss wanted privacy for his call, he would ask.

"I need to speak with you." The caller's voice was so loud, Ethan could hear it clearly.

"Is this Paul Harris? How did you get this number?" Ackerman barked.

"Look, things are happening—"

"I said, who gave you this number?" Ackerman insisted.

"L-Lucy." The mayor's panic was evident.

"Damn. What do you want?"

"Chief Booley has accused me of doctoring deeds at the Elkhead County Records Office in order to help you."

"He said this out of the blue? Why?"

"I'm being forced to fire him."

"Who gives a shit?" Ackerman's lip curled in a sneer.

"Lucy said you would help."

"I don't see that this is any of my business."

"If Booley knows about me, then he knows about you, too." The implication being that the ex-police chief would tell the authorities that Ackerman didn't own the mineral rights to Molly's Mountain.

None of this was a revelation to Ethan. He had assumed the deal had been secured either through bribery or forgery. It was how Ackerman did business. He knew the right people and was a man of unlimited funds. He could get whatever he wanted. And when things didn't go to plan…that was when Ethan stepped in.

Ackerman's eyes narrowed. "I have a man on the ground who'll take care of it." He nodded toward Ethan.

"What are you going to do? I don't want to be part of a murder." The mayor's voice had climbed another octave.

"Then why did you kill Ben?" Ackerman was gauging the weakling's reaction.

"I-I-I didn't. That wasn't me."

"So you say."

"Are you going to kill Booley?"

Ethan couldn't believe the residents of Hopefalls had voted for this idiot. Hadn't he ever heard of plausible deniability?

Ackerman rolled his eyes. "Murder is messy. I don't kill people. This Booley character is just shaking you down. He wants a payoff. I'll take the money I pay him out of your share."

Ethan knew that was a lie. Ackerman used coercion to get what he wanted, but he didn't like to be on the receiving end and always dealt with blackmailers the same way. If the past were anything to go by, the police chief would soon be dead. And if the mayor didn't dig deep and find a backbone, he would die, too. If only because he was too spineless to be trusted.

"Did you murder Ben?" The tremor in Harris's voice rang out loud and clear. This man really didn't have the stones to be part of the Syndicate.

"No, you idiot, I didn't murder Ben," he shouted down the phone. His face was red with anger. "Why the hell would I? We can't move forward now he's dead. His estate could be tied up for years. But I'd be tempted to kill the person who did him in."

Ackerman disconnected and threw the phone on the coffee table. "I want the police chief taken care of immediately."

Ethan stood and smiled. This was what he'd been waiting for. "And the mayor?"

"Not yet. We might still need him." Ackerman rubbed his stubby hand over his jaw. "The trouble is the damn environmental studies are kicking my butt on this. Who cares it there's some precious plant on North's land? If I had my way, I'd burn the whole damn place to the ground."

"Let's call that plan B." He knew how to set fires. They were fun, but they didn't give him the same high as slicing and dicing.

"See if you can blame this police chief's death on the neighbor."

"Morgan?"

"That's the one. If I can't mine the tantalum from Molly's Mountain, then I might be able to tunnel to it from his ranch."

"Rumor has it that he needs money and is desperate to sell," Ethan supplied.

Ackerman shrugged. "And if he's in jail, I'll get it for a bargain."

Ethan headed for the door.

"Do you like this Morgan guy?" Ackerman asked.

Ethan stopped with his hand on the doorknob. "I don't like anyone, you know that, but I'd screw him if he were inclined. Unfortunately, he isn't."

To say he enjoyed killing would be to underestimate his euphoric reaction to taking a life, but there were two things he refused to do, even for the Syndicate. He would never kill a child and he refused to rape anyone. It wasn't good business. The police were more apt to hunt down criminals who killed children, and rape was just messy. Luckily for him, the Syndicate was unlikely to ask him to perform those crimes. They were strictly about money, which suited him perfectly.

Ackerman nodded his understanding. "I might need you to fake it with Lucy."

Ethan stopped again. Lucy Portman was a founding member of the Syndicate. There was no way Ackerman could order her death without a consensus from the other members. "When will you know?"

"It'll take me a few days to arrange a meeting, but something has to be done. Her sex addiction is getting out of hand. And I can't believe she gave that sniveling idiot my phone number." He thumped the arm of his chair. "None of us complained when she invited her husband to join the group. Marshall was successful in his own right. But the man had a soft streak. We all give to charity. It's expected. But Marshall took it a step further and got personally involved. The whole fiasco last winter with Dr. Wilson was Portman's doing. Now the world knows about that damn solar panel."

Ethan didn't say anything, just stood there with his hand on the door handle. Adrenalin zinged through his veins. Two murders.

Ackerman droned on. "And now she has another man in tow, and she gave the moron my phone number. I'll have to dump this phone and get another one."

None of Ackerman's bluster mattered. All Ethan needed were his instructions. "Am I to assume my role as a protester causing public mischief is over?"

"Tired of sleeping in a tent and wreaking havoc on Hopefalls?" Ackerman raised an eyebrow in question.

Ethan shrugged. It wasn't the tent that got to him. It was the withdrawal. He hadn't carved anyone in months. The fact that Ben North had been killed while he'd been cooking eggs and pretending to care about the environment irked him. He wanted to see blood spurt from a body. He needed the high of knowing he had the power of life and death over another human being.

"We'll be leaving this God forsaken backwoods soon. Be prepared to go at a moment's notice," Ackerman said.

"Of course." He bowed his head in a fake show of humility. "You'll contact me about Lucy?"

Ackerman waved an arm, dismissing him as he walked to his bedroom.

Ethan exited the room, excitement pulsing through his body. He was going to kill someone. He couldn't wait.

Chapter Twenty-Two

Tim smiled as Logan opened the front door to Dana's house. "How are you?"

Dana had called him and left a voicemail, asking if she could talk to his dad. He could've phoned her back, but he wanted to see her, pursue her. Everything had changed last night. He had seen who she really was. She wasn't just a cop. She was a warrior for justice, and he had yearned for justice for most of his adult life. That revelation came to him at three in the morning. He hadn't slept. Visions of her had ravaged his mind. With her, he could see a future, a home, and the family he'd always wanted. If someone had told him a week ago he'd be interested in having a relationship with a Hopefalls policewoman he would have thought they were crazy, and yet here he was, standing at her door.

Logan grunted, his sleepy eyes blinking. He mumbled something unintelligible, his slim frame sagging as if staying upright was too much work. Blue hair stuck out at odd angles. He wore a crumpled, old T-shirt and a pair of sweatpants.

Tim followed the teen into the kitchen and took a seat at the table. Logan grabbed a jug of orange juice from the fridge.

The table was piled with an assortment of newspapers, sketches, and dirty dishes. He picked up a black drawing of a bear. The amount of effort that had gone into the artwork was impressive. Thousands of minute pen strokes merged to make the final picture. He guessed it was Logan's work. He could be wrong, but somehow he couldn't imagine direct, practical Dana taking the time to draw. "It's Monday. Aren't you going to school today?"

"Sure, what time is it?"

"Eight."

"Shit, I'm late." Logan left the juice on the counter and hurried down a short hallway that presumably led to the bedrooms.

"I'll give you a ride if you like," Tim shouted after him.

"What are you doing here?" Dana called from behind a dark stained wood door that was in desperate need of painting.

"Good morning to you, too." Tim smiled, imagining her in a state of undress.

"Did you get my call?" She strode into the kitchen, wearing a white T-shirt and a pair of jeans. Her hair was damp and her skin pink as if she'd just climbed out of the shower.

He pictured her naked with water cascading over her breasts. His body reacted to the image. He was grateful his position at the table hid his erection from her. "You want to talk to Dad," he said, reaffirming her message.

"Is that a problem?" She placed the juice in the fridge and turned to face him, her hands on her hips. She glared at him, her nipples poking through her shirt, daring him to reach out and touch them.

He stood and closed the distance between them. He bent his head to whisper in her ear. "Maybe you should reconsider getting pissy with me because it's a real turn on, unless you want me to kiss you again. Or maybe you like the idea of me stripping you naked. Would you like me to suck your nipples?"

She licked her lips as her skin flushed. Her gray eyes focused on his crotch like a laser-guided missile. His breath hitched. He itched to touch her and feel her silky skin.

He turned away, thinking to put some distance between them, but she grabbed his arm and spun him around. She stared up at him, her mouth slightly parted.

He'd intended to seduce her with sweet words, but they lodged in his throat. His body ruled his mind. His urgent need overwhelmed his common sense. His mouth brushed over hers. Her lips parted, warm and inviting. He couldn't believe this was happening. He'd thought about it since the moment they'd met at the police station but considered her out-of-bounds. After last night, everything had changed. His tongue swept inside, claiming her for his own. A frisson of excitement zinged through his veins as he pushed her back against the refrigerator.

Her hands made their way under his T-shirt. The feel of her touch on his overheated flesh sent a rush of blood to his penis. His rock-hard cock pushed painfully against his zipper. He tugged up her shirt and shoved aside her bra. There was no subtlety to his actions. He clamped his lips over her nipple and sucked it into his mouth.

She arched, pushing deeper. He yanked her bra down on the other side releasing her other breast, massaging it.

"Hey Mom, have you seen my sketchbook?" Logan called from his bedroom.

The shout was more effective than a bucket of cold water. Tim jumped back and took a breath, fighting to control his lust.

Dana froze, her eyes wide.

Logan was home. The last thing he wanted was to have her kid walk in while he made love to Dana up against the fridge. Besides, this was all happening a lot faster than he'd planned. No, that wasn't true. He'd made his decision. Dana was the one for him. As far as he was concerned, there was no way they could move too fast, but he wasn't so sure about her feelings.

She'd been through a lot last night. There were things she had to sort out. He would be patient and go at her pace. "Why do you want to see my dad?" He stuffed his shirt into his pants. His voice sounded thick, which wasn't such a surprise considering he was still semi-erect. "He's sick and confused, and I don't like the idea of people badgering him."

She rearranged the straps of her bra so she was covered and tugged at the bottom of her top, smoothing it down. Her hard nipples poked through the fabric. "Everything that's going on here connects to Jack."

He distracted himself by tidying the table, hoping to hide his condition. "In what way?" He carried the dirty dishes over to the sink.

"The gun Ben was shot with was purchased jointly by Ben and Jack. By the way, who purchases a gun with someone else? I've never heard of that before."

He stuffed the plates into the dishwasher. "I think they considered it an investment. It was a limited edition. They never used it for target practice."

She rammed her arms into her leather jacket and did up the buttons, covering her breasts. Under the circumstances, it was probably best he couldn't see them. "What happened to it?"

He shrugged. "As I said, I was ten. I was into horses, football, running, and video games. What were you doing at that age?"

"Knitting."

"Really?" Now, that was a surprise. She was too tense, too active. He couldn't imagine her sitting still for long. He straightened and faced her. "Do you still knit?"

She smiled, still standing by the fridge, watching him, her gray eyes staring at his chest. "No, I turned twelve and moved on to make-up and boys and forgot all about it."

He wished they could talk about everyday things instead of death and drama, but unless they dealt with Ben's homicide, it would hang over them just like Alice Hayden's car accident had haunted him. He wanted a future with her and didn't see that happening unless he was cleared of Ben's murder. Until this homicide was solved, there would never be anything serious between them. He didn't want a fling. He wanted a chance at a real long-term relationship. "Okay, so apart from the gun, there's nothing else that leads back to Dad."

"Yes, there is. There's you, Tim. Everything Booley did to you was to get back at your dad because your mom picked him."

Tim flashed to the image of his mother's sad eyes as they glistened with tears. "I think Booley hurt Mom more than anyone else." She had lost him at fifteen. He hadn't realized until the death of Caroline, his fiancée, just how much the loss of a loved one would hurt. He hadn't died, but he was gone from his mother's life, and the time they'd missed could never be recovered.

"No argument from me there. If he'd done that to Logan, I probably would have killed him." She flexed her fingers as if she were getting ready for a fight.

"Have you called the authorities?" Tim said, changing the subject. He didn't want to think about the pain his mother had gone through.

"Yes, I called Montana's Attorney General, the Elkhead County prosecutor, and the Granite City-Elkhead County Police Department and left messages with all three. Once I've talked to them, I'll have to take a step back and leave them to it. I'm not a cop anymore." She frowned as she looked down at her hands. She'd been a policewoman for twelve years, all her adult life. She was probably adrift and didn't know what to do next. That was the real reason behind her wanting to see Jack. She needed something to take her mind off the events of last night and the reality of being unemployed. That worked for him. He wanted nothing more than to spend time with her and get to know her.

She straightened away from the fridge, pulling herself up, dismissing whatever thoughts had clouded her mind. "The nurse said he's more lucid after his morning exercise. I thought he might be able to tell me more about the gun."

"As you just said, you're not a cop anymore," he pointed out, wanting her to know her limitations.

She blushed. "No, but I will be again. It's all I know. It's who I am."

He understood. He used to feel like that about the Rangers, but he'd left to care for his dad and had found a new life.

Logan appeared. He was wearing a pair of black jeans and a black T-shirt with a tear down the middle. His long hair slanted over his eyes. "Can I still get a ride?"

"Sure." Tim pointed to Dana. "Do you have any coffee?"

"She makes crappy coffee," Logan said as he opened the front door.

Dana caught up with her son and kissed his cheek. "I'll pay attention to the scoops and the cups this time. Listen, come straight home tonight. We need to talk."

"About what?"

"What we're going to do now that I'm out of a job."

"I don't want to fucking move again." Logan headed for Tim's truck. He climbed in and slammed the door after him.

Tim walked to the driver's side and leaned in the open window. "I understand you're upset, but when you talk to your mom like that, it really pisses me off."

Logan shrugged. "This has nothing to do with you."

He had a point. Logan's relationship with Dana was none of Tim's business. But Tim didn't like the attitude, the lack of respect, and he especially didn't want Logan to think that it was okay to behave that way in front of him. Plus, if he was to have a relationship with Dana, he needed to get along with her son, and that wasn't going to happen if the kid didn't show his mother some respect.

"You're right. How you and your mom get along is none of my business, but I find it offensive when you behave like that in front of me."

Logan's lip curled in a sneer. "Like you said, it's none of your business."

"Get out of my truck." Tim gritted his teeth, his patience at an end.

"Why?"

"I'm not giving you a ride to school." He walked to the passenger side and yanked the door open.

"But I'll be late."

"You should've thought of that before you mouthed off. Get out." Tim pointed to the sidewalk, resisting the urge to grab his scrawny ass and haul him out.

"Fuck." Logan unbuckled his seatbelt.

"There you go again, swearing."

"I have a right to be angry. You don't know what it's like being the son of a cop. I never have any friends. If I behave, everyone thinks I'm a suck-up. And if I'm bad, everyone thinks I'm doing it to be a snitch."

"Why do you care what other people think?"

"That's rich coming from you."

The kid had him there. He'd felt the weight of the unproven allegations levied against him. They had been an oppressive burden. "You're right. I like it that people know I didn't kill you aunt—"

"Great aunt."

"Whatever."

Logan really was a smart-ass.

"My point is, I always had friends who knew the real me and liked me for myself. Be yourself. Some will hate you, others will like you." He grinned at the kid. "I mean, they won't like you that much because you're a real pain in the butt, but you'll get by."

Logan sighed and headed to the house. "I'll go and apologize to my mom."

"You're supposed to say sorry to me," Tim called after him.

Logan stopped and turned on his heel. "Why?"

"You swore in front of me. I don't like it." Tim struggled to keep a straight face.

The kid smiled. "You'll get over it."

****

In a town as small as Hopefalls, nothing was far away, and they reached the school in less than five minutes. The square building with a playground on one side and a football field on the other hadn't changed much since Tim's time there.

Logan tensed and didn't move to get out. Instead, he sat deep in thought.

"You're going to be late for school," Tim urged.

Logan kept his eyes on the floor, not looking up. "Mom seems tough, but she's not. If you're just playing around, looking for a good time, go elsewhere or I'll—"

"You'll what?" Tim wasn't going to let Logan threaten him, but at the same time he respected the kid for standing up for his mother.

Logan stared at Tim. His blue eyes were almost the same color as his hair. "I know you're tough, but she's my mom. I'm asking you not to mess with her. She's a good person, and she doesn't deserve—"

"Listen. I'm not going to promise to back off. I like your mom, but that doesn't mean something's going to happen."

Logan frowned. "So you're not interested?"

"I didn't say that. I have no idea what's going on between us. It's not up to me, and it's definitely not up to you. A gentleman should always leave the choice up to the woman."

Logan nodded as he absorbed that bit of wisdom and then stared out the window. "My dad did a real number on her. She fell in love with him, and I think he might have loved her…us, but he loved partying and drugs more."

Dana had mentioned she gotten pregnant as a teen but hadn't given any details.

"Where is he now?"

"He died when I was three from a drug overdose."

Tim inhaled. It had taken a lot of guts for Logan to have this man-to-man talk with him. It was only fair he be honest in return. "Look, your mom's a strong woman with a mind of her own. If a relationship develops between us—great, but you should know I come with a lot of baggage. I'm drowning in medical bills. Whatever happens, I can never marry her. Not because I want to play the field or anything like that. I can't saddle someone else with my debt. Plus, we're getting ahead of ourselves. We haven't even been on a date. And I have no idea if she's interested in me. I can promise I'll treat your mom with respect, and I'll be straight with her."

Logan held out his hand. "Good enough."

They shook hands. Despite the hair and the grouchy demeanor, Logan was a good son.

"Hey kid, one piece of advice," Tim said as Logan opened the passenger door.

He hesitated, half out of the truck. "What's that?"

"If you want to fit in, get a haircut."

"The hair thing again." He'd obviously heard it before.

"People here are very set in their ways. Once they get to know you, they'll like you."

"You sound like my mom."

"I'm not saying you shouldn't be yourself. I'm saying learn how to compromise. Cut it short and keep the blue."

Logan smiled. "I'll think about it."

Chapter Twenty-Three

Dana took a long last sip of her coffee as they drove along the Hopefalls Highway, heading to Shady Pines in Granite City.

She put a hand to her stomach to quell the queasiness that erupted every time she thought about last night. Everything in her life had changed. She might not have been emotionally fit for the position, but at least she'd had a job and a direction. Today she was out of work, and it looked like they would have to move.

One thing was sure; she should be looking for employment, not coming to talk to an Alzheimer's patient. Her motivation was a mystery, even to her. Was she visiting Jack because she wanted answers to Ben's death? Or was this just an excuse to spend more time with Tim? He'd kissed her this morning with an intensity that took her breath away. She'd never felt anything like that before. And when he looked at her it was as if he were caressing her with his gaze. She wanted to touch, explore, and discover every inch of his body and feel his warm skin under her fingertips. If it hadn't been for Logan, she would have made love to him right there on the kitchen floor.

But what about Ben's murder? Tim was still a suspect, and if she wanted to continue to serve in law enforcement, she couldn't be associated with a man suspected of murder.

Besides, this was all too soon. She'd only known him a couple of days and was already wondering what it would be like to lie next to him sweaty and complete after a bout of lovemaking. She suppressed a groan. She wasn't a game player. If she liked someone, she let him know.

She'd only had two relationships since Oliver's death. Both of them had been serious, or so she'd thought. But she hadn't introduced either of them to Logan. She'd kept her dating world separate from her home life. That was impossible with Tim. Dear God, Logan had practically introduced them. There was no division here, and she doubted Tim would tolerate her keeping an important part of her life from him.

She sighed as she watched the forested wilderness go by. She needed to get her act together and make the mental transition from cop to…what? She didn't know how to do anything else.

"You know you can find a different career," Tim said as if reading her mind.

"It's all I know. If I'm not a cop, I don't know who I am." Her coffee burned like acid in her stomach at the idea of not being a policewoman.

"What about the gun thing?"

"What gun thing?" she said, pretending she didn't have a problem.

He squinted at her as he slowly shook his head and then turned his gaze back to the road. "Who did you kill?"

The question should have surprised her, but it didn't. He knew she was lying, which made sense. He'd seen what a mess she was when she'd pulled her gun on him. And he was way too perceptive not to know what her reaction meant.

She shut her eyes, remembering every detail from that fateful night. "I was called to a bank robbery. His name was Alex Rowe. He walked into a bank wearing a vest wired with explosives and carrying a handgun. When things went south, he used a teller as a hostage and tried to walk out." She could picture him, sweating, screaming threats, with his gun pointed at the woman's head.

"And you shot him." He stated a fact, but to her it was so much more.

She'd trained and practiced at the firing range, making sure she was a good shot. But shooting at targets was very different from shooting at people. She continued, unable to stop. "He tripped. The teller ran. He raised his gun to shoot her."

"And you took him out so he couldn't kill the teller. Sounds justified."

"That's what my bosses said, but it was all fake." Her throat felt thick, constricted.

"Fake? What do you mean?"

"The gun wasn't loaded, and the explosives weren't real. He couldn't have killed anyone. I shot an unarmed man." She tried to keep the emotion out of her voice, but it still wobbled.

"Shit." He steered the truck to the side of the road and pulled her into his arms. He wasn't making a pass. He simply hugged her, giving her comfort, seeming to understand her torment.

She held him for a long time, saying nothing. She wanted to cry, but all her tears had been shed months ago. She would never know what motivated the robber to aim at the teller. It was possible he'd meant to kill himself, or perhaps it was a reflex. It was something she had to learn to deal with.

He rubbed his big warm hand down her back. It was as if he understood, and maybe he did.

"Did the same thing happen to you?" She turned to stare at the forest, embarrassed about her vulnerability. She forced herself to face him.

He shook his head, frowning. "No, my problem is worse than that."

"Worse?"

"I can kill without caring." He sat up in his seat, staring ahead unseeing.

"It must've been kill or be killed in Afghanistan."

"Yes, but I changed after Caroline died. I was a machine. It wasn't pretty. I didn't realize what I'd become until I was out." His voice was flat, as if he were reciting a grocery list.

"That's why you carry a knife." It was his way of avoiding confrontation. He was right. People were more scared of knives than guns.

He nodded. "It makes it harder to kill. With a knife, you're in close quarters. You can see the guys face and look him in the eye. You have to really mean it."

She nodded. After her experience, she understood. Taking a life should be difficult.

He guided the truck back onto the highway. His admission should've made her like him less, but it didn't. He'd been open and frank about who and what he was. He'd stated the facts, not to brag, but to let her know he understood.

No wonder she hadn't slept last night. It wasn't the town meeting or Booley's attack afterward. The kiss they'd shared in the diner parking lot had replayed through her mind. That and the fact he hadn't gotten angry when she'd been pissy with him after the fight. He'd wanted to help. Granted, she didn't need his help, but his intention had been good, and she'd snapped at him. She'd been upset because he had undermined her authority. Police officers were helped by the public every day, so why did she have such a hard time with it? Because she was a woman and she'd been up against Booley, a misogynist who believed she was incapable of defending herself.

Tim seemed to take it all in his stride. He'd served in Afghanistan. He had experience subduing and searching insurgents, people suspected of terrorism. The constant threat from the local population and IEDs must've been overwhelming. But his service to his country had taken its toll. It had changed him. What kind of man would he be if he'd never joined the army? His experiences in the Rangers had given him a unique understanding of death and danger. On the occasions when Booley had confronted him, he'd shown restraint. But Dana had gotten a glimpse of the hardness, the ability to inflict harm at will. And yet, he dampened his steely core with compassion and charm. He was a man of conflicting traits. She suspected he had a gentle nature but had become deadly through necessity. The contradictions in his character drew her like a lodestone. He was both tough and caring.

She'd sensed his discipline when he'd walked into the Hopefalls Police Station three days ago and had suppressed her attraction because she'd seen him as her enemy. But she couldn't think of him in those terms, not anymore. She trusted and respected him. That bit of self-awareness came as a surprise, but it shouldn't. He'd saved Logan, he'd wanted to protect her from her belligerent boss, and he cared for his father. He was stronger than her, better trained, and had admitted to being able to kill at will, and yet she felt no fear.

The only thing standing between them was the fact that he was a suspect in a homicide investigation. That had been Booley's doing, and she wouldn't let it continue. Tim deserved a life where he didn't have to live under a cloud of suspicion. For his sake, she would find out who killed Ben North.

Chapter Twenty-Four

Dana signed in at reception and then walked with Tim to Jack's room.

Jack Morgan sat in an armchair facing the door, a glass of water on the table next to him. He glanced at Tim, but there was no sign of recognition.

"Hi, Dad." Tim kissed his father's head. "This is my friend, Dana. She'd like to talk to you."

Jack's watery gaze flickered to the photos on the wall by the bed and then back to Tim. "My son's a good boy."

Tim stepped back and sat on the bed, his arms folded across his chest, his posture rigid. To a passerby he might seem relaxed, but she knew he wasn't.

Dana pulled a visitor chair over and sat next to Jack. "Yes, he is. He has a good heart."

"He does." Using the back of his hand, Jack wiped the drool that ran down his chin. "Are you the one?"

"The one what?"

"The one for him. My wife, Georgina, married me despite the fact I was a rancher. She didn't like the country. Said it was too far away from everything, but she stayed. Do you know why?"

"Tell me." She welcomed the chance to hear about the good times at the Morgan ranch.

Jack smiled, and for the first time, his eyes sparkled. "Because she loved me, and then when Tim came along, she loved him, too. We wanted more children, but that wasn't meant to be. Five miscarriages." He held up his hand, fingers wide. "Five. Each one broke her heart. In the end, I said enough. We had each other, and we had Tim. We should be happy with what God gave us. I wonder now if I did the right thing. It was selfish." He thumped the table hard. The glass of water toppled and spilt, splashing liquid down the side of his chair and across the carpet.

Dana righted the glass and looked around the room for something to mop up the mess. She now had an idea of just how strong Jack could be. He was thin, probably a mere shadow of his former self, but he could still do some damage. That was why he needed special care. A home care aid would never be able to control him.

Tim mopped up the spill with a white towel that looked as if it came from the bathroom.

"Was Ben your friend?" she asked.

"For years. He likes to drink. I had to go and take his guns away from him when he was drinking. I didn't mind him firing at the trees, but he tried to drive his truck into town. Drove straight into the ditch."

He stopped talking and stared into the distance, his mind presumably lost in a moment from the past.

"What happened then?" Dana urged as she moved the small table out of the way so Tim could soak up the water.

"I went to pull him out, and what did I find? Guns, that's what. Not a hunting rifle and a handgun like most people. He had a whole arsenal of weapons."

"What was he going to do with them?" And where were all these weapons now that he was dead?

"Kill Booley. Not that I blame him. Booley was always a lying, cheating son of a bitch."

"Did you tell the chief?" Dana straightened in her chair. Mrs. Anderson had talked about Booley's dislike for Jack, but no one had mentioned Ben's hatred of Booley. If there was a rivalry between the two men, then that was relevant to the investigation.

"Of course not. He would've arrested Ben and charged him. I couldn't have that."

"Why not?"

Jack grunted and then said, "Ben was my friend. And the chief, well, he knew Ben's secret."

"What secret?" Dana fought to keep her voice smooth and calm.

"The name of Ben's mistress."

Dana put a hand to her mouth. So Ben had hated Booley, but how did Booley feel about Ben? She also couldn't imagine the old, stooped man she'd known having a mistress. "Do you know who she was?"

Jack shrugged. "No, it wasn't my business. As long as Booley stayed away from my Georgina, I didn't care."

"So what happened to the gun you and Ben purchased together? The limited-edition Colt six-shooter with the horse on the handle."

"I gave it back to him. You look just like your mom." The change of subject caught her by surprise. She stared at him for a minute. Her mom was a tiny woman with dark hair. They had never looked alike. She took after her father's family—tall, strong, and blond. "My last name's Hayden. I look like my grandmother."

"My son didn't have anything to do with it. He didn't kill Alice." Jack surged to his feet. "You get out of here. I won't let you take him away."

Dana tipped her chair as she backed away. The conversation had turned so fast. In Jack's disjointed mind everything made sense, but to her it had come out of the blue.

Tim stepped between them. He placed his hands on Jack's upper arms, holding him in place.

"I won't let you take him," Jack roared.

"Get out of here. I'll meet you at reception," Tim said over his shoulder.

Dana backed out of the room, unable to tear her gaze away from Jack. One minute they were talking, and the next he had changed into an angry, confused man.

The sound of weeping echoed through the hallway as the old man collapsed into tears.

She inhaled. The heartbreak in Jack's sobs was another reminder of how much pain Booley had caused to an innocent man and his family.

Chapter Twenty-Five

Finn eyed Kennedy as they sat in their government-issued Ford SUV outside the office of Caleb Millar, the lawyer who'd been handling Ben North's case. Millar's office was only a few blocks from downtown Granite City. This corner of town was run-down. A homeless man slouched in a nearby doorway, presumably asleep, and the stench of rotting garbage filtered into the car.

"It's a beautiful morning," he said, trying to lighten the mood.

"Yep." She avoided eye contact with him as she opened the door of the SUV. Everything about her, from her posture to her expression, was tense, coiled tight. He didn't need to be a graduate of the FBI's course in non-verbal body language to know she was pissed at him.

Finn stayed in his seat, knowing Kennedy would mirror his action and remain in the vehicle. "You've only used one-word answers since we left the office. Say what's on your mind."

She tugged the door closed. "You shouldn't be involved in this investigation."

"Why not?"

"There's a possible connection between Ackerman and the Ben North homicide case in which your best friend is a suspect. Your involvement will compromise this whole investigation."

"You can wait in the car if you want."

She shook her head. "No way. We're FBI. We always work in pairs."

"I was only going to ask Ben's lawyer to share the details of the Eminent Domain case. It might have a bearing on Ben's homicide, and it might not. But we have to see if there's a connection to the Syndicate. We know they have nothing to do with Tim. And for all we know, Ackerman's interest in mining is just business—"

"Big Business."

"Yes, but there's nothing wrong with that. We'll do what we always do—we'll investigate, follow the evidence, and see where it leads."

"Okay, but I want everything done by the book." She tugged on the door handle, ending their conversation.

"You should take the lead," Finn said as he joined her on the sidewalk.

"Really?" Kennedy narrowed her eyes.

"Sure. You know what you're doing. I'll back you up."

"Okay." She pointed at him. "But no looking over my shoulder."

Caleb Millar seemed out of breath when he opened his office door. He looked more like a university student than a lawyer. He wore shorts and a T-shirt with sweat stains under the armpits. "Sorry, I haven't showered. My first appointment isn't for another hour. I live upstairs, so I figured I had time to work out. What can I do for the FBI?"

"We're looking into a possible connection between Ben North's case and public corruption," Kennedy announced.

"I was sorry to hear about his death. I liked him." He momentarily spread his hands wide, palms up, a gesture that suggested openness.

"What can you tell us about him?" Kennedy sat in a chair in front of the desk and nodded for Caleb to take his seat opposite.

"I can only share what's already public knowledge. Third Estate Mining, known in legalese as the condemnor, claimed they owned the mineral rights to whatever is under Ben's land." Millar's hands moved as he talked. The more movement, the more likely it was he was being honest.

Kennedy pulled a note pad and pen from her jacket pocket. "I thought the power of Eminent Domain only applied to the government."

"Not in Montana. According to the law, Eminent Domain can be used for commercial enterprise. It clearly says that private entities are explicitly granted the power of Eminent Domain, including mining corporations. Third Estate Mining argued that opening a mine and providing good paying jobs would invigorate the economy in this part of Montana."

Kennedy scrawled the information on her pad and then said, "The police talked to the district attorney. He said the process of Eminent Domain has never been stopped, which means Ben was going to lose his land."

Millar nodded. "Yes."

"Can you explain?" Finn asked. He wanted to make sure he understood who all the players in this case were.

"It's the right of the State to claim land to build a road, a school, or even put a power line through someone's property. It's part of our constitution and is normally used for the public good."

"So the State can just come and take someone's home?" Finn stood behind Kennedy with one hand resting on her chair.

"No, there's a legal process that has to be observed, and just compensation must be made. This is America. You can't force someone out of their home without paying them."

"But Third Estate Mining doesn't want to build a road or a school. They want to build a mine, which ultimately benefits the mining company. What would they be mining?" Kennedy asked, shifting her chair forward so Finn was forced to let go.

"Columbite–tantalite, otherwise known as coltan. It's a mineral electrical conductor that's used in laptops, smartphones, and other devices. It's actually very rare. There's only one other coltan mine in North America, and that's in Canada."

Kennedy jotted down the name of the ore. "So there's a lot of money riding on this?"

Millar stretched back in his office chair and interlaced his hands behind his head, a sign of confidence. "I would imagine, yes."

Kennedy looked up. "How was Ben doing in this legal process?"

Millar rocked forward and placed his elbows on the desk. "Third Estate Mining offered Ben double what his property was worth, but he refused."

"He probably had nowhere else to call home," Finn said, but why he felt the need to justify the old man's actions was beyond him.

Millar nodded. "Third Estate Mining had filed paperwork. We were due to appear in court in three months. It was complicated by the fact that Ben claimed Third Estate was lying about owning the mineral rights."

"Explain that," Kennedy demanded.

Millar shrugged. "It's not unusual for the surface rights and the mineral rights to be separated. When the state of Montana settled the land a hundred years ago, they could have separated the rights. Most people aren't aware that they don't own what's beneath their property."

"What about Ben?"

"He had a deed that proved he owned both the mineral and surface rights."

Kennedy fidgeted in her seat, making herself comfortable. "But I thought you said Third Estate Mining had documentation proving their case."

"The problem with cases like these is tracking the paperwork."

Finn propped himself against a large filing cabinet, feeling more at ease. Ben North had been a good judge of character. Everything about Caleb Millar seemed open, honest, and straightforward, which was unusual for a lawyer.

"Do you think someone forged their documents?" Kennedy asked as she scribbled in her pad.

"Not necessarily. Ben's deed was from 1885, when his great-grandfather migrated to Montana. The mineral rights could've been sold off after that. There have been instances where a landowner splits the estate in their will or sells off the mineral rights without their descendants knowing."

"I take it you're investigating," Finn said.

"I was, yes. In the Granite City–Elkhead County Records Department, I found a document that showed Ben had sold the mineral rights a year ago to Paul Harris."

"The mayor of Hopefalls?"

"The very same."

"We'll need a copy of that."

Millar tugged at his bottom lip with his teeth, as if deciding on the best course of action. Then he shrugged. "As I said, I liked Ben. If this case is what killed him, then he would've wanted justice."

"By the way, do you know who owns Third Estate Mining? I've never heard of them," Kennedy said, changing the subject.

"I wondered that, too. It took me a while, but I managed to trace ownership back to another company, Pent Up Media."

"Pent Up Media? The multinational media giant that's owned by Lance Ackerman?" Kennedy scribbled the name down.

"That's the one."

"What now? Who inherits Ben's land now that he's dead?" Finn moved closer to Kennedy.

"Hold on a second. Ben's will is in the safe." Millar disappeared into the back room.

Kennedy swung around as soon as he was out of earshot. "Will you sit down. You're driving me nuts, hovering behind me."

"I'm on the other side of the room."

"You're still behind me." She ground her teeth as she talked.

"There's only one chair." Finn had never seen her so agitated.

She pointed across the room to a metal office seat that was positioned near the front door. "Grab that one and pull it over."

Finn did as he was told, sitting next to Kennedy.

Millar walked back into the office, an open file in his hand. "Ben donated his land to the National Wilderness Preservation System, which is run by The National Park Service, with the proviso they form a nature preserve to safeguard Molly's Mountain wilderness."

"Will that stop Third Estate Mining?"

"Not on its own, but he also found an endangered plant, the water howellia."

"So the claim on Ben's land has collapsed."

"Not collapsed so much as in limbo. First Ben's estate has to go through probate, then if Third Estate Mining still want the land, they'll have to deal with the federal government, and the wheels of bureaucracy are slow."

"What about money? Did he have any accounts?" Kennedy rose and stood behind Finn. Whether she was standing behind him intentionally, to prove a point, or if she just needed a change of position he couldn't say.

"There's nothing else with a monetary value, but there was a letter." Millar flicked through his file until he found what he was looking for. "I sent it by registered mail this morning to a Timothy Morgan at Wind Valley Ranch in Elkhead County as per the deceased, Ben's, request."

Shit. Finn resisted the urge to loosen his suddenly too-tight collar. Why had Ben North written to Tim? Kennedy was right. He was too close to this case.

"Do you know what was in the letter?" Kennedy placed her hand on the back of Finn's chair. It was as if she were silently saying *I told you so.*

"No, it was already sealed."

Finn stood to leave. "Was there a reason you sent it registered? That'll take a lot longer than regular mail."

"It'll take ten to fourteen days for delivery." Millar looked him in the eye. "I chose the best service for my client. I don't know what's in the envelope. I paid for the extra security you get with registered mail because I want Morgan to receive the letter exactly as Ben intended, and considering the circumstances of Ben's death, I stand by my decision."

Finn headed for the door. He needed to get out of here and call Tim. Kennedy followed and then halted and grabbed Finn's arm, stopping him. She turned to Millar. "How did he pay you? We can't find any bank accounts in Ben's name."

"Normally, in Eminent Domain cases, I work on a contingent fee basis. But Ben insisted he pay me up front. He wanted to keep his land, and he needed to be sure that I would fight for him to stay rather than be paid for negotiating the sale."

"But you said no one has ever stopped the process."

"That's right, but just because it's never been done, doesn't mean we shouldn't try."

"So how did he pay you?" Finn stepped closer, realizing the importance of Millar's answer.

"Cash. He walked in here with a bag containing twenty thousand dollars and asked me to take the case. I gave him a receipt if you need to see it."

Kennedy nodded. "Yes."

The young lawyer rummaged through his desk. "Someone gave me a car as payment once. I don't mind as long as I can pay my bills." He handed a small, narrow blue-covered book to Kennedy.

"Did he say where he got the money?" Finn asked as Kennedy flicked through the pages of the receipt book.

"No, and that wasn't the only payment. His case was expensive, as you can imagine."

"And you didn't ask?" Using her smartphone, Kennedy took photos of the receipts.

Millar grinned. "Do you know the trick to being a good lawyer?"

Finn shook his head. "No."

"It's knowing what not to ask."

****

"Go ahead, say it," Finn said as soon as they reached the SUV.

"I've already said it, and I'm tired of you ignoring me." Kennedy took the keys from his hand, opened the driver's door, and slid the seat forward.

"We have to investigate the possibility that the Syndicate exists. And if they do, are they a criminal organization?" Finn stood for a moment. How could North's case be linked to the Syndicate? Then he walked to the passenger side and climbed in, his mind muddling through the information Caleb Millar had shared. "Lance Ackerman. He's the link."

"State your case." Kennedy buckled her seatbelt.

"We know he's connected to Lucy Portman—"

"For all we know, that could be innocent."

"You're right. We have no proof, but what about Paul Harris, the mayor?"

Her light brown eyes met his. "I have no problem believing he's involved in North's homicide, which once again is out of our jurisdiction."

"I think the cases are linked."

"How?"

"The mayor of Hopefalls, Lance Ackerman, and Lucy Portman were all having dinner together."

"Portman and Harris are lovers."

It wasn't a question, but Finn answered it anyway. "I agree. But why was Ackerman there?"

She turned to look at the old commercial building that housed Caleb Millar's office. "We need to have some professional division in this case."

"Some what?"

"We're going to give Ramirez all the information we got from Millar. Let him question the mayor of Hopefalls and Tim Morgan. That way you haven't tainted the investigation."

Finn nodded. He would rather question Tim himself, but there was no way Kennedy would go for that.

She started the ignition. "He also needs to find out how the mayor paid Ben for the mineral rights."

"What?" Finn frowned.

"Ramirez can't find a bank account for Ben, so how did the mayor pay him?"

"Good point." He should've thought of that. He must be getting slow. No, that wasn't it. He was distracted, first by Michael, and now Tim.

"We've delegated work to our friend in the Granite City-Elkhead County Police Department. What do you have in mind for us?" Finn asked.

Kennedy grinned and put the SUV in gear. "We're going to question Ackerman."

Chapter Twenty-Six

Dana hung around in the lobby of Shady Pines waiting for Tim. Jack had been pretty agitated when she'd left the room, so it would probably take a while for him to calm down. His outburst was fast and terrifying and explained why he needed special care.

She'd been waiting about ten minutes when the security guy strolled away, heading down a hallway to the left, coffee cup in hand. Dana took the opportunity to look in the sign-in book.

Yesterday, she'd been a police officer and would've charmed the guard into letting her examine the visitor's log. She normally didn't get much resistance because there was a certain amount of authority and trust that went with the badge. Today she was just a regular person.

She pushed the loss of her job out of her mind as she flicked through the pages, searching for Jack's name. Tim visited on a regular basis, which wasn't a surprise. There were a few entries for Zoe Harris and Mrs. Anderson. She thumbed through the sheets, finally finding Ben's name. He had visited Jack twice. The first time a week before his death and then again two days before he died. She had no idea why this information was important, but her gut told her it was. Somehow Jack Morgan was the key to discovering who killed Ben North.

She moved closer to the exit, antsy now that she had uncovered the information. She wanted to talk to Zoe and Victoria about their visits to the senior's home. Maybe they had seen or heard something unusual. She should also give this information to Detective Ramirez. He would probably have something to say about her recent behavior. He would definitely have a lower opinion of her, but it was what she deserved. She'd own up to her actions and then deal with the consequences.

Her phone rang, and she stepped outside to take the call.

"Dana, I need to talk to you." Mrs. Anderson's voice rang with the same authority all old-fashioned teachers possessed.

"Is anything wrong?"

"Yes, everything. We can't find the mayor, Booley's disappeared, and you've resigned—"

"What do you mean he's disappeared? He's in jail."

"He was allowed out on bail this morning. No one's seen him since he left the police station. Now tell me, what were you thinking, resigning like that?"

"I was thinking that I don't want to work for a corrupt police chief."

"I understand." Mrs. Anderson sighed, and Dana could picture her rolling her eyes. "The plan was to have Booley resign, not you."

"Plan? What plan?"

"The council has known for some time that Booley is as crooked as a corkscrew."

"Why didn't you fire him?"

"Paul wouldn't hear of it." Mrs. Anderson was all but shouting, her anger apparent.

"Paul Harris, the mayor, insisted you keep Levi Booley on the payroll?"

"Yes."

Dana was quiet as she thought about the circumstances of her initial employment. She had heard about the job through Joe Freeman, who had kept in touch with her father. Joe was also a member of the council. "But you're the town council. You insisted Booley hire me. Surely, you could've overruled the mayor and forced him to get rid of the chief."

"We had no proof, and the law states we can't fire someone without good cause. The town can't afford to get sued."

"Why didn't you pull me aside and tell me this two months ago?"

"We didn't want to give you any preconceptions. We figured if there was anything, you'd find it."

"But I haven't been looking. I've been using all my energy to deal with the chief's workplace abuse without punching him. I've been working twelve-hour shifts and coping with an unhappy teen. You should have informed me of your suspicions. I could have been collecting evidence, talking to the State's attorney. I take it you don't suspect Shelly or Xavier, I mean Officer Robinson."

"Shelly could never find any evidence of wrongdoing. And we weren't sure about Officer Robinson until last night."

"Let me get this straight. You suspected Xavier was corrupt too, but when he arrested Chief Booley, you realized he was honest."

"Yes, plus Shelly speaks very highly of him."

"I haven't talked to Xavier this morning. Do you know what charges are going to be laid against Booley?"

"You haven't asked?"

"I called Montana's Attorney General and appraised them of the situation. They'll send someone to look into it. But I decided to keep my nose out of it. Alice was my aunt. Anything I say is tainted. Their investigators will be talking to everyone."

"Booley was charged with disorderly conduct."

"Damn, why wasn't he charged with assault or attempted assault?"

"Don't swear, dear, it's unbecoming," Mrs. Anderson scolded. "I'm only repeating what Shelly told me. If you want more information, you'll have to talk to her."

"Sorry." Dana blushed. She hadn't been chastised like that since she was ten. "Hopefully, Booley isn't hiding in the shadows, waiting to exact his revenge on the citizens of Hopefalls."

"We don't know where he is, and we don't care. He covered up a crime, your aunt's death, and caused untold damage."

"Has anyone seen Eva Bryant? She should probably be held for questioning."

"No, and the diner hasn't opened. No one's heard from her."

"Maybe she disappeared with her uncle."

Mrs. Anderson made a clucking sound. "It was a bad day for this town when he was hired."

It would take months, if not years, to cope with the fallout of Booley's duplicity, which was not something she wanted to deal with in a phone call. "So, what can I do for you?"

"The town council had an emergency meeting this morning. We voted unanimously for you to take over as police chief."

"And the mayor's okay with this?"

"He's gone, too."

"Gone where?"

"We don't know. I'm the council president. In the mayor's absence, I have the power to presume the duties of acting mayor. Do you want the job or not?"

"How about I become acting police chief?"

"You don't want a permanent position?"

Dana did, but what good was a police chief who couldn't fire her gun. She needed to get her act together. "It's not that I don't want the job," she hedged, "There's a lot of upheaval right now. I'll be your interim chief until the dust settles."

Mrs. Anderson sighed. "You're probably right. We'll do it your way and revisit the matter at a later date. Come over to the town hall and—"

"I can't. I'm in Granite City visiting Jack Morgan. I can come in when I get back to town, but first I need to talk to the Granite City-Elkhead County police."

"Is it a personal or professional visit?"

Who she met in her personal time was her business. And she refused to discuss her suspicion that Jack Morgan was an integral part of the North homicide. At the same time, she didn't want to alienate her new boss. "A bit of both, I suppose," she said, deciding on a vague answer.

"Very well. Call me when you get back to town." Mrs. Anderson disconnected.

Dana stifled a laugh. She didn't have to find another job and uproot Logan. Plus, she would have a chance to get to know Tim. Her insides fluttered as she remembered the kiss they'd shared yesterday evening and then again this morning. The idea of exploring his body and feeling his naked chest against hers sent a frisson of excitement coursing through her veins. She inhaled, reigning in her thoughts.

Tim exited the facility. Once again, she was struck by his long, lean physique and the way he moved with a purpose, a directness, which she now realized telegraphed his internal strength. He was a man of integrity and honor. Those traits were an integral part of him and added to his magnetic charm.

He stopped in front of her. "Why are you smiling?"

"I'm the new temporary Hopefalls Police Chief." Without thinking, she threw her arms around him.

He whooped with laughter, hugged her, and swung her around.

Before she knew what was happening they were kissing. She didn't know who started it. He slipped his tongue between her lips, deepening the embrace. She responded by tugging him closer.

She'd had a restless night, imagining what it would be like to lay with him, to experience his weight on top of her as they moved in the same synchronized rhythm, the sensation of his skin against hers. She wanted to grab the knife from his belt and slice his clothes off.

His hands cupped her face, as he continued his onslaught. The way he held her, touched her, made her feel cherished.

He pulled back, hesitated a moment.

She expected to see regret in his gaze, but all she saw was tenderness and caring. His big thumbs caressed her cheeks. He opened his mouth to speak, but she stopped him with a small peck on the lips. She didn't want to talk, didn't want words of love. She wanted him to show her how he felt.

He seemed to understand. His mouth met hers as his tongue swept inside. This kiss was more than core deep; it was a linking of mind, body and soul. She was his for the taking.

His warm hands moved down her spine, stopping at the small of her back.

She wrapped her arms around his waist and yanked him closer.

The siren of an ambulance driving into the facility parking lot blared into her consciousness. She pulled away, her breath coming in short gasps.

She was gratified to see that he, too, was breathless. He stood close, looking down at her, his eyes glazed.

She wished they were in some secluded place where they could indulge, but they weren't. She'd been a hair's breadth away from being charged with public indecency.

She plunged her hands through her hair in frustration. He made her want to forget about everything and drag him to bed, any bed would do. Come to think of it, the truck would work. God. She needed some serious help. Maybe she should think about enrolling in Sex Addicts Anonymous. "You are really bad for me." She tried to laugh but the only sound she could make was a husky cry.

His mouth quirked into a lopsided grin, which revealed a dimple. "I like to think I'd be really good for you." This was his real smile, not the one he showed his customers, but the real him, the man beneath the polite layer of charisma. He lowered his head so they were almost touching. "When I get you alone, there'll be no stopping."

She closed her eyes as her pulse raced. That was exactly what she wanted. Her nipples pushed against her T-shirt. She needed him, needed to continue what they'd started. She knew she was allowing her physical craving to control her, but she didn't care. She'd never felt this strong primal attraction before. It was overwhelming and all-consuming. It overrode her common sense and destroyed her ability to think logically. The only way she could regain some restraint was to give into her mad sexual desires. Today. She would take him back to her place before Logan got home from school. It was eleven now, and she had one more stop to make. Hopefully, it wouldn't take that long.

Chapter Twenty-Seven

"Jack was good until the conversation led to Booley," Dana said, hoping a change of subject would bring her some much-needed control. They walked toward Tim's truck in the Shady Pines parking lot.

"They never did get along, and now he associates the name Booley with all the pain I caused when I ran away." He turned to stare at the facility grounds.

"You don't blame yourself, do you?"

"I have days when I do, yeah." He grabbed the door handle, avoiding her gaze. He obviously didn't want to discuss what had to be a painful memory.

"It wasn't your fault. You were set up."

He opened the door, saying nothing.

He wasn't going to talk about it. She understood, but at the same time she wanted him to confide in her and needed him to trust her enough to share his trauma.

Hah. Two days ago, she'd trailed him across the state because she believed he'd murdered his neighbor. There were no shortcuts. She would have to earn his trust, just as he'd earned hers.

"Can you drop me off at the police station on the square? I need to see Detective Ramirez."

"You know they have this wonderful invention called a phone. You should try using it sometime." He smiled, but once again it was his polite mask, not the real smile that revealed his dimple.

"It won't take long. I want to apologize in person for interfering in the case, and I need to tell him about the changes in the Hopefalls Police Department."

"Will this job work for you? You know with your…your…" He shrugged, not finishing the sentence. But then again, he didn't have to. She knew what he was trying to say.

"I think it'll be better."

"How?"

"As chief, I will have more paperwork and won't be on patrol unless it's absolutely necessary. Plus, I'm only the interim chief. This position will give me time to get my act together and figure out my limitations." A year ago, she would have thought nothing of using her SIG Sauer to defend herself and the citizens in her care. Now she had "limitations."

He negotiated a left turn, heading toward downtown. "I know you're having a hard time with what happened in Spokane, but you're a cop. You're not trained to kill. You're trained to defend, and that's what you did. You stood up to Booley in the name of justice, and you're going to make an excellent police chief." He placed his free hand over hers, offering her his strength and support.

She stared out of the window, watching the city streets go by. He was right. She wasn't trained to kill. She was an investigator. Maybe that was the reason she couldn't let Ben's death go. She turned her palm up so they were holding hands. "Ben spoke to your father before he died—"

Tim sighed. "I don't want Dad disturbed by this. Is there any way to leave him out of it?"

She shook her head. "It's unavoidable. Ben was shot with a gun that was jointly owned by your father. I'm amazed Ramirez hasn't been to see him, but I'm going to suggest he talk to Zoe Harris and Mrs. Anderson first."

"Why them?"

"They've visited your father on more than one occasion."

"I was terrified of Mrs. Anderson when I was in second grade. I would try everything I could think of to get her to like me, and nothing worked." He smiled at the memory.

Mrs. Anderson had retired before Dana attended school, so she'd never experienced her as a teacher. But she understood what he was saying. Even as a retiree, Mrs.

Anderson was a strong, dynamic, fearsome woman. "And now?"

"She's the same. Tough and uncompromising, but thank God she's one of the good guys."

"Amen to that." Dana stared out of the window the rest of the way to the police station. She was certain Jack had something to do with Ben's Homicide, but the pieces just didn't fit together. What if the gun had nothing to do with Ben's death? Ben had the Colt. His death could have been a spur of the moment thing, something unplanned. The gun was lying there, waiting to be used. She wasn't sure about that. Would a fancy Colt six-shooter, limited-edition, be lying around fully loaded? She didn't know enough about Ben or how he stored his weapons. There were so many questions, and she didn't know the answers to any of them.

Chapter Twenty-Eight

Detective Ramirez met them in the lobby. He shook Dana's hand first and then addressed Tim. "I was just about to call you."

"Me?"

"Do you have time for an interview? It shouldn't take long."

Tim nodded and then frowned.

Ramirez led Dana to his desk. Although she had never set foot in the Granite City–Elkhead County police station, it felt familiar. Desks were crowded into the middle of a large central area, with interview rooms around the edge. The sound of officers talking on the phone, the slang used, and the sight of handcuffed suspects sitting with their arresting officers reminded her of her time in Spokane.

"What can I do for you, officer?" Ramirez pointed to a metal chair with a vinyl seat positioned next to his desk.

Dana made herself comfortable. "I'm replacing Levi Booley as the Hopefalls Interim Police Chief. Actually, I resigned last night when it became obvious that Chief Booley had used his position to cover up a probable manslaughter and victimize an innocent man."

Ramirez whistled through pursed lips and then smiled. "That's a lot of information. I heard rumors this morning there was a big to-do last night, but no one has shared any details. Congratulations."

Dana smiled and nodded. The idea of being chief was both new and terrifying. "As I said, I was on my way here to talk to you. I need to apologize for interfering in your case."

His brow wrinkled. "How did you interfere?"

"Under Chief Booley's orders, I tailed Tim Morgan around on Saturday and Sunday. It was a waste of time."

He gave a curt nod, acknowledging her words but didn't comment on them. "It's interesting to hear Booley's been fired."

"Why's that?"

"He was on the phone this morning, demanding I detain Morgan for Ben North's homicide. I told him to butt out of my case."

"Did Booley say where he was? The town council wants to talk to him."

Ramirez shook his head.

"In the interest of being completely honest, you should know I've just come from Shady Pines Care Facility. Shady Pine's was my idea, not the chief's."

Ramirez pinned her with his assessing gaze. "What were you doing there?"

"I was visiting Jack Morgan."

"I hear he has Alzheimer's."

"That's right, but he's a bit less muddled after his morning exercises. He told me Ben came to see him. I checked the sign-in book and, sure enough, Ben was there twice. The last time was just two days before he died. You might want to speak to Zoe Harris and Mrs. Anderson. They were there around the same time, so they might know something."

Ramirez scribbled the names in a notepad. "Thanks. Anything else?"

"Jack said he gave the fancy Colt to Ben."

"So when Tim said he hadn't seen it in years, he was telling the truth."

"Yes, but the gun's just a prop, something to distract us." She tugged at the ends of her hair, realized what she was doing, and brushed it back off her face.

Ramirez smiled. "You're wasted as a small-town cop, and you're right. He died of a heart attack brought on by poisoning."

"It was the white powder on his face, wasn't it?"

Ramirez tapped his keyboard, bringing up the report. "Devil's breath, yes."

"Is that a new street drug? I've never heard of devil's breath."

"It's used by gangs, primarily in Columbia. They blow it in the faces of their victims. It takes away free will. People have been known to lead the criminals back to their homes and give them their belongings. There have even been cases where the target's go to an ATM and withdraw all their money."

"So, in effect, they help the perpetrators steal their valuables?

Ramirez nodded. "Yeah."

"Do the victims know what they're doing?"

"Yes, but they can't stop themselves."

"Dear God." Dana put a hand over her mouth, shocked at the consequences of having a narcotic like devil's breath hit the streets.

"It can stay in their system for a week, and it plays with the mind. The devil's breath causes a bad high, which includes nightmarish hallucinations and self-harm. It's pretty awful stuff."

"Are you telling me someone used a South American hallucinogen to poison Ben?"

"That's exactly what I'm saying."

"If this stuff is used to control people, then we have to assume someone wanted to have power over Ben, but why?"

Ramirez tapped his fingers on his desk. "Maybe they wanted him to sign something, perhaps an authorization to mine Molly's Mountain."

Dana pictured the protesters at the gate of Ben's Land. "That question leaves a wide pool of suspects. Half the town wanted that mine."

"Okay, let's approach this from another angle. Do you know anyone who's been to Columbia?"

Dana shook her head.

"How about drug dealers?"

"I'll have Xavier do the rounds, but it's a small town. If something this exotic was available, someone would have said something."

"And you haven't had anyone hospitalized with these kinds of symptoms?"

"Nothing." She had hoped the ME's report would help discover who had killed Ben, but instead it had given her a new set of questions and no answers.

****

When Ramirez had finished his conversation with Dana, he had escorted her to the reception area and offered her a cup of coffee while she waited for Tim to be questioned. There had been camaraderie between them, an understanding.

With Tim, Ramirez was all business. The detective led him, in silence, to a cubicle-sized interview room.

"Do I need a lawyer?" He took in the scuffed, gray walls. The only furniture was a table and two chairs. A bar ran down the middle of the table, presumably to give the police a place to attach a suspect's handcuffs.

Ramirez narrowed his eyes. "I don't know, do you?"

Tim wasn't playing games. "Tell me what this is about, or I'll insist on a lawyer, and we will wait until she gets here before I answer any questions."

The detective sighed and flexed his fingers as though he were giving himself time to decide the best course of action. "What did Ben want to talk to you about?"

"I don't know. He left a message. He didn't give details." He buried his frustration. He knew from talking to Finn that the police repeatedly asked a suspect the same question in order to trip him up. All he had to do was keep his head. He hadn't done anything wrong.

"How did he sound?" Ramirez snapped the question out like rapid gunfire.

"Old. We talked about this when you interviewed me in Hopefalls. What's changed?" Damn it, the only reason he was even considered a suspect was because of Booley.

"Ben sent you a letter."

"What? How do you know?"

"He gave it to his lawyer to mail to you in the event of his death."

"What? Why?"

"I was hoping you could tell me." Ramirez was calm, in control. Which was only natural considering he knew what was going on.

"Ask the lawyer. Can't he tell you?" Tim had a hard time wrapping his head around this latest piece of information.

"No. It was already sealed."

"And you can't interfere with the US mail."

"If something criminal is going on, I can."

"I don't know what to tell you. Ben obviously wanted to talk to me about something. But seeing as I didn't have a chance to see him before he died, I have no idea what it was about." Tim ground his teeth together. He wanted to scream, yell, and rage against the injustice, but he held his tongue. Lashing out would only make things worse.

"Do you know what's in the letter?" Ramirez asked.

"No idea, and no, I didn't kill him, and I definitely didn't murder him over a stupid gun."

"We will need to see the letter when it arrives. I can get a warrant—"

"That won't be necessary. I have nothing to hide."

"Whatever Ben North wanted to talk to you about must've been pretty important. If you think of anything or come across some knew information, let us know. Thank you for your cooperation." Ramirez stood, nodded goodbye, and left the room.

Tim stared after him. The door was open. He wasn't in handcuffs. He was free to go for now, but he was obviously still a suspect in Ben's murder.

Chapter Twenty-Nine

Finn enjoyed the feel of warmth on his back as he stood in the sun outside the upscale Sharp's Inn and Resort, the most expensive hotel in Granite City.

Kennedy joined him, staring up at the red brick building with masonry dating back to the end of the nineteenth century. "Lance Ackerman probably won't even speak to us."

"We can ask. What's the worst that can happen? Besides, it was your idea to talk to him." It was a beautiful day, and he wasn't going to let Kennedy's apprehension get to him.

"I know, but I have this feeling we're about to get sued."

Finn looked her in the eye. "What's our motto?"

Kennedy straightened, standing to attention. "Fidelity. Bravery. Integrity."

"So?" He wanted her to fill in the blanks and understand they had to do this because it was the right thing to do, even if they got sued.

Kennedy frowned. "Are we displaying bravery or integrity?"

He smiled. "Both. Let's go."

They headed toward the hotel.

Finn continued to make his case. "We know the Syndicate is real, and I have a hunch that something is going on here that's bigger than Ben North's homicide and more important than the acquisition of Molly's Mountain—"

"You think the Syndicate are involved."

It was a statement more than a question, but he answered anyway. "Yes, I do."

"Do you really think Ackerman's going to admit being part of an alliance of billionaire businessmen? And what is their goal? To control the world? Do you know how crazy that sounds?"

"Yes, I know it sounds nuts, but what if it's not so much about the world as it is about money?"

A doorman opened a polished brass door as they approached.

"Explain," Kennedy demanded.

"What if they want to manipulate events so they can make more money?"

"Let's say you're right, and there's a group of rich businessmen trying to gain control of industry and policy makers. Where would they start?" Kennedy pressed a button to call the elevator to the lobby.

"We know they were behind Marshall Portman's attempts to stop Marie Wilson's solar panel—"

"Because everyone would be off the grid."

"Yes, and the power and oil companies would fold."

Kennedy gave a low whistle. "That's a lot of money right there. But Ben North's homicide doesn't connect."

"Doesn't it?" The elevator doors dinged open, and they stepped inside. Finn pressed the button for the top floor. "Ackerman owns Pent Up Media. People believe what the news outlets tell them. Do you remember that security guard who found the bomb in the stadium and the press said he'd planted it himself?"

"That was years ago. That poor guy got crucified."

"He was a hero who was condemned because the newspapers ran with a sensational, but false, story."

She pursed her lips. "I don't get the relevance."

"Owning the newspaper and television outlets isn't enough these days. You have to own the Internet too, because no matter what the papers say, there'll be someone on social media contradicting them."

"Still?" She wasn't convinced.

Finn held up his phone screen so she could see it. "I did some research on the way over here. Tantalum, which is extracted from coltan, is mainly used to manufacture capacitors. Millar wasn't kidding when he said the stuff was rare. It's a conflict mineral, which is primarily mined in the

Congo. There is a shortage caused by an embargo over human rights violations."

"So you're saying this stuff is more valuable than gold."

"Imagine if you controlled a major ingredient needed to make computers and smartphones."

"Are we talking about a bid to take over the tech companies?"

Finn nodded. "I think so."

"But like you said, it wouldn't matter. You could make all the smartphones you want, and it wouldn't make a difference because you can't control the net."

"I'm not so sure. If you had a monopoly on the manufacture of all computers, smartphones, and other data-collecting equipment, you could put a backdoor in every device, a portal that would allow access without the user's knowledge." He tapped his phone with his knuckle. "What if Lance Ackerman and his friends had the power to use our phones to listen in on our conversations? There would be no more freedom. All law enforcement investigations would be compromised. There would be no such thing as doctor-patient confidentiality. And all he has to do to achieve this goal is to take Molly's Mountain from Ben North."

Kennedy paled as the scope of Finn's idea sunk in. "Special Agent Callaghan, you're the scariest man I ever met."

The penthouse suite was situated on the fifth floor at the end of a short corridor that resembled the interior of a castle with red brick walls and lamps that looked like medieval torches.

"I have a weird, itchy feeling that's telling me there's going to be a whole shitload of trouble coming down the line," Kennedy said as they stood outside Ackerman's hotel room.

"Do you want to wait in the car?"

"No, but watch what you say. If Ackerman is part of the Syndicate, then he has a man in the FBI who can access evidence. We need to tread carefully."

Finn nodded. She was right. He couldn't charge in. He had to remain professional and not let his personal connection to the case make him tip his hand. "I'm going to ask Ackerman about Third Estate Mining interests in Montana and see what he says."

"Okay. Keep your questions general. We'll gauge his responses and go from there, and do not ask him about Portman."

"Lucy or Marshall?"

"Neither of them. If they are connected, we cannot let them know our suspicions, and you cannot run with your control-the-world theory."

"Actually, it's my control-the-money theory, but fair enough." Finn knocked and stepped back, his hand on his weapon. It wasn't that he expected trouble, but he liked to be prepared.

Lance Ackerman answered the door himself, which was a surprise. "What do you want?"

Finn expected a man of his means to have a servant and bodyguard in tow. He flashed his credentials. "I'm Special Agent Callaghan and this is Special Agent Morris. We'd like to talk to you about your interest in Molly's Mountain."

"What took you so long? I've been expecting you since North's death." Ackerman shuffled to a large dining area near the full-sized kitchen. The hotel room was larger than Finn's apartment. There was a living room with three overstuffed leather couches. A large screen TV hung over a brick fireplace. From his vantage point near the door, Finn could see two other rooms, one on either side of the living room. The one on the left held a study with another couch.

Ackerman sat at the table, a plate of scrambled eggs and toast in front of him. His large stomach didn't allow him to get close. He pointed to the chairs at the table. "Take a seat. I have diabetes so I have to eat."

Finn sat opposite Ackerman. Kennedy stood behind Finn.

"What can I do for you?" Ackerman bit into a piece of toast and proceeded to chew without closing his mouth.

Finn instinctively looked away, not wanting to see the mouthful of partially digested food. Then he caught the glint in Ackerman's gaze. The billionaire was playing with him, purposely being as disgusting as possible so that Finn would turn away. It could be a tactic to prevent him from gauging Ackerman's body language and facial expressions. He forced himself to stare at the obese man.

Kennedy cleared her throat and moved to stand next to Finn. She retrieved her notepad from her pocket. "Mr. Ackerman, we were wondering if you could give us some advice."

"About what?" He took another bite. Crumbs fell over his distended belly.

"Mining." Kennedy fixed her shrewd gaze on Ackerman.

Ackerman stopped eating and pushed his plate away. "What about it?"

"We understand that as the Eminent Domain law stands, land can be taken for economic enterprise."

"It's not an ideal way to do business, but there are times when you have to pull out the big guns. Normally, in these circumstances, both parties reach an agreement out of court. One that, I believe, is mutually beneficial." He rested his arms on his bloated stomach and spread both hands wide with fingertips touching. It was a sign of supreme confidence.

"But that didn't happen with Ben North," Kennedy pointed out.

"No, it's a pity." Ackerman flipped one hand palm up, an indication of openness. "But I can see where he's coming from."

"You can?" Kennedy's brow crinkled.

"Sure. All he had was that mountain. He had no family, no wife, and nothing to do except sit on that mountainside and watch the sun go down on his life."

"So what happens now that Ben's dead?" Kennedy continued, turning the subject so they could get the information they really needed.

Ackerman stretched back in his chair, his hands holding his braces, thumbs up, another action that relayed self-assurance and status. Ackerman thought he was better than them. No surprise there. "Nothing. Ironically, Ben's death has called a halt to the proceedings."

"So North's death has stopped you acquiring Molly's Mountain?" Finn needed confirmation on this point.

"Potentially. It's definitely delayed the project. Ben's estate has to go through probate that'll probably take a year, if not longer, depending on whether he left a will or not. If he didn't, it could take years."

"So you haven't benefited from recent events?" Kennedy repeated the statement as a question, forcing Ackerman to clarify his position.

"No, it's put us in a legal limbo."

Kennedy scribbled a note in her pad. "Thank you for your time."

Finn stood. "Just one last question. How did you know there was coltan on that site?"

Ackerman froze in his seat. Slowly one hand rubbed the back of his neck, signaling discomfort. "Paul Harris, the mayor of Hopefalls, approached me. He owned the mineral rights."

"And you purchased them from him."

Ackerman nodded. "That's right. He'd done all the research. He used to be a landman—"

"Landman?" Kennedy's features were blank, revealing nothing. This was the same information they'd received from Ramirez, but it would be interesting to hear Ackerman's version.

"They investigate mineral right ownership. You know, go through the county records and that sort of thing." Ackerman stopped rubbing his neck and went completely still. "Harris led me to understand this was all kosher."

Finn smiled, reassuring him. "I'm sure it is. We just needed to understand how Ben came to be in this situation.

Kennedy was silent all the way to the SUV. As soon as they were inside the car, she said, "Shit, he was a good liar."

"When did he lie?" Finn asked, wondering if she'd picked up on the same tells.

"The mayor. Ackerman rubbed the back of his neck when he mentioned Paul Harris."

"I agree. And he stiffened again at the end when he said it was all kosher."

She propped her elbow against the door, resting her cheek against her fist. "That statement was intended to give us Harris as a suspect and take the spotlight off Ackerman. Plus, he didn't move at all when he said it."

"Agreed, it was a dead giveaway." Most people gesture less when they were lying. Ackerman had been a statue.

"So what now?" Kennedy asked.

"Legally, I don't think there's much we can do. All roads lead back to Paul Harris." He was almost certain Ackerman had engineered the situation so Harris would be blamed. He decided not to share his opinion with Kennedy. She was already irritated with him over this case. Voicing his conjecture would only add to her frustration.

Her eyes narrowed as she slanted her gaze toward him. "You think Harris was set up and is going to take the fall?"

Once again, her insight floored him. He could lie, but there was no point. She would see through him. Finally, he nodded. "The thought had occurred to me. Let's get some lunch and then look into the paperwork."

"Paperwork? You hate paperwork."

"I do, but you're right, we can't charge in. We have to build a case, and there are a lot of questions that haven't been answered."

"Yes, and the first one on my list is how does Lucy Portman fit into this?"

Finn shrugged. "Maybe she's just a broker. You know, a matchmaker?"

Kennedy started the car. "So who approached whom?"

"Ackerman's already said Harris approached him. That could be true—"

"Or Ackerman could've found out about the coltan under Molly's Mountain." She shoulder-checked and then pulled into traffic. "Then he told his friends in the Syndicate about it, and Lucy introduced him to her lover, Harris. Then what? Did Harris forge the deeds to Molly's Mountain or did he legitimately buy them?"

Finn winced as she changed lanes suddenly, narrowly missing another vehicle. "I don't know. We need evidence."

"I guess we're doing paperwork then." She stepped on the gas, heading to the Dumb Luck Café.

Chapter Thirty

Dana held her kitchen door open for Tim, all too aware that he stood a little too close. She could have backed away but didn't.

He had been quiet on the drive back to Hopefalls, seemingly lost in his thoughts. Her body didn't care about his mood. She'd once read that a woman's sexual appetite was affected by the hormones estrogen, progesterone, and testosterone. If that was true, they had a lot to answer for. Being in the enclosed truck, she had become fixated on his scent and his hands. The way he held the steering wheel fascinated her. Seriously, what sane woman would become obsessed with a man's hands? She needed to stop daydreaming about what it would feel like to make love to him. They would have sex, and she would be able to think again.

This wasn't like Eva wanting to use him. Dana genuinely liked him. Not only had he saved Logan, but he had also listened to her and understood what she was going through. He was kind, compassionate, and brave, and possibly her only friend.

"What time does Logan finish school?" His gold eyes wandered the room, taking in the peeling wallpaper, the green appliances, and the mess. She hadn't tidied up before she'd left. It hadn't occurred to her. She'd been focused on talking to Jack, and nothing else had mattered.

"He won't be home for an hour." Her skin tingled as he reached around her to close the door.

"Good." He backed her up until her butt was against the fridge. He didn't touch her. He didn't have to.

Every nerve ending, every molecule in her body, was charged, ready to ignite. She wanted him, wanted to touch all of him. She imagined straddling him on the kitchen table.

"What are you thinking?"

She tilted her face up so she was staring into his eyes. "Why?"

"You groaned."

She ran a finger from his corded neck down to the top button of his shirt. "I was thinking how much I'd like to use your body for my personal pleasure."

"I don't know if I can allow that. You haven't even bought me dinner yet."

"Playing hard to get?"

"A man has to have standards, and if I allow you to use my body, then you might not respect me in the morning."

She laughed, throwing her head back.

He kissed below her ear and then trailed kisses down her throat.

She tugged at his shirt, pulling it free of his jeans.

His mouth found hers. His tongue plunged between her lips. She hadn't thought she could become more aroused. She was wrong. The combination of his hands under her shirt, stroking her back, and his sweet, warm mouth on hers made her crazy. She fumbled with the buttons of his shirt, tearing the last few open, wanting to feel his skin and run her hands over his taut, naked chest, but he had other ideas. He tugged at her T-shirt, flipping it over her head. Then he stopped and stared at her. With one finger, he pushed down her bra cup and stroked the nipple, which showed its appreciation by thrusting upward as if begging for more attention. Heat flooded her body. A thousand electrical impulses hummed through her veins, accumulating at the apex of her thighs.

He placed his hands under her buttocks, picked her up, and carried her to the kitchen table. She pushed the mess aside as her butt touched the surface.

His mouth closed over hers again. His tongue slid inside to twine with hers as he unclipped her bra and tossed it aside. Then his thumps played with her sensitive nipples.

The intensity of her reaction stunned her. It was as if her body was on fire.

It wasn't enough for her to sit on the table and let him touch her. She needed to participate, wanted to excite him and feel his warm sex in her hands. She fought with the stiff button of his fly.

His mouth closed over her breast. She cried out as her body reacted, arching, thrusting out her chest while pushing her pelvis closer. This was happening so fast.

He continued his onslaught. One hand slid under her butt, pressing it against the bulge of his penis.

She managed to undo the button and then slowly slid his zipper down, wanting to feel him writhe within her. Her hand enfolded his penis.

His mouth found hers. Their tongues curved together, searching, exploring, igniting. The erection in her hand grew even more engorged.

He tore at the zip of her pants in a frantic attempt to rid her of her cumbersome bottoms, tugging them off, and throwing them on the floor.

He plunged inside. She arched, feeling stretched, her body shocked at his intrusion. It was as if she'd touched a live wire. Every part of her, every nerve was raw, tender, and ready to shatter. At the same time, it felt right as if she were home.

He stilled, putting his forehead to hers. "I can't move. If I do, I'll come."

An involuntary sob escaped her lips. He couldn't stop now. She needed…needed…more.

She sat on the table impaled by his penis. His arms were clamped around her. She wanted to flip him over so she was on top and in control, but she couldn't move.

She contracted her vaginal muscles, clenching his penis.

He arched, thrusting himself deeper.

She clenched again.

"God." He thrust harder, faster.

And then she was lost in a maelstrom of sensation as he drove her closer to the edge. He pressed her down so she lay on the table, exposed and vulnerable. She rearranged her legs so they dangled over his shoulders, the position forcing him deeper still. She was so close, so near, and yet she couldn't go over, couldn't find completion.

He continued his onslaught, his hands resting on the tabletop, pinning her knees against her shoulders. He thrust faster, driving, pushing her closer. He sucked her nipple into his mouth, and she was lost. A light flashed behind her eyes. She pulsated around him, her body erupting in a flood of quivering spasms as her orgasm spun out of control.

****

It was a while before she was able to move. Tim was bent over her, his head resting on her chest. Finally, she ran a hand over his hair, reveling in the feel of his soft mane, damp from exertion. "I need to get up."

With a groan, he stood.

She followed, pushing off the table, shaking so much she was surprised her knees supported her. She snatched her clothing from the floor. Quickly, she climbed into her underwear. Had she moved too fast and allowed her own desires to take control? She'd only known him for three days. Yes, she considered him one of the good guys, and obviously their attraction was mutual, but she had never jumped so quickly into bed with anyone. There was so much they didn't know about each other. Plus, he was still a suspect in Ben's death. If this continued, she would be forced to choose between her career and him, and she wasn't ready for that level of commitment.

Her doubts must've shown on her face because he hooked her chin with his index finger. "I didn't plan this."

That was true. She was the one who'd rushed things, who'd invited him back to her place. This was her plan. Her face flushed. "Was this a mistake?"

He zipped his fly and stared down at her, his eyes serious and hard. "No. This was not a mistake. This was going to happen. It just happened sooner rather than later."

"What do you mean?"

"We are in a relationship." He poked the air with his index finger to make his point.

"We only met three days ago."

"So?" He shrugged into his shirt.

She tugged her top over her head, not bothering with her bra. "What I'm trying to say is that we don't know each other." *And you're a person of interest in a murder investigation.*

"Don't we? I know everything about you that's important. You are a woman who would rather move and relocate your son than be dishonest. The small stuff we'll learn over time."

He was right, despite Booley's accusations, and his attempts to blacken Tim's name, she did know one thing about him that stood out. "You saved my son from a bear, and you came to report that bear to your worst enemy because it was the right thing to do. You must've dreaded walking into the police station."

He shook his head. "You have no idea."

Her past boyfriends weren't like Tim. He was intense and serious whereas, by comparison, they had been downright casual. "Look, it's been years since I had a boyfriend. I got carried away, and I'm not good at relationships."

"Meaning, it's been years since you've had sex?"

She nodded.

He narrowed his gaze, his golden eyes twinkling. "How many years?"

She inhaled. "Three. Can we forget about this and start over?"

He stepped closer, pulling her into his arms, grinning. "I could say yes, but I'd be lying. And I don't want to forget. You and I are real. That's just the way it is." He touched his lips to hers in a chaste kiss and then turned to the clock on the stove. "Logan will be here soon. I should get going."

She placed a hand on his chest. His shirt hung open, allowing her to enjoy the feel of his course hair under her fingers. Her hand wandered to a scar on his right side under his ribs. He'd been shot. Xavier had told her when he'd looked into Tim's background, but knowing he'd been wounded and seeing the scar were two different things. When she touched the mottled flesh, she realized how close to death he had come.

He snagged her hands, pinning them to her sides. "Oh, and you should know, wearing a white T-shirt and no bra is a real turn on."

Before she could react to his statement, his mouth covered her breast through the fabric. She wrapped one leg around him, willing him to take her. Heat flooded her body. She wanted him to make love to her again, wanted to lose control and go wild. Next time she would be on top.

She groaned, and using every ounce of strength she possessed, she pulled her hands free and shoved him, telling him, without words, it was time to go. No matter how much she wanted him, she was still a mother, and she had responsibilities. Besides, she needed time to think. Yes, she wanted sex, but a relationship was a totally different thing. "You need to leave before we get carried away again. That would be bad."

He gave her a slow, sexy grin, one that revealed his dimple. "No, it would be good, real good." Then he waggled his eyebrows.

"How good would it be to have Logan walk in to find us doing it on the kitchen table?" They probably could fool around, but she needed time to decompress and deal with everything that had happened today before her son arrived home. They had things to discuss, and she didn't want visions of sex with Tim to interfere with her concentration. Who was she kidding? The thought of trailing her hands over his taught, muscled buttocks would probably be distracting her all evening and into the night.

He did up his shirt, walked to the door, and grabbed the handle. She put her hand over his to stop him from opening it. She poked him in the chest. "The next time, if I start screaming, don't stop me."

Beads of sweat formed on his forehead. "Damn, I'm not going to get any sleep."

She smiled as she closed the door after him. She might not know what she wanted, but playing with him and getting the last word was fun.

****

Dana stared at her son and his friend, a girl whose name she couldn't remember. She'd tidied the kitchen, taken a shower and changed, emerging from her bedroom just as Logan came home. She forced herself not to look at the kitchen table, pushing her memories of sex with Tim aside.

"Mom, say something," Logan insisted.

She couldn't believe the difference Logan's new haircut made. It was short at the sides, the top a little longer and gelled into blue spikes. "You're so handsome."

"Mom!" Logan blushed.

"Sorry, I didn't mean to embarrass you, but it's the truth."

"So you like it?" the girl said. She was stunning with dark eyes and high cheekbones that hinted at a Native American heritage.

Dana held out her hand. "Hi, I know we've met, but I can't remember your name." The girl looked to be older than Logan, but Dana reserved judgment. Sometimes teenage girls seemed older than they were.

The young woman stared at the floor, obviously embarrassed. "I'm Mia Trahan. You've had my dad in the drunk tank."

Dana smiled, hoping to put Mia at ease. "You're not responsible for your father."

"Yeah, my dad's a druggie," Logan added. "I mean he was a druggie. He's dead."

"I'm sorry." Mia seemed genuinely distressed by Logan's statement.

Logan shrugged. "It's okay. I never knew him. He died of an overdose when I was a baby."

"Did you cut Logan's hair?" Dana said, changing the subject. Normally she didn't mind talking about her choices as a teen. It gave kids hope to know they didn't have to get everything right the first time. But she wasn't in the mood to rehash her past, especially when there was so much happening in the present. She'd hoped taking a cold shower and changing her clothes would have helped her feel more balanced and less out of control, but they did nothing to rid her of the deep, elemental need that coursed through her veins. She wanted Tim again the way a drug addict wanted their next fix.

Mia nodded. "It was fun. He has good bone structure."

"You did a great job." Dana smiled as she tried to focus on the conversation.

"I'm hoping to study hairdressing. I'm trying to build my portfolio so I can get into a good school. I want to learn the latest techniques and get a job in one of the top salons. Then I'd like to open my own shop, but I need to learn the business first." Her large oval eyes glowed.

"What grade are you in?" Dana asked. This girl was leaps and bounds ahead of Logan. She had a plan, an attainable goal.

"Eleven."

"I wish I'd had my act together when I was your age. Could you cut my hair sometime?"

Mia tilted her head, viewing Dana's hair from different angles. "Someone really did a number on you. Where did you go?"

"Jezebel's in Granite City. They came highly recommended."

Mia shrugged. "I'll make a note not to apply there for a job. I don't want to be associated with a bad stylist."

Dana blinked. Even someone in grade eleven could tell she had a bad haircut.

Mia shucked off her backpack. "I have my scissors and your hair's already wet. I could do it now. It won't take long. I just need to tidy up the ends and even it out."

Dana dragged a chair to the middle of the kitchen. "Okay."

"How'd you feel about a pixie cut? You have a slim face, so you could carry it off."

Dana sat in the chair. "Go for it."

A few snips of the scissors later and Mia was done.

Dana felt her head. God, it was short.

Logan snapped a picture with his phone. "Here. It looks good."

Dana examined the photo. It was shorter than she was used to, but it did look better.

Logan grabbed Mia's hand. "I want to show her the mural I'm painting in my room, okay?"

Dana nodded. Was there something between Logan and Mia, or were they just friends? It was hard to tell. *Damn.* Logan knew the basics of sex. She'd badgered her father until he'd talked to him about it. If he got a girl pregnant, then he was going to have to take responsibility for his actions. Not like her ex. She made a mental note to have a little chat with him later. It was just so easy to get carried away.

Talk about the pot and the kettle. She was the one who'd lost control today with Tim. *Damn it.* No, it took both of them to have sex. He'd wanted it just as much as she had. She had to remember that. Plus, he'd said they were in a relationship. Umm, she wasn't sure how much stock she could put in that. Wasn't it true that men said things after sex to make a woman feel better? They needed to slow things down, if only for her peace of mind. She'd drive to his place tomorrow and have a chat with him. But first things first, she needed to call Mrs. Anderson and figure out what was going on with the police department.

Mrs. Anderson picked up on the first ring. "Hi Dana."

"How'd you know it was me?"

"I have call display, dear." Of course, she did. If there was one thing Dana should remember, it was that the retired teacher was as sharp as a butcher's knife.

"I was wondering if you still wanted me to be the temporary police chief."

"Oh yes, very much. Unfortunately, we can't find the mayor or Booley to inform them of our decision."

"They're both still missing?"

"Yes."

"Have you informed the police?"

"I'm doing that right now."

Dana smiled. "Okay…I meant Officer Robinson. He's a top rate policeman, and I have absolute faith in his abilities."

"That's good to know." Mrs. Anderson obviously wanted Dana to take the lead.

"I'm happy to help, but you do understand that I quit. I don't have a badge or a weapon. Technically, I need to be sworn in again."

"And we need the mayor for that," Mrs. Anderson added. "You see our problem, don't you?"

"I do. I'll call Xavier now."

She put down the phone. So two out of the three people who'd been present at the scene of Ben's homicide had disappeared. Could their disappearance have anything to do with Ben's death, or were they simply reacting to last night's meeting?

She strode to the kitchen table. Magazines and newspapers were piled neatly on one side. She opened her laptop and typed in *devil's breath*. A list of articles appeared on the screen. She clicked the first one, opening it. A member of the scopolamine family, it was made from the seeds of the angel's trumpet, technical name *brugmansia*. There was a photo of a beautiful shrub with flowers in white, gold, and pink. The rest of the article just repeated what Detective

Ramirez had told her, including the fact that it was predominately found in Columbia.

She did another search, typing *brugmansia* and Montana. The plant didn't grow wild in Montana but was distributed worldwide as a houseplant.

She just couldn't see Booley poisoning Ben. Levi Booley was a bullyboy pure and simple. He would shout, beat, and berate someone, but those traits didn't require any skill, thought, or subtlety. Of course, blowing devil's breath into Ben's face didn't require a lot of technical know-how either. How close would you have to be? Within a foot? Two feet? She couldn't see a crotchety old man like North allowing Booley within ten yards, let alone two feet. The same could be said of the mayor, especially when she considered he was Third Estate Mining's biggest supporter.

She slammed her laptop shut, opened the dishwasher, and started filling it with the dishes from the sink. It was stupid of her to want to solve Ben's homicide. She didn't have access to all the facts. Plus, she had enough on her plate, taking over the police department and dealing with Logan. The truth was she was looking into the investigation to avoid thinking about a tall sexy ex-Ranger who, up until yesterday, she had suspected of killing Aunt Alice.

Chapter Thirty-One

Ethan Moore stared at the man in the white hat. Ethan had changed his appearance since the last time they'd met. He'd been pretending to be a protester then. But his mission was to cause a disturbance and give the environmentalists a bad name.

Since then he'd shaved his beard and wore a blue top-of-the-line suit, coupled with a white well-cut shirt and a Hermes tie. His rough, worn-in hiking boots were the only exception to his business attire. But he had a pair of Dolce & Gabbana shoes in his Jeep, which was parked on one of the trails at the bottom of the mountain.

Booley looked like an old-time cowboy instead of the police chief of a one-horse town. His cigarette glowed in the twilight. Soon it would be completely dark. Ethan smiled at the Chief's stupidity. Most people meeting a stranger for the first time, especially when negotiating blackmail, would have chosen a public place. But this idiot had picked Molly's Mountain.

Ethan's hand itched to pull his knife from its scabbard. He wanted to slice at the old man's flesh, watch his skin split neatly open and blood spurt from the wound.

"What can I do for you?" Ethan wondered if Booley would recognize him. He wanted to give the impression he was the personal assistant to a billionaire.

"It's what I can do for you that's important." Booley took a last puff from his cigarette and then extinguished it under his foot.

"And what is that?"

"Paul Harris thinks he's smart, but I know he forged the deed to Molly's Mountain."

"That's quite an accusation. Can you prove it?" Ethan wondered if this was a waste of his time.

Booley pulled an envelope from his pocket and shoved it into Ethan's hand.

There were bank statements, photocopies of yellowed documents, a glossy photo of Harris and Lucy Portman naked in what was presumably the mayor's bed, and a picture of Lucy Portman, Mayor Harris, and Lance Ackerman having dinner together. "What am I looking at?"

"Proof that Harris didn't pay Ben for the mineral rights, and that he and your boss have been meeting to discuss Molly's Mountain."

"This means nothing. Ackerman's an influential man. He meets people. This get-together was in a restaurant. There's nothing cloak and dagger about it. As for the rest, I think if the mayor had committed a crime and faked some documents, then you should take the matter up with him," Ethan said, not caring if the chief liked it or not. His job was to gather any evidence that could lead back to Ackerman, kill Booley, and plant the knife on Morgan.

Booley rubbed his hands along his thighs, revealing his uncertainty. Ethan wanted him to make his pitch. He would let Booley think a deal could be made. Then, at the last moment, when the Chief thought he'd succeeded, Ethan would take his life. It wouldn't be quick. He wanted to enjoy the shock in his eyes, then the despair, and finally acceptance as his life slipped away.

"I'll go to the police with what I have," Booley spat. His hands curled into fists, clearly showing his anger and frustration.

"I doubt that."

"Are you prepared to take that chance? North was murdered. Something like this will add Ackerman to the pool of suspects."

Ethan suppressed a smile. "What do you want?"

"A million. That's not much money to your boss, but it's enough for me to start a new life."

"I'll need all your devices, everything you've got." This point was non-negotiable. Once the Chief was dead, the authorities would go through his electronics looking for clues.

"I only have a laptop and a phone. I can't get the computer until tomorrow."

"Tomorrow it is. Meet me here at noon." Ethan headed for the trail that would lead to his car. Soon he would get to slice his knife into human flesh.

Chapter Thirty-Two

Dana nursed her cup of coffee and hummed with appreciation as she sat at the desk she shared with Xavier. The first cup of the morning always tasted the best. She wore her jeans, a T-shirt, her leather jacket, and runners, not her police uniform. Booley was a jerk, but she wouldn't take his place until he'd been fired and had a chance to collect his stuff. Besides, the mayor was still missing, so she couldn't be sworn in.

Xavier slumped into a chair opposite her. Large, dark circles shadowed his eyes.

"When was the last time you slept?" Dana took another sip of her coffee. She hadn't slept much herself, but that was because she kept picturing Tim pressing her up against the fridge and then taking her on the table.

"I've had some naps here and there." His voice was flat and dull.

"It's been too long," Shelly called without looking up from the report she was entering into the police computer.

"When was the last time you were home?" Dana asked.

"I get home every day to shower, but I haven't slept in my bed since Friday." He rubbed a hand over his face.

"Damn, Xavier. You shouldn't even be driving, let alone walking around with a gun."

"Send him home," Shelly added. She was much more verbal now that Booley was gone.

Xavier closed his eyes and then forced them open. "I'm not arguing with you. Are you back?"

"Unofficially, I've been asked to take over as interim chief."

"About time," Shelly added.

He grinned. "I was called into a council meeting. They asked me how I felt about it."

"What did you say?" Dana was intrigued. The town council hadn't interviewed her, which struck her as odd. But then again, she'd been out of town all day yesterday so maybe they would sometime in the future.

"I told them if they kept Booley, I was looking for another job. If you were chief, I'd stay." Xavier tapped a finger on the desk to make a point.

"Thank God for that." It was good to know she had his support, but then she'd suspected she would. He was a young, idealistic cop. There was no way she could see him putting up with a corrupt chief. She pushed her mug aside. "Before I send you home to sleep, I want to talk about Booley and Mayor Harris."

"They're missing," he stated.

Shelly stood and walked over to join them. "There was a voicemail from Detective Ramirez saying he wanted to speak with the mayor regarding Ben's homicide."

Xavier's eyes widened, the news making him more alert. "Really?"

"He was at the crime scene when I got there," Dana added.

"You think he shot the dead body?" Xavier had obviously been appraised of the ME's report.

Dana shrugged. "There were three people at the cabin, and any one of them could have shot the body, or it could've happened before they arrived like they said. But I can't imagine Booley or Harris getting close enough to administer the poison."

Xavier nodded. "I see your point. Ben was an ornery old man. You'd do him a favor and chase trespassers off his land, and you wouldn't even get a 'thank you.' He'd just slam the door in your face."

"He was a little nicer to me—"

"Ben had a softness for women." Shelly stood in front of them with her hands on her hips. "When he first came home from Vietnam, he had a string of girlfriends before he finally settled down."

"Really?" Dana was shocked. It was hard to believe the old man had been a womanizer. Then another question occurred to her. "What do you mean by 'settled down'?"

"He started seeing one woman."

Xavier rested his elbows on his knees. "But he never married?"

"She was already married and wouldn't divorce her husband," Shelly said.

Dana stood and pointed to Shelly to take her seat. "When was this?"

Shelly made herself comfortable, her short, round legs not reaching the floor. "The late seventies, maybe early eighties."

Dana paced to the closed door of Booley's office and then swung around to face them. "We need to track down Ben's girlfriend and her husband."

Shelly put a finger to her lips, thinking. "If I tell you this, it has to be in confidence. It can't go in any police report."

Dana strode back to the desk. Her thoughts were clearer when she walked. "I can't promise. It might have a bearing on the case."

"It doesn't."

"It might," Xavier added.

"Okay, just don't write it down for now," Shelly pleaded. "For me."

"Tell us." Dana started pacing again.

"Victoria Anderson." Shelly put a hand to her mouth, seemingly shocked by her own words.

Dana gasped. Mrs. Anderson, the retired schoolteacher, who'd told her off for swearing, had been having an affair with Ben. "How do you know?"

"Booley—"

"She was the mistress. Jack stopped Ben killing Booley because he knew the name of his mistress," Dana said, putting the pieces of Jack's story together.

"Back then she was a very beautiful woman. Booley threatened to tell her husband if she didn't sleep with him, too."

Bile rose in Dana's throat. "That's awful."

"The Andersons had been living separate lives for a while by then. He was a gambler, couldn't be trusted with the grocery money. So Victoria told Booley to tell him. She loved Ben and didn't care who knew."

Dana stood in front of Shelly and Xavier, her hands on her hips. "It sickens me to know that a police chief of Hopefalls was blackmailing someone in order to extort sexual favors from them." She addressed Shelly. "How did you work for him for so long?"

"I've been collecting information and sharing it with the council, but I never could find anything that would lead to criminal charges."

"What about the husband? Where is he now?" Dana asked.

"He's dead. They reckon he killed himself over his debts."

"When was this?

"Ten years ago."

That dismissed him as a suspect. "Why didn't Victoria and Ben ever marry?"

"She never said, but I suspect they were both set in their ways."

Victoria hadn't mentioned her relationship with Ben. Did she feel sorrow over his death? Did her affair give her a motive to murder him?

And then there was Booley. The man was an abomination. She squared her shoulders. She didn't care if Booley knew he was fired or not. She was the head of the Hopefalls Police Department, and he would be charged.

"Shelly, we need to make finding Booley and Harris a priority. Can you ask the volunteer search and rescue to help us with this? Also, can you put out a call for volunteers to go door-to-door in Hopefalls? That'll help us cover more ground."

Shelly walked to her desk. "On it."

Xavier stood. "What do you want me to do, boss?"

"Has Mrs. Harris filled out a missing person's report?"

He shook his head. "No, the only reason we think he's missing is because we can't find him for town business. We haven't heard a peep from her."

"Okay, I'll follow up with her and then join the people searching door-to-door. I'll also see if I can narrow down the last place and time they were seen. Once we have a timeline, we can go from there."

Dana picked up the keys to Xavier's cruiser and shoved them into his hand. "Go home and get some sleep. You're no good to me in this condition."

He gave her a weak smile. "On it, boss."

The minute the door closed behind him, the phone rang. Dana grabbed it. "Hopefalls Police."

"This is Joe Freeman."

She remembered the postmaster demanding Booley's arrest on the night of the town meeting. "What can I do for you?"

"I just saw Booley heading west on the Hopefalls Highway."

"Towards Wind Valley Ranch?"

"Yep."

Butterflies erupted in her stomach when she pictured Tim, tall and sexy-as-hell. There was no way he would put up with any more intimidation from Booley. If he were forced to protect himself, he might end up on the wrong side of the law, and she couldn't allow that.

"Thanks. I'll check it out." She disconnected and then told Shelly about the call. "So now we're only looking for the mayor. I'll deal with Booley. I need my weapon and a set of cuffs."

"They're in the chief's desk along with your badge."

Dana opened the door to the small office and stopped. All the files and papers from Booley's desk were sprawled over the floor. The laptop that normally sat on his desk was gone. "Shelly, has anyone been in here?"

The older woman peeked over Dana's shoulder "What the hell happened?"

The drawers of the filing cabinet were wrenched open, file folders sticking out. The room had been searched, but by whom?

Dana stuck out her arm, preventing Shelly from entering. "Was this door closed when you arrived this morning?"

Shelly nodded.

Dana grabbed a pair of latex gloves from her desk. "Call the state police. Tell them what's happened. We need a forensic team to go over his office. I called them yesterday, so they probably have a detective on the way."

"Are you going in there?" Shelly asked as she grabbed the phone.

"I have to get my badge and gun. Then I'm going to Wind Valley to stop Booley." The idea that Booley was going to harass Tim further filled her with rage. There was no way she would allow this persecution to continue.

She tugged open a drawer and found her badge, a set of cuffs, and her SIG Sauer. "First time's a charm."

It was a reflection of the ex-chief's state of mind that he hadn't bothered to secure her handgun in the weapon's locker. She closed the door behind her and headed out of the station.

Chapter Thirty-Three

Dana's heart beat hard against her ribcage as she negotiated the long, bumpy trail that led to Tim's house. She was nervous after yesterday. She'd had sex with Tim because she believed it would rid her of her core-deep lust, a kind of face-your-fears strategy. The pulsating need that reverberated through her body told her it hadn't worked.

The road curved. The white-capped mountains, the yellow fields, and the lush green forests came into view. They were jarring in their beauty. She remembered the photo of Tim on Jack's wall. His childhood had been happy, probably idyllic, until Booley had ruined everything.

Tim walked out onto the deck as she parked in front of the house. His hair was mussed from sleep. He yawned and scratched his flat stomach, an action that drew her eye to his shirtless torso. She almost moaned as she remembered running her hands over his hard muscles, her fingers exploring his bullet wound. There were other scars she hadn't noticed yesterday. A knife wound to his right shoulder and another near his left hip.

"I'm here in my official capacity," she said as she climbed the porch steps.

He blinked sleepily. "Are you here to arrest me?"

She imagined him in bed. Her skin heated at the idea of cuffing him to the bedpost. She pushed the thought away. "No, Booley was seen heading out this way. I wanted to make sure he wasn't causing any trouble."

The rat-a-tat-tat of gunshots punctuated the air.

Dana's hand automatically went to her weapon. Another round of shots rang out. She drew her SIG and followed the sound.

"No, wait," Tim called after her.

She ignored him, racing to the left side of the house. With her SIG aimed, she marched toward a man with shoulder-length black hair. He wore earmuffs. His right hand held a firearm, aiming at a target, which was tied to a bale of hay.

"What the hell?" Dana stared at this new person. She'd imagined Tim was up here alone. He wasn't. She'd thought she'd gotten to know him in the last few days, but she'd been wrong. She didn't know him at all. She was aware of the facts of his past, but that was all they were—facts. She wasn't privy to the day-to-day details that made up his life.

The dark-haired man put his Glock 19 on the table in front of him, which held six handguns, neatly lined up in a row, along with boxes of ammunition. Then the stranger turned and smiled at her, one hand holding onto a cane the other up in a show of surrender.

Tim stood by her side. "I'd like you to meet Michael. He's staying with me for a few days."

She stuffed her gun into her holster. She had reacted, with no hesitation, no doubt. She'd believed Tim was in trouble and she'd responded. She'd also reigned in her reaction when she'd realized there was no danger. And she didn't feel shaken or traumatized. Come to think of it, she did feel more centered, as if she had found herself again. But why and how that change had occurred she couldn't say. Maybe it had something to do with standing up to Booley. At the town hall, when she'd thrust her badge at Booley, she'd known exactly who she was and what she stood for.

Michael distracted her when he tugged the earmuffs from his head and placed them on the table. He held out his hand. "You must be Dana."

Tim's brow furrowed. "How do you know her name?"

"Finn told me." Michael grinned, revealing a set of perfect, white teeth. He was an exotically handsome man with high cheekbones, a tanned complexion, and straight black hair.

Tim rubbed a hand over the stubble on his chin. "I need coffee."

"Good idea. It should be brewed now." Michael limped toward the house, using his cane for support.

Dana slowed her stride to match his. "What happened to you?"

"I was hit by a car." Michael kept his gaze on the uneven ground in front of him.

Dana grimaced but said nothing.

Once they reached the house, Michael hobbled through the kitchen, making a beeline for the couch where he gently lowered himself into place. "The soft cushions are easier on my butt."

"Is there anything I can do?" Dana stood in the kitchen. The first floor of the house was one large room with the spaces divided by the furniture rather than walls. There was also a wide archway that marked the divide between the kitchen and living room. She'd expected the interior walls to be made of log, but they were plastered. The living area had been painted white. The color, along with the picture window that faced the valley, gave the room a bright, open feel. The same couldn't be said for the kitchen. The cabinet doors were nicked and scarred with age. Wallpaper covered in citrus fruits was yellowed and peeling.

Despite the disrepair, the room was neat and clean, a lot cleaner than her place.

"Why don't you join me in here," Michael called. "Tim will bring us coffee."

She glanced back at Tim, mainly to see if he was okay with Michael's order.

He smiled and nodded. "You might as well get it over with. Just to warn you, there'll be questions."

Dana made herself comfortable in an overstuffed, brown leather armchair with brass studs running down the front seams.

"That's Tim's chair," Michael said as he shifted in his seat to lean on his right side.

Dana just smiled. If Tim had said that, she might have moved, but she had the feeling Michael was testing her. Why he would do such a thing was beyond her, but she always listened to her gut when dealing with people.

"So, Finn tells me you're a cop," Michael began.

"Yep." She decided to keep to one-word answers.

"And you're investigating Tim."

"No." That was the truth as far as it went, although, Tim was still a suspect.

"Finn said you were smart."

Dana just shrugged. It was a statement that didn't require an answer.

"Are you going to answer me?"

"I have."

Michael smiled. "Tim, your girlfriend won't talk to me," he called.

Tim appeared in the archway. "You mean she won't let you interrogate her."

Michael looked sheepish and then grinned at her. "You handled yourself well."

It was a game with no malice or spite intended. Michael might be hurt, but he still wanted to protect his friend. Tim had been dealt a lot of hurt by the Hopefalls Police Department, so she couldn't blame him. "Actually, I'm here because I got a call that Booley was heading in this direction and I wanted to stop him before he caused any more trouble. Have you seen him?"

Michael shook his head.

Tim put a tray on the coffee table. It contained three mugs of steaming coffee, a jug of cream, and a plate of muffins. The muffins looked a little too healthy for her liking. They were small bits of carrot and some kind of green stuff in them. She took a sip of coffee. It was rich, aromatic, and exactly as coffee should taste, unlike her blend of tar with cream and sugar.

"Good muffins." Michael licked his fingers. "Try one."

Dana took a small bite. The muffin was moist, sweet, and delicious. "Umm, did you make these yourself?"

Tim opened his mouth to speak, but Michael interrupted. "Yes, he's a great cook. If fact, he's the homemaker of our group. He makes a wonderful Thanksgiving dinner. We always spend holidays at Tim's."

"Who do you mean by we?" Dana had no idea Tim had friends, and a social life she knew nothing about.

Michael opened his mouth, but it was Tim's turn to interrupt. "You've met Finn, and David was at the police station with Marie. Then there's David's twin sister, Sinclair. She works for Child Seekers International, so she doesn't get home much. I think that's it."

"He's forgetting me." Michael gave a mock bow from his seated position.

Dana laughed. "I think he's ignoring you."

Michael shrugged. "My point is that Tim here"—he waved his arm at Tim, who rolled his eyes—"is an excellent cook, and he cleans up after himself. He's perfect husband material."

Dana felt her cheeks burn.

"Shit, Mike." Tim shook his head.

Michael's demeanor changed. His gaze was hard and steady. "Don't call me Mike."

Tim grinned. "You earned that one for embarrassing Dana."

Dana's face grew hotter.

The phone rang in the kitchen, saving her from further awkwardness. Tim answered it. "Dana, it's for you."

Dana glanced at her cell phone as she walked to the kitchen. No signal.

"We need to talk to you." Even on the phone, Mrs. Anderson's voice made her stand to attention.

"I got a call that Booley was heading out to Wind Valley, so it'll take me a while to get back."

"I know where you are. I called you."

Dana rolled her eyes. Dear God, could she get any more stupid? Thanks to Tim, no sleep, Booley running amok, a missing mayor, and a strange, injured Native American, she'd become completely distracted. She needed to tackle one thing at a time. First on her list—deal with Mrs. Anderson. "Is this an emergency?"

"No, we would like to talk to you about your swearing-in ceremony and the mayor's absence."

"I'm on my way." She needed to make her position official if she was going to get stuff done.

Tim was waiting by the door with a to-go mug as she hung up. He still wasn't wearing a shirt.

She placed a hand on his chest, giving into the urge to touch him. "Walk me to my car."

He held her hand as they stepped outside.

She stopped and gazed into his hazel eyes. "About yesterday—"

"I know you think it was a mistake, but it wasn't. At least not for me." A muscle in his jaw twitched. She got the impression he wanted to say more.

"I just-just…" Just what? She'd enjoyed every minute of it, but what now?

He stood, staring at her, waiting for her to gather her thoughts.

Finally, she said, "I got carried away. Everything's going so fast."

He wrapped his arms around her, drawing her into his embrace. "Don't worry, next time we make love, I'll take it slow." His lips brushed against hers.

It wasn't what she meant, and he knew it, but talking about it wasn't going to change what had happened. She reached up, burying her hands in his hair and tugged him closer, deepening the kiss, exploring him with her tongue. Once again, she was hit by a jolt of passion so strong her knees almost gave way.

It wasn't just his mouth that caused desire to penetrate so deep she was almost drunk with it. It was the feel of his hot, hard body pressed against her. Her breasts tingled as she rubbed against him in a mimic of lovemaking.

When she brushed his nipple with her fingers, he gasped into her mouth and thrust her up against the car. Breaking the kiss, he trailed kisses and licks down her throat.

"I wish you didn't have a house guest." She arched her neck to give him better access.

"He's only here for a few days, then he's moving on." His hands stroked her butt, sending quivers of pleasure to the apex of her thighs.

"Good." Dana placed her hand flat on his chest, forcing him back, his heart beating against her palm.

He tilted his head to the side. "Actually, I thought your place might be better. It takes too long for you to drive out here."

"What about Logan?" She couldn't have her son come home to find her in bed.

"He goes to school, doesn't he?"

A warm hum tingled down her spine at the thought of Tim in her bed. "It would have to be on my lunch break." That way Tim would be long gone before Logan got home.

He pressed his lips into a thin line. "Everyone would know. There are no secrets in a small town. Would you be okay with that?"

Unsure of her answer, she directed her gaze to the yellow fields. She wanted to continue to see him, wanted more sex, but as far as she knew, he was still a suspect in a homicide investigation. But she didn't believe he'd killed Ben. If she thought for one minute he'd committed a crime, she never would have made love to him, but would the residents of Hopefalls feel that way? If she only had herself to consider, she wouldn't have cared, but she had to think about Logan.

He hooked her chin, forcing her to look at him. "I've already told Logan that our relationship won't lead to marriage. My finances are a mess, and I don't want you to take that on."

She poked his chest, shoving him back a step. "You talked to Logan about marriage?"

His mouth fell open. "Yes, I thought it would be good to be honest—"

"Did it occur to you that I might have some input?" How could they discuss something this important without her?

"Logan and I were having a man to man—"

"Who cares? I'm the one who has to put up with you, not him." She was all but screaming now.

Tim seemed genuinely surprised by her reaction. "I was just trying to—"

"Trying to what? Undermine me. I'm an adult. You don't get to choose for me, and neither does my son. I'll decide who I marry, not you. And if our relationship…" She used air quotes for the word "relationship" because she had no idea what was happening with Tim, but they weren't at that stage, yet, no matter what he said. "If it gets to the marrying stage, then I will determine whether or not to take on your debts. Got it?" She was a firm believer in the old saying— *start as you mean to go on.* If there were any important decisions to be made about her life, she would be the main contributor.

There was something in the quirk of his lips that suggested he might be on the verge of smiling.

"Are you enjoying this?" She glanced down.

His erection pressed against the zipper of his jeans.

"This is a turn on for you?"

He shrugged, not bothered by her accusation.

He shouldn't find pleasure in her anger. She could feel the slow boil of rage simmering to the surface. "What the hell's wrong with you?"

He held up his hands in a show of submission. "For the record, everything you do turns me on. I can't help it." He grinned. "And the idea of you cuffing a suspect—oh man. I could stay up all night fantasizing about that."

She smacked his shoulder. "I'm not responsible for your infantile fantasies." Although, she had daydreamed about cuffing him earlier—not that he needed to know that.

He grabbed her shoulders and looked her in the eye. There was no sign of teasing now just the intensity of his gaze. "Actually, I told Logan the same thing yesterday."

Her mouth fell open. "You discussed our sex life with my son?"

"No, nothing like that. He had a man-to-man chat with me. He wanted to make sure my intentions were pure. I thought he might have mentioned it, but I can see by your reaction he didn't."

When would this role reversal with Logan end? He was worried about her. It should be the other way around. She should be the one questioning his friends, especially given his history of choosing to associate with pond scum. She shook her head. "Not a word."

He released her and stepped closer. "I made it very clear that what happens in our relationship is up to you. I know you're worried we went too fast yesterday. We can slow it down and get to know each other, if that's what you want." He tilted his head to the side. "I like your haircut. It suits you."

It was an obvious attempt to change the subject, and she went with it, if only because she internally winced at the knowledge that Logan had seen the attraction between her and Tim. "It's short."

"It's cute and sexy as hell." He bent his head so his warm breath tickled her ear. "I wonder if it will get spiky when you're hot and sweaty in bed after we make love."

She groaned. The vision of them naked in her bed with the sheets tangled around them was almost too much. She had gone from being mad at him to being aroused in sixty seconds flat. *Damn.* "I thought you said we could take it slow?"

He laughed and then said, "And I meant it, but I never said I'd play fair."

There was no way she would win this round. He had the advantage because she was compromised by her attraction to him. A strategic withdrawal was probably the best she could do. "I have to go. Mrs. Anderson is waiting for me."

"And I have an appointment with a lady who owns acreage on the other side of Hopefalls. She's thinking of going organic and wants some details on pricing." He backed up as she opened the car door and climbed in.

The truth of the matter was she didn't want to slow things down. Hadn't they just talked about where and when they would have sex? She'd just been blindsided by his admission that he talked to her son about marriage. The sex she could deal with; the two of them planning her future, without her, was another matter.

He'd also enjoyed taunting her. Well, two could play at that game. "There is one thing I have to ask before I go," Dana called through the open window.

"What?"

"When you talked to Logan, you said your intentions were pure?"

He nodded.

"They better not be too pure. I carry cuffs, and I'm not afraid to use them."

He moaned.

She laughed as she put the car in gear and drove away.

Chapter Thirty-Four

Ethan Moore rode across the bumpy fields of Wind Valley Ranch. There were no vehicles in front of the house and no sign that anyone was home, which was perfect. He'd placed the dripping Ka-Bar knife in a large bag to preserve the blood. Now all he had to do was plant it in Morgan's house. He couldn't leave it in an obvious place. Maybe he could put it in a heating vent or the freezer. Yes, the freezer would be perfect. It would look like Morgan had tried to hide it. At the same time, freezing the bloody knife would preserve the blood and prove Morgan had killed Booley.

He felt as if he'd experienced a hundred orgasms, and in a way, he had. The high he got from a kill was unlike anything he'd ever experienced.

Booley had been something special. Who knew the old man had so much fight in him. It had been a pleasure to slash at him again and again and watch the police chief struggle against the inevitable. His denial had lasted longer than most. He just wasn't able to wrap his mind around the fact that he had been wrong in his assessment of Ethan. He kept thinking he could win. It wasn't until the end that his eyes registered the truth—Ethan had been toying with him.

He parked the ATV. Tonight, when the job was done, he'd sit in his hotel room and go over every detail. He never kept mementos. To do so would be foolish. He was the only person who knew how many people he'd killed, and he wanted to keep it that way.

He grabbed the blade from the bag and stomped up the steps, not bothering to be quiet. He tested the door—unlocked—and took a step inside.

"Who the fuck are you?" A Native American sat at the kitchen table, a Glock 19 handgun aimed at Ethan's chest.

"I'm-I'm—" *Shit, think, think.* "I'm a friend. Morgan said I could use his bathroom to wash up after hunting."

"You've got about five seconds to get out of here before I kill you." He stared at Ethan as he sat straight-backed in the chair. His hard, unblinking dark eyes showed no sign of hesitation or uncertainty. His hand was steady, no nervous tremor, and his breathing was calm and regular.

Ethan had no doubt this man would put a bullet in him. He put his hands up. The action made the blood from the knife drip down his arm. "I'm going. I don't mean any harm. He backed out, closing the door after him.

He headed back toward Molly's Mountain. What the fuck was he going to do now? He could drive away and then backtrack and try to kill the bastard. No, that would raise more questions. The idea was to blame Morgan for Booley's death, get rid of him that way, but that was shot to hell. He tried to remember everything he had seen in the kitchen. The man, the gun, and the phone on the table. The gun wasn't the biggest problem. It was the damn phone. Whoever that guy was, he'd probably called for backup the moment he'd seen Ethan driving across the field, which meant help was on the way. Booley's body was lying up in North's shack on Molly's Mountain, waiting to be discovered. There was no way he could plant the evidence on Morgan. Thank God, he had a plan B ready to go.

Chapter Thirty-Five

Finn placed his coffee and the bag containing a Rueben sandwich and a cookie on his desk. It had been a long, hard morning, maybe the longest of his career. When he added it to the nightmare he'd faced yesterday afternoon after interviewing Ackerman, he figured he was due a pay raise.

"How did it go?" Kennedy asked, glancing up from her computer screen.

"I would rather face a thousand ax-murderers than go back there again."

"Stop being so melodramatic. It was only the county records office."

"Records before 1984 are not computerized. I had to search through hundreds of documents."

Kennedy swiveled in her seat to face him. "Did you find anything?"

"I found the original deed for North's property dated first September 1898. But that was as far as I got. It's like the lawyer said, the land could've been divided and split since then. I need to go through Ben's genealogy and work up a family tree. Then I'll have an idea who to look for."

"Did you get the deed Mayor Harris sold to Third Estate Mining?"

"Yes."

"Great, I got a copy of Ben North's handwriting from his lawyer. We'll send them to the Questioned Documents Unit at Quantico." She pointed to an evidence bag.

Finn filled out a label. "It'll be interesting to see the results."

"Do you think Harris tricked Ben out of his mineral rights?" Kennedy used her thumb and forefinger to twirl her pen.

"Or faked the documents. Either way, he must think it's a lock. Ben's elderly with no money. How does he prove they'd been stolen? You heard Millar—once the Eminent Domain process starts, it's impossible to stop." He snapped on a pair of latex gloves. He'd sealed the papers in a bag the moment he'd found them at the Elkhead County Records Office, but he liked to ensure all procedures were followed to prevent contamination.

He placed the suspect deed into the secure courier package. "So all Ackerman has to do is legally buy the mineral rights from Harris and start the process. It didn't matter how much money North gave his lawyer. The chances of him winning were slim. The only thing they didn't count on was someone killing North."

Kennedy fixed her astute gaze on him. "You really don't think Ackerman or Harris killed him?"

"I think they're capable of it. I just don't think North's death was in their best interest." Finn sealed the envelope.

"So whose idea was it to steal Molly's Mountain, Ackerman or Harris?"

He threw his gloves into the garbage. "My money would be on Ackerman. Somehow, he discovered this mineral, coltan, is under Ben's property. He approaches Paul Harris—"

"A landman."

"Who's also the mayor of a dying town." Finn opened his lunch and took a bite of his sandwich.

"And you think Harris was desperate enough to go along with him? I don't know about that. I looked into Harris's background."

He swallowed, without tasting, and then said, "What did you find?"

"Nothing. He's never been arrested. He has no criminal record. He's never even had a speeding ticket."

"Maybe he got in over his head. We know he's Lucy's lover, and Ackerman paid him a fortune for the rights. Sex and money can be a powerful motivator."

Finn's phone played the funky jazz tune. Damn. He had to remember to change his ringtone.

"Finn."

The curtness in Michael's voice made him snap to attention. "What's wrong?"

"Some guy was here. He had a bloody knife. Said he was a friend of Tim's."

"You don't think he was?"

"Called him 'Morgan.'"

"What were his exact words?" Finn had no doubt Michael would be able to recall the conversation word for word.

"'I'm a friend. Morgan said I could use his bathroom to wash up after hunting.'"

"Shit." Tim never allowed anyone to call him Morgan. It was Tim, Timothy, or Mr. Morgan, never just Morgan. "Have you called Tim?"

"He's next after you."

"Okay. I'm on my way."

Kennedy stood near the door, waiting. She was armed and wearing her raid jacket.

"You caught that?" Finn grabbed the car keys.

"Michael's in danger?" She swung the office door open, heading to the SUV.

Finn marched after her. The idea that a man with a bloody knife had turned up at Wind Valley Ranch sent chills through his spine.

Chapter Thirty-Six

Tim grabbed his rifle and his backpack, which contained a new can of bear spray. His Ka-Bar knife, as always, was in its scabbard at his waist.

"I'm coming with you." Dana stood at the kitchen door, staring at the drops of blood on the floor.

"You should wait for—"

"Who? The police. I am the police. If anything, I'm the one who should be going after this lunatic, not you." She stood ready, one hand automatically resting on her weapon.

"You're out of your jurisdiction," he countered, hoping she would leave him to pursue the freak who'd showed up at his door.

"I can make a citizen's arrest and then take the suspect to the Granite City- Elkhead County police." She had him there. Not a surprise considering she was trained in law enforcement.

Tim had stopped at the Hopefalls Police Station after his sales call, hoping to have lunch with her. After Michael phoned to tell him about the man with the bloody knife, they'd rushed to Wind Valley together. His instinct was to shield her, although he doubted she would appreciate that. "I was going to say the FBI. Someone needs to guard Michael."

Her brow creased. "Michael? Why would he need protecting? This is about you. This guy knew your name. He came to your house."

Michael limped into the kitchen. "She's right. You need backup. Finn will be here soon."

Tim didn't like the idea of Dana getting caught up in this mess, but she was a cop. Her job was to put herself on the line of fire to safeguard those in her care. If they were to have a future, then he had to learn to deal with that. Finally, he nodded, and grabbed the key for the ATV and then turned to Michael. "What did this guy look like?"

"I was sitting down so my perspective might be off. He was Caucasian and as tall as you...and slim."

Tim remembered stopping to warn the protesters about the bear. "Did he have a beard and a wool cap?"

"No." Michael shook his head. "He had no distinguishing features, just the knife."

"Who were you picturing?" Dana asked.

"One of the environmentalists camped at Ben's gate." Tim closed his eyes, trying to recall the details of his encounter. "Moore...that was it, Ethan Moore."

Dana jotted the name in her notepad. "I think I've seen him around town. He was one of the last protesters to leave Molly's Mountain, and he was at the town hall meeting on Sunday night. Why would he come to your house?"

"I don't know, and the guy I'm thinking of has a beard, but he could have shaved." Tim shook his head. "He struck me as being ex-military. He eyed Michael. Thank God, he'd done some target practice. "Maybe we should wait until Finn arrives."

"The asshole headed across the field toward Molly's Mountain," Michael said. "He was out of view once he reached the forest."

"What if he doubled back and is waiting for us to leave?" Tim reasoned.

"Will someone tell me what's going on?" Dana said through clenched teeth.

Tim inhaled a long, calming breath. "I'm not sure. Michael here is ex-army CID. Someone is trying to kill him. Finn asked me to take care of him for a few days until he could figure something out. I didn't ask for details."

She grabbed the keys from his hand and headed for the ATV. "Okay, it's need to know. I get it." She pointed to Tim. "You stay here and keep an eye on him. Booley and the mayor are missing, and I have to go after the man with the knife. I can't have him running around the county, stabbing people."

"I'm coming, too." Tim snatched the keys from her hand.

She grabbed them back. "No. Stay here and watch out for your friend. I can handle this."

"No one's saying you can't, but I can track him. I know the land and I know how to obey orders."

"What about Michael?"

Michael shoved a walkie-talkie into Dana's hand. "I'll radio you if there's a problem. If he comes back, I won't ask any questions. This time I'll shoot to kill."

Tim stared at Dana. "I'm coming. We can either go together or I'll trail after you on the other ATV I have in the barn." The truth was there was no other ATV. He'd sold it a long time ago. He felt a small twinge of guilt about lying to her, but he couldn't let her go alone. If anything happened, he'd never forgive himself.

****

Dana hopped off the back of Tim's ATV as they pulled up to the river that marked the divide between Molly's Mountain and Wind Valley Ranch. Dana had her misgivings about Tim aiding in the pursuit of the suspect. The legal ramifications didn't bother her. The criminal code stated she could order a person to help in securing a pursuant. No, she was worried about Michael. They had assumed this situation was about Tim, but what if they were wrong? She pushed her doubts aside. Tim was right, she couldn't track someone through the bush. She needed his help. Once they had the guy with the knife in custody, they would figure out who he was after.

Tim moved forward, his rifle to his shoulder. Falling back on his Ranger training, he was focused, lethal. He headed toward the off-road vehicle parked nearby. She drew her weapon and followed. There was nothing on the ATV except a smear of blood.

The rustle of leaves in the trees was deafening as the treetops bent, pushed by the gusts of wind blowing off the Cabinet Mountains. Surprisingly, Dana and Tim were protected from the worst of the squall by the forest.

Using her smartphone, she snapped some pictures of the blood smear and the off-road vehicle, being sure not to touch. "Why do you think he left this here?"

Using the strap, Tim slung his rifle over his shoulder and studied the ground. "My guess, he's heading to Ben's cabin." He pointed to a narrow track that started on the other side of the creek and led up the mountainside. "It would be faster to run up the trail than drive to the bridge on the highway."

He hunched down to take a closer look. What he saw, she couldn't say. Maybe there was a blade of grass out of place or a snapped twig, but nothing stood out to her. He pointed to the river, raising his voice to be heard above the wind. "He went across the creek. We'll have to wade across and pick up his trail on the other side." He grabbed the bear spray from his pack and glanced at her belt.

She assumed he was checking to make sure she was armed. She holstered her weapon. "Don't worry I'm ready."

"That won't take down a bear." He thrust the can at her. "If we meet one, use this."

Dana nodded, clipping it to her belt next to the radio, and then followed him across the waterway. Once they were on the other side, he shrugged into his backpack and snapped the waist belt in place, securing the load. "The tracks lead up towards Ben's cabin."

Do you think he could've doubled back? He might be waiting to ambush us." She tugged on the straps of her pack, making sure they were secure.

He scanned the area. "That's a chance we'll have to take."

"I suppose it depends on his endgame. What's his goal? Does he want to kill us or is there something else going on here?"

He hunched down to examine the dirt floor of the forest. "He was moving fast, following the trail. We can reassess if I see any sign he stopped or deviated from the path."

"Lead the way." She didn't like the idea of being behind Tim. She was the cop. She should call the shots, especially when trailing a suspect, but she had absolutely no tracking skills.

Running up hill for forty-five minutes was harder than she imagined. It was made worse by her belief that Tim slowed to keep pace with her. At those times he made a show of checking for signs that they were still on the right path.

Tim put an arm out to stop her as they reached the crest of the mountain. "Shush."

A chemical smell assailed her, burning her throat—gasoline.

They were nearly at the top. Ahead of them was a rocky ten-foot escarpment. Ben's cabin was on top of the ledge. A dirt track lay to the right. She'd driven up the same trail the day they'd discovered his body.

Crouching low to the ground, she crept to the driveway. They would have to follow it to reach the house. She would've preferred to stay undercover and advance without being seen, but it wasn't possible. The topography of the land saw to that. They reached the flat outcrop. Bits of yellow crime scene tape billowed in the wind. Whether it was torn or cut, she couldn't say.

She unclipped her pack and slid it off, not wanting to be burdened with the cumbersome load. Tim did the same.

With her weapon raised, she approached Ben's cabin. Tim stayed close behind. The front door was wide open. She was twenty feet away and could see the back of a tall, slim man as he emptied the contents from a red plastic gas can over Ben's couch.

"I think that's Ethan Moore," Tim whispered.

She nodded, acknowledging his words without engaging in conversation. Blood splattered the walls of the house. The assailant must've knifed someone and then decided to hide the weapon in Tim's house to implicate him. But who did he kill?

She stretched, standing on tiptoe, but was too far away to see anything. "I can't let him start that fire and destroy the evidence," Dana whispered.

Tim's lips pressed into a thin line. "You are not going in there."

"Yes, I am."

"Okay, I'll come with you."

"No, I need you to wait outside in case he doubles back around and traps us.

He rubbed his chin and then aimed his rifle at the door. "Okay, go ahead. I'll cover you."

"How good are you with that rifle?"

"I'm a Ranger—a trained marksman."

Of course, he was. He was probably more capable of handling this situation than her. But it was her job to stop the psychopath. "I'm going to arrest him.

Tim readied his weapon, resting the butt against his shoulder.

They moved forward in unison with her in the lead.

Chapter Thirty-Seven

She stopped on the first step. Booley's body, or rather what was left of him, was sprawled across the floor of the cabin. "Dear God." Nothing in her career as a policewoman had prepared her for the horrific mess. She instinctively looked away, but then spotted two handprints planted on the floor, a large red oozing mass next to it.

She wanted to leave, to get away from the stench of blood, death, and gasoline. She resisted the urge to suck in a deep breath and focused on the task. "Where did he go?"

"I don't know," Tim's monotone was nothing more than a whisper.

"Stay here and cover the exit."

He didn't answer, but then she didn't expect him to. He'd been a soldier and had told her he knew how to obey orders.

She moved forward, gun raised and ready. Without stepping in the blood, she entered the cabin, scanning the surroundings, clearing the house. There was no sign of Moore, but the kitchen window was open. Maybe he'd heard them coming and fled.

A creak in the floorboards made Dana swivel around. Tim stood behind her. She sighed and lowered her weapon. "I told you to wait outside."

"I couldn't let you walk in to this massacre alone."

She appreciated his need to protect her, but it wasn't necessary. "What if he doubles back and blocks our exit?"

"What if he's waiting in here to ambush you?" Tim stepped toward her.

"You know she has a point." The man she knew as Ethan Moore stood behind them, blocking the door. He flicked open a lighter. He must've escaped out of the window and snuck around the house, trapping them.

Dana aimed her SIG. "Close the lighter and throw it on the ground behind you."

Ethan smiled. "I don't think so. If you shoot me, I let go, and this whole place will go up in flames. My death will be quick." He shook his head, his smile mocking. "But yours…yours will seem like an eternity of pain."

Tim put down his rifle, laying it carefully on the couch. His gaze hard and cold as he stared at Moore.

A lump formed in Dana's throat. He was surrendering. How could he? There was no doubt in her mind that Moore was going to kill them. They couldn't give up. They had to stand their ground. Dana straightened her arms, strengthening her stance. "Back up."

Without a sound Tim, launched himself at Moore, grabbing the lighter. The momentum threw them out of the cabin and down the steps. The lighter landed on the ground behind him.

The two men exchanged blows, moving fast. They rolled to their feet, still trading punches.

She followed them outside and aimed her weapon at the pair but couldn't get a clear shot. She knew from her experience as a beat cop that stepping in the middle of a brawl was a great way to get hurt. Then she saw the glint of a blade in Moore's hand and another as Tim drew his Ka-Bar. This wasn't a brawl—it was a knife fight.

Tim grabbed Moore by the neck, shoved him back, and stabbed him in the gut, the jabs fast, and calculated.

Moore didn't react. It was as if he didn't feel the thrust into his stomach. Instead, he twisted, trying to get to Tim's midsection. Tim curled, bending in, forcing Moore to pierce his shoulder blade.

They broke apart, circling each other like wolves. Both of them were bleeding, Tim from a deep gouge that sliced his upper back while Moore held a hand to his stomach.

Dana stepped between the men, holding her weapon on Moore. "Put the knife down—" Part of her wanted to pull the trigger. He was a crazed killer who had carved up her boss, but she couldn't bring herself to do it. Was this hesitation part of her problem? No. It was like Tim said, she wasn't a killer. She was a cop. She was supposed to arrest the bad guys, not shoot them. This wasn't like before. Moore didn't have a hostage. She had the gun, which meant she had the advantage. "Ethan Moore, I'm arresting you for the murder of Police Chief Levi Booley.

"Dana, get out of the way," Tim growled.

She ignored him and focused on Moore. "Drop the knife. I will shoot you, but I'd rather charge you."

Moore smiled, slicing the air with his blade, his other hand on the stab wound to his side, which dripped blood. "That's the difference between us. I'd rather kill you."

"That's not going to happen." She realized she didn't need to repeat her threat. She would shoot Moore. She wasn't scared. She wasn't nervous. This was kill or be killed. "Drop the knife."

Moore just smiled. His injury obviously wasn't that serious.

A rustle in the bushes behind Moore caught her attention as a huge grizzly stomped into the clearing.

"The smell of gas mixed with blood was probably too much for her to resist." Tim sounded calm, controlled. "Dana, back away slowly."

Moore swung around. "Shit."

"Dana." Tim grabbed her shoulder, tugging her backward.

Once she was level with him, they stepped back in unison. She holstered her weapon and grabbed the bear spray, never taking her gaze off the bear or Moore.

They reached the edge of the escarpment. Below them was a ten-foot drop.

"What now?" Dana asked.

Moore swiped the lighter off the ground and sprinted for the house.

The bear charged.

Tim shoved her over the edge.

She flailed, trying desperately to protect her face from twigs and pine needles. She hit a tree trunk, bounced, and hit another tree as she tumbled in a free fall. Tim grabbed her hand, almost yanking her shoulder from her socket. He dangled upside-down his legs wrapped around a branch. She hung in midair, gasping for breath.

Blood leeched down his arm. "We need to keep moving. Can you reach the ground?"

She glanced down. The crumbling dirt of the forest floor slanted beneath her. The angle was steep, but if she accounted for that, there wouldn't be a problem. "Yes, I can."

"Okay, jump."

She landed, slid on the loose ground, but managed to use a tree trunk to stop.

Tim had no problem getting down. He grabbed a branch and released his legs, gracefully lowering himself until his feet touched the forest floor. Without a word, he started down the mountain, slipping and sliding, choosing the fastest path.

"Do you think going over the ledge will stop the bear? Dana panted after him. Her legs were shaky, which she hoped was a result of the adrenalin rush and not fear.

"No." The knife wound to his shoulder blade caused blood to ooze down his left arm and back. He was leaving a scent trail that would be easy for the bear to follow.

"Maybe it went after Moore. He was wounded, too."

Tim shrugged, but kept moving, working his way down the mountain.

"Do you think it's the same bear?"

He stopped and turned to her, his chest heaving. "Probably, but I don't know for sure. It's hard to tell one bear from another, and no one's going to take notice of distinguishing features when she's charging at you."

A loud whoosh sounded. A column of smoke billowed above the trees. Ethan Moore must've set light to Ben's cabin.

Tim shoved the keys for the ATV into her hand. "Go warn everyone about the fire."

She shook her head. Tim needed to back off. She now understood what he had told her yesterday by the side of the road. He could kill. Not everyone had that ability. It wasn't that he wanted to kill, but he was capable of taking a life. If he crossed paths with Moore, he would end him. But she didn't want Moore dead. It was her duty as a police officer to arrest him for Booley's murder and then hand him over to Ramirez for questioning in Ben's Homicide.

"No, I'm going after Moore." She unclipped the walkie-talkie and bear spray from her belt. "Tell Michael about the fire and the bear. He can use the landline to call the Hopefalls Police Station."

He grabbed the radio from her and clicked the call button. There was no signal, just static. He stared at her for a moment as if deciding something. "I need to go back up the mountain to make the call."

They ran, retracing their steps, heading toward the fire and the bear.

He swiped at the sweat on his forehead with the back of his hand. "What makes you think Moore didn't die in the inferno?"

"The fire's a distraction, and it could've scared away the bear. But he's still alive. It's what I would do if I wanted to cover up a murder. Remember the gasoline? It was all over the house. And then there was the lighter. This was always part of his plan."

He tilted up his head, squinting at the sky. "In these dry conditions, with the wind driving it, the blaze will hit the town soon."

"All the more reason for you to talk to Michael." She had her weapon and her cuffs. She was all set. "We need to split up. What's the fastest way to get to the trails at the bottom of the mountain?"

"What makes you think he's heading for the trails? Why wouldn't he just use the ATV?"

"It's a possibility, but I don't think so. That vehicle has no registration tag or license plate. If I saw him driving down the road, I'd pull him over. He probably drove here with the off-road vehicle in the bed of his truck or in a trailer."

He gazed at the ground and then scratched his cheek, frowning. She could tell he didn't like the idea of her hunting through the forest for a knife-wielding madman.

Finally, he said, "You'll need to head north. Keep the sun behind you. As you get closer to the bottom of the mountain, maintain your course, with the creek on your left. He turned and then disappeared into the brush, ending their conversation as he vanished, blending into the wilderness.

Chapter Thirty-Eight

Tim climbed the escarpment and peeked over the edge. The bear was nowhere in sight, but that didn't mean she wasn't close. Bears were known to dig through the remains of a campfire, looking for any food that wasn't completely burned. But this was so much more than a campfire. All that was left of Ben's cabin were a few burning timbers. Tall, yellow-orange flames licked at the trees behind the house, and massive plumes of smoke wafted high into the sky. Tim tried to listen for Moore and the bear but couldn't hear anything above the wind and the crackle and roar of the inferno.

Luckily for him, the gusts blew the fire northeast, away from him. It was like having an invisible shield protecting him, but he knew from experience the wind was fickle. It could change directions without notice. He needed to call Michael and then track Moore. There was no way he would leave Dana to deal with that crazed killer. He'd known she wouldn't back down. That's why he had told her to follow the creek because it intersected with the Hopefalls Highway. She could track it until she reached the road. And if the fire did turn her way, she could take cover in water. He hadn't exactly lied, but he hadn't told her the truth either. He planned to track down Moore and kill him. Dana was all about justice. She would try to arrest him and bring him to trial, but Moore was a different kind of monster. The idea that he would slice her sent a chill down Tim's spine. He would do anything to save her, and if that meant lying, so be it.

He levered himself up and over the edge and then clicked the button on the radio, scanning the area as he talked. "Mike can you hear me?

"Don't call me Mike."

He ignored Michael's rebuke. "I need you to call the Hopefalls Police Department. Tell them Ben's cabin is on fire. The wind is blowing from the southwest, pushing the fire straight for town."

"I see the smoke, and I heard you loud and clear. Making the call."

"They also need to be on the lookout for Ethan Moore. He killed Levi Booley." Tim spotted the bear tracks heading south into the bush.

"Just to confirm. Levi Booley, the police chief, is dead." He could hear the surprise in Michael's voice.

"Affirmative." Tim crossed the clearing, heading for the burning remains of the cabin. "Dana has gone after Moore. I think my truck keys are on the kitchen table."

There was a moment of silence. "Yes, they are."

He didn't get too close, but instead checked the ground leading away from the ruins, looking for any droplets of blood. "Meet us at the bridge where Molly's Creek meets the Hopefalls Highway."

"You want me to drive. I don't know if I can."

"You have to. The fire could trap us. We need an out." The wind ceased, causing him to be engulfed in wafts of smoke. He choked and coughed, momentarily blinded by the gray-yellow haze. Then everything cleared as a blast of cold, clear air blew over the mountain.

"Got it. Calling Hopefalls now."

Tim clipped the walkie-talkie on his belt. He didn't need to ask Michael how long he'd wait. He knew his friend would do everything humanly possible to save them.

He crouched down, inspecting the dark, oozing droplets. He figured Moore had flicked the lighter into the gas and then jumped out of the loft window. He probably hadn't used the front door or the kitchen window because of the bear. It would've been at least a fifteen-foot drop, but that wouldn't be a big deal to an athletic killer like him. Tim ran after him, tracking the beads of blood, hoping Moore wouldn't cross paths with Dana before Tim could catch him.

****

Dana scrambled through the undergrowth, keeping the stream on her left so she wouldn't get lost. The fire consumed the forest on her right. Yellow, red, and gold flames dance and licked at the trees, making them crackle and hiss. The noise was so loud she couldn't hear her own gasps. Sweat trickled down her back. Every cell in her body told her to run for safety and get away from the raging inferno. Hunting Moore had seemed like the right thing to do, but she didn't have the skillset to track a man through the forest. She'd insisted on hunting him down because she couldn't live with the idea of a psychopath like Moore escaping. From what she'd seen of Booley's body, she would guess Moore took pleasure in killing, and if he wasn't stopped, he would murder again.

She wished she had Tim's experience in the wilderness. There was a thought. How much wilderness expertise did Ethan Moore have? He obviously wasn't a harmless protester, and he'd set fire to the forest so he didn't care about the environment. Did he have anything to do with Ben's homicide?

A loud, sharp whistle caught her attention. She turned toward the sound and spotted Tim in a clearing a hundred yards up a slope, away from the creek, and closer to the fire. Her heart did a little flip, and she sighed with relief. He was safe, and with his help, she could hunt Moore.

He waved and headed toward her, inching down the steep incline. A swirling mass of smoke enveloped him, obscuring him.

The smoke cleared in time for her to see Moore kick Tim in the stomach, launching him through the air. He landed in a clump of shrubs.

Her heart stopped. She couldn't let Tim die. Before she could think about her reaction her SIG Sauer was aimed at Moore's chest. "Stop," she yelled. But the thunderous rumble of flames and splintering wood drowned out her voice.

Moore rushed at Tim, a long deadly blade in his hand ready to strike.

Tim surged to his feet in time to block Moore's thrust with his elbow.

Smoke hid them, again. Dana scrambled up the slope, grabbing at roots and spiky shrubs with her free hand, never taking her gaze from the spot she'd last seen Tim.

The wind shifted. Tim rolled to the side, his hand going for the knife at his waist.

Moore neared, preparing for another kick. Tim grabbed Moore's heel with one hand while slicing at the back of his ankle with the other. Moore didn't react, which suggested Tim had stabbed his boot. Tim stabbed again. This time Moore tensed and tried to pull away. Then he changed tactic. Using his good leg, Moore jumped and twisted, yanking his injured leg out of Tim's grasp. The knife was still lodged in Moore's calf. Tim had lost his weapon.

Dana raised her weapon to shoot, but another waft of smoke obliterated them from view. She sprinted closer, trying desperately to see through the yellow fog.

The haze cleared. Tim rose to his feet. Using his foot, he kicked a branch off the forest floor and caught it in his right hand.

Moore charged, pulling his knife arm back, ready to strike.

Dana aimed and fired.

Moore crumpled to the ground.

She'd shot him. This wasn't like before. There was no second-guessing, no uncertainty. She had stopped him. That was her job, to protect those who couldn't protect themselves. She hadn't hesitated, hadn't faltered. She had no doubts about her actions. Ethan Moore had murdered Booley and been intent on killing Tim.

Tim? Where was he? She was about to call his name when he appeared by her side. He bent over, resting his arms on his knees, gasping for breath. "I knew you could do it."

She patted along his torso, checking for broken bones. "Are you hurt?"

He straightened. "No, just bruises. You?"

She stared at Moore's body as he lay on his side ten feet in front of her, blood flowing freely from a wound at his head. "I need to see if he's alive."

The loud crack of splintering wood sounded, followed by the crash of a falling tree.

Tim grabbed her hand and tugged her down the incline toward the creek. "We need to go," he shouted in her ear so he could be heard above the roar of the wildfire.

She pulled her hand out of his grasp. "I need to check his vital signs. If he's alive, then we'll drag him out of here and he can be charged."

A thunderous snap reverberated through the forest as another tree splintered. Tim threw her down the slope away from the inferno. They rolled, eventually coming to a stop at the bottom of the incline.

Dana righted herself. She stared up at the mass of flames and smoke.

Tim wrapped an arm around her waist, yanking her farther down the slope. "You have to leave him. We're out of time. Michael is meeting us at the bridge." It didn't feel right abandoning Ethan Moore's body, but they had no choice. They slid down the incline toward the stream.

She hadn't realized she was so close to the road. Tim was safe. They had a way out of here. For the first time in a long while she was grateful she was a good shot.

Chapter Thirty-Nine

Tim released a deep breath as his truck skidded to a stop at the roadblock created by Officer Robinson. The police cruiser was parked sideways across the street at the four-way stop in the center of town. A low-lying plane flew overhead, dropping red retardant on the forest and the houses on the west side of Hopefalls. Fire trucks screamed past, their sirens blaring as they headed to the fire.

Cars loaded with boxes, suitcases, valuables, and other personal treasures filed into the eastbound lane of the highway, heading away from the fire, and to the safety of Granite City. It was the only option. All the other roads led into the wilderness. It would be all too easy for civilians to become trapped. Once in Granite City they could go in multiple directions to escape the blaze.

Tim climbed out of the vehicle. Sweat coated his body and his dry tongue smacked against the roof of his mouth. They were lucky. Michael had been waiting for them at the bridge. The heat from the blaze was devastating. The fact that Tim had managed to drive through it, and the three of them had emerged unscathed was nothing short of a miracle. It was an experience he never wanted to relive.

One glance at Dana told him she was in the same condition. Her short blond hair was soaked from root to tip, and her shirt stuck to her body, accentuating her shape.

Michael sat stone-faced in the back of the truck. If he was in any pain, he didn't let on.

Dana slid out of the pickup and headed toward Officer Robinson. "Fill me in."

Tim trailed after her, not ready to leave her side. The fire, Ethan Moore and the fear she might get hurt, or worse, chilled him to the core. Moore took pleasure in other people's pain. He'd seen the euphoric delight in Moore's eyes when they'd been locked in combat.

Officer Robinson cleared his throat and then said, "The Montana Department of Natural Resources and Conservation has issued an evacuation order."

"How many people have left?" Dana was in full cop mode now.

"I don't know. I've been busy stopping sightseers."

Tim joined them. "Sightseers?" He couldn't believe anyone would want to get close to a forest fire.

Dana thumped her fist against the roof of the cruiser, her frustration evident. "Those idiots who drive to a disaster area so they can see it or take a picture because they think it won't kill them."

Officer Robinson pointed toward the police station. "I have Shelly coordinating the evacuation. Volunteers are going door-to-door, making sure everyone is out."

"I can help," Tim offered.

"Me, too." Michael carefully eased out of the vehicle.

Dana pressed her lips into a thin line as her gaze fell on Michael's cane.

Michael grunted and then said, "I wasn't thinking of anything that involved moving. I can help with the phones and organizing shit."

Dana nodded. "I can take you to the police station, but Shelly's in charge, and if she tells you to get lost, you're on your own." She then sat sideways in the driver's seat of the cruiser and grabbed the radio. Shelly, this is Dana. I'm okay. You?"

"Oh, thank God." The older woman's voice crackled over the line.

Dana didn't bother with niceties. "How's the evacuation going?"

"Slow. Buses have left the school with all the kids accounted for."

"Was Logan with them?"

Xavier waved his hand in front of her face, interrupting her. "Yes, I put him on there myself."

She smiled, relieved. "Thanks."

The radio buzzed, and Shelly answered, "Yes. He's fine. I have Joe and Victoria helping the older folks. Everyone else is leaving of their own accord. I have everywhere covered but The Heights."

Dana keyed the mic. "Copy. Stand by." She looked at Officer Robinson. "That makes sense. It's up on the hill out of the way. Plus, it's the least populated area."

Officer Robinson stared up the road that led to The Heights. It was deserted. "The only local who lives there is the mayor. The rest are holiday homes, and there's no way to tell if those owners are visiting or not."

"Speaking of the mayor..."

Officer Robinson shook his head. "No, there's still no sign of him."

Dana spoke into the radio. "I'll cover The Heights. I'll—"

Tim put his hand over the receiver. "No damn way are you going up there alone."

She took her finger off the mic button and stared at him. "I'm a cop—"

"And we just encountered a knife-wielding maniac—"

"Who's dead."

He crouched down in front of her. "I get it, but we just went through a heap load of crap, and I'm not ready to have you go off on your own." He knew he needed to learn his boundaries when it came to her job, but he couldn't do that right now. He was too emotional, too raw. When Moore had attacked him the second time, he'd feared for Dana. If Moore had taken him out, then who would protect her? The fact that she had saved him and hadn't needed protecting didn't matter.

She cupped his face with her hand. "You got stabbed. You need to go and get stitched up."

She had a point. Dried blood caked his shoulder blade and down his arm. The pain wasn't too bad, and his ribs were just bruised. He'd been hurt worse.

She patted his face and then pushed his good shoulder. "Plus, I'm pissed because you lied to me."

"When did I—"

"Follow the creek? Are you really going to tell me you didn't point me in that direction because it was safer? While you hunted Moore."

Shit. He didn't realize he'd been so transparent. He probably should apologize, but he couldn't. Given the choice, he would do it all over again. "What do you want me to say? I'm not sorry. Most of the time I'm laidback. I don't sweat the little stuff, but I'm still deadly. And you"—he poked her shoulder for emphasis—"don't have to go it alone. I'm here for you, but it only works if you take the help that's offered. You wanted to go after Moore, but I couldn't let you die. I will always have your back, no matter what."

Her eyes glistened. "I never thought—"

"Ethan Moore is a killer who knows how to use a knife. So do I." It was as simple as that. She would have to decide if she could accept him. He knew he was a man of contradictions. He was easygoing by nature, but life had taught him how to be tough and how to kill. And some lessons couldn't be unlearned.

She stared into the distance for a moment and then nodded. "You still need medical attention. I can drop you and Michael off at the police station. You can wait for me there."

"No." He shook his head, his answer emphatic.

She opened her mouth to argue.

He stopped her by putting a finger to her lips. "I get it. This is what you do. And I respect that, but you saw the cabin, what was left of Booley's body. I was scared. I thought that freak would hurt you. I'm just not ready to let go. Give me this one. Let me go with you. Besides, you left your cruiser at the ranch so we need to take my truck. I go where it goes."

She gave him a small smile. "Okay, but as soon as we're done, you're getting stitched up."

"I promise."

She keyed the mic again. "I'm dropping off a friend at the station. His name is Michael. Tim will come with me to The Heights."

Chapter Forty

Tim's big truck was surprisingly easy to handle. Dana drove up to the heights, mainly because she needed to be in control. Tim's words at the roadblock had unsettled her more than she wanted to admit. She hadn't realized she had been trying to do everything herself, but his words rang true. It wasn't that she had anything to prove; it was more a question of trust. She had never trusted the men in her life, not after Oliver had dumped her. But she was no longer a pregnant teenager, and Tim was nothing like Logan's father.

Tim was asking—no, demanding—she give more of herself. He hadn't ordered her. He was just so unreserved and relentless in his care of her. How could she resist? And why would she want to? The answer was simple—she didn't. She'd been getting in her own way, putting up roadblocks.

No, that wasn't technically true. She'd tried to keep him at arm's length because he was a suspect in Ben's homicide. But she was now convinced Ethan Moore had killed Ben. Later she would sort through the why and the how of the case. For now, all she wanted was to clear the town, get Tim the care he needed, and check on Logan.

She fished her smartphone from her jeans and put it on speaker. She only hoped Logan was in an area that had cell service.

He picked up on the first ring. "Mom, are you okay?"

"Yes, I'm fine." She wouldn't mention Ethan Moore, Tim's injuries, or the fire. She simply needed to hear Logan's voice, know he was okay, and reassure him. "I'm going to help with the evacuation and then leave. Where are you now?"

"I'm on the school bus. They said they're taking us to a school in Granite City. We're going to be fed and housed in the gym."

She hated the idea of him going through this alone. He wasn't a little kid and he didn't need her around, but still, this was an extreme situation. If she couldn't be there with him, she hoped he had someone he could count on. "Are any of your friends with you?"

"Most of the kids went with their parents. Those of us who were left were put on the bus."

Her chest tightened as guilt threatened to suffocate her. From the corner of her eye she saw Tim roll his eyes, but he said nothing. Logan was manipulating her, trying to make her feel guilty, and it worked.

"As I said, do you have any friends on the bus?"

"Yes, Mia's here."

"Good, I like her."

"Yeah, me too." Logan's voice had softened.

"If you want, I can come pick you up now so you don't have to spend any time at the school." That wasn't true. She had to help the citizens of Hopefalls, but she could call someone in the Granite City–Elkhead County Police Department and see if they had anyone who could collect him.

"No, that's fine. I'm good," he assured her.

She tried not to laugh. He wanted to stay with Mia.

She said goodbye and disconnected.

Tim grinned as he straightened in the passenger seat. "Shame on you."

"What?"

"You knew he wanted to stay, and you didn't call him out for trying to guilt you."

She laughed. "Let him try. I figure he's allowed to get a few jabs in. I haven't made it easy for him over the years."

"You mean being a cop or a single mom."

"Both."

Dried blood crusted the left side of Tim's back and down his arm. His dirt-covered face was also bruised with one eye swollen, and the way he held his left arm across his chest bothered her. "Your ribs are broken, aren't they?"

He stared ahead, not meeting her eye. "No, they're just bruised."

"How do you know? You could be hurt worse than you realize."

"I'm not in enough pain to have any broken bones." He straightened and then winced. "Mostly, I just ache."

She shook her head. "I should have taken you to get checked out."

"We've been through this."

"Damn it. I know you're tough, but you're still human. I want you in one piece, whole and healthy."

His hazel eyes slanted to her. "I like you, too." He grinned, making her breath hitch. Damn, the man was fine.

Dana parked and forced herself to concentrate on the task at hand. "There are only eight houses. Let's split up. We'll stay within yelling distance."

"Most of these places look empty." Tim seemed tired. The adrenalin crash was probably hitting him now. She felt it herself, but probably not to the same degree. It wasn't just the fatigue and exhaustion. Even if he'd had no injuries, he would hurt all over.

She climbed out of the truck, eager to finish and get him the medical care he needed. "You're right. They probably are empty except for the mayor's house. I'll start there. You go to the one next door."

He nodded and jogged up the street, keeping his left arm close to his chest.

Dana walked up the rocky path that led to the large log house the mayor called home. Mrs. Harris opened the door as she approached. She was wearing jeans, a turtleneck, and a windbreaker. Casual clothes. And yet she still managed to look as if she'd just stepped off the cover of a magazine. A small yappy dog barked and ran out. It bounced around Dana's legs, snapping and whining. Zoe did nothing to discipline the little beast. Instead, her cold, hard gaze settled on Dana. "I'm not leaving without Paul."

She spun and flounced back into the house, dismissing her. The nasty dog trotted after its master.

Dana wasn't sure what to make of Zoe's demeanor. They'd had a good relationship until recently, not close, but always respectful. Things had changed on the night of the town meeting when the police chief's deceit had been uncovered. Maybe she was angry because she agreed with Booley's assessment of Tim. Whatever the reason for her change in attitude, Dana couldn't leave her to burn to death or be suffocated by smoke.

She followed Zoe into a bright, airy living room. "Where is the mayor? The town council has been looking for him."

All the furniture looked to be expensive with antiques artistically placed on end tables and the mantle. A huge plant sat in the arch between the living room and the kitchen. Garish, frilly curtains were drawn back, allowing light to stream through a wall of windows. On a clear day, she would've been able to see Molly's Mountain. All she could see now was a gray plume of smoke that stretched hundreds of feet into the air.

"He's away on town business." Zoe waved a dismissive hand as she sat in a chair positioned to take advantage of the view.

Dana tried to reason with her. "Then you can leave without him."

"That's out of the question. Paul would expect me to stay."

Dana closed her eyes, burying her frustration. Then she strode to the window and pointed at the wildfire. "Look. There's not going to be a town if they can't get this fire under control."

The dog scratched at the backdoor.

"One second. If I don't let Missy out, she'll make a mess on my new hardwood floor." Zoe rushed to give the little beast access to the yard.

Her gaze fell on the large plant. It was massive, with hanging flowers of pink and orange that reminded her of ornate bells or maybe…trumpets. She gasped. This was the angel's trumpet. She recognized it from pictures on the Internet. What did the article say? The seeds of the *brugmansia* were used to make the drug, devil's breath. Had Zoe or the mayor caused Ben's death? She was getting ahead of herself. After all, what motive could they possibly have? Ben's homicide had delayed the mine. That couldn't be in their favor.

"I see your admiring my houseplant." Zoe stood next to her.

A chill ran down Dana's spine. The flower by itself wasn't enough to arrest Zoe, but as the investigating officer, Ramirez would want to know about it. He had information Dana didn't and, besides, this could be nothing. For all she knew, there were lots of people in Hopefalls with deadly shrubs in their living room. They were sold all across America as houseplants, for God's sake.

Act natural. Even as she thought the words, she remembered her initial gasp. Had she telegraphed her suspicions? "I'm doing up my grandmother's house. I'd love to get a plant like this. What's it called?"

"They call it the angel's trumpet because of the shape of the flowers." Zoe ran a perfectly manicure nail over a pink petal. "It's widely available at any garden store."

Damn. Dana walked to the front door. She tried not to look at the plant or display any facial cues. Details flooded her mind. Zoe visited the nursing home. Had she overheard Ben talking to Jack? But what had she heard? Why would she poison Ben? Dana needed to leave *now* and call Ramirez before the fire destroyed the evidence.

She reached for the door handle. "If you're not going to evacuate, then I should leave. I have a lot of people to help."

Zoe followed her. "Before you go, there's something I want to ask."

Dana turned. "Yes."

Zoe removed a Smith and Wesson 9 mm from her jacket pocket and thrust it into Dana's ribs. "You know, don't you?"

Chapter Forty-One

"We're going to walk to your car," Zoe said through clenched teeth. Her unblinking eyes were hard and cold.

"The police know you didn't mean to kill him." Dana held her hands in the position of surrender as she stepped through the door, Tim's truck directly in front of her.

Zoe stayed close. "Stop." She freed Dana's SIG Sauer from her belt and threw it across the lawn out of reach. Then she nudged Dana, silently, ordering her to walk. "I didn't kill anyone. Everyone knows Tim Morgan killed Ben North over that stupid Colt."

"No. The police know Ben was already dead when he was shot." All Dana had to do was keep Zoe talking. Hopefully, her common sense would kick in and she would realize the insanity of her actions. With any luck, she would become distracted and drop her weapon, or she might see the futility of kidnapping a cop. "The medical examiner's report says that Ben died of a heart attack, which was triggered by poisoning, specifically *brugmansia*, extracted from the plant known as the angel's trumpet. The same one you have growing in your living room."

"It's only in the living room for the winter."

Dana stopped and turned to stare at her captor before continuing on. The position of the plant wasn't important, but it was a good indication of Zoe's warped state of mind. So much for her common sense and sanity. The woman was unhinged.

They had made it to Tim's truck. "I'm going to reach into my pocket for the keys," she shouted, hoping Tim could hear her. She didn't want him to get shot trying to save her, but at the same time she needed him to go for help.

"No, I'll do it. Which one?

"My front, left side."

Zoe jammed her weapon hard into Dana's back as she reached from behind and slid her hand into the pocket. She retrieved the keys and placed them in Dana's raised hand.

"Don't try any funny business. I will shoot you." Zoe stood with her feet wide. Both hands held the Smith and Wesson steady, her gaze locked on Dana. There was no hesitation and no doubt about Zoe's intent.

She opened the passenger door. "Get in here and slide over. That way I can keep an eye on you."

Dana climbed across the seats. She needed to stall for time. Sooner or later Tim would notice she was in trouble and sound the alarm. "What will your husband say about all this? Does he know you killed Ben?"

Zoe waved the gun. "Once this is over, he'll lose interest in that whore and come back to me. Start driving and don't try anything clever."

"What whore? Does she have a name?" Stalling hadn't worked, and now they were in the truck. The engine had a loud rumble. Tim had to have heard her start it up.

"Paul's hooked up with some rich bitch called Lucy Portman. She's the one who got him into this Molly's Mountain deal. He thinks I don't realize what he's up to when he says he's away on town business, but I know."

"How?"

Tim was making his way through the trees, heading toward the mayor's house. Dana made herself look straight ahead. There was no telling what Zoe would do if she spotted him.

"I tailed him. I saw them fondle each other under the table. He even followed her into the ladies' washroom. It was disgusting. Enough talking, drive."

Luckily, Zoe was too caught up in her own story to notice Tim running for the truck.

"Where am I going?" Dana did a U-turn as smoke wafted over the street, covering everything with a yellow-gray haze.

"Molly's Mountain."

"But it's on fire."

Zoe smiled. "Yes, it's a good place to get rid of a body. Don't you think?"

Chapter Forty-Two

Tim dashed through the forest. The road curved down the hillside in a multitude of switchbacks. He decided on a direct route through the trees. He cursed as he tripped and slipped, but allowed the momentum to carry him down, skidding on his butt. He ignored his throbbing shoulder and sore ribs. He righted himself as he reached the bottom of the hill. He didn't know if he'd missed the truck or if it was behind him.

His eyes watered, his lungs burned, and his mouth tasted like he'd swallowed the smoke from a thousand campfires.

He tensed as he neared Officer Robinson's patrol car. It was a reflex born out of years of fear. For most of his life, he'd been scared of the Hopefalls Police Department. Booley was his boogieman. He'd stolen Tim's childhood, his home, and threatened his freedom. Now Booley was dead and Dana was in trouble.

Officer Robinson stood in the middle of the road, a red bandana wrapped around his face. Tim ran toward him, nearing the four-way stop sign that marked the center of Hopefalls. His black Ford pickup drove past. Dana was taking her time. Good.

The young cop waved his arms, his actions telling Dana to stop.

Tim hoped she would slow down as she approached Officer Robinson, but instead she sped up and then veered to the side.

The officer jumped out of the way, landing behind his cruiser.

Dana swerved back onto the highway, heading toward Molly's Mountain and the fire.

"What the hell?" Officer Robinson stood, staring after her.

"The mayor's wife is in the passenger seat." Tim reached the roadblock.

The policeman spun around to face Tim. "But she nearly hit me."

Tim opened the passenger door of the cruiser. "Dana probably did that to get your attention. From what I could see, Zoe Harris has a gun on her."

Officer Robinson's jaw dropped, then recovered and sprinted for the vehicle. "Let's go." He put the car in drive and raced after the truck.

Tim tried to picture Dana's face. She hadn't looked in his direction. She'd stared straight ahead, not making eye contact. She'd been protecting him.

****

Finn sped toward Hopefalls. They'd been halfway to the town when they'd heard about the fire. A low-flying aircraft zoomed overhead, making it feel more like a warzone than a town in mandatory evacuation.

Traffic on the other side of the highway was bumper to bumper. Emergency response vehicles sped ahead of him, their sirens blaring.

Kennedy played with the knobs on the radio, tuning in the scanner. Curt professional voices echoed over the air, relaying the coordinated effort to fight the wildfire.

She froze, listening. "It's on Molly's Mountain. That can't be a coincidence." She scooped her phone from her pocket. "I'll try calling Michael."

Finn navigated through the deserted town and headed for the police station, hoping to touch base with Officer Hayden and the rescue workers.

"The line's dead." Kennedy hit the disconnect button. "Do you think this fire was set so someone could get to him and kill him?"

"Let's not get ahead of ourselves. We only suspect his life is in danger. There have been no attempts to kill him." If only his emotions matched his words. His gut told him

Michael was in danger. If the Syndicate hadn't figured out his true identity yet, they would—soon.

He parked in front of the police station. "Let's see if they have more information. You never know, this could've been caused by a careless campfire or a cigarette thrown from a car."

The station was empty except for an older woman with short gray hair and Michael. They sat side by side, each of them talking on landline phones, which made sense when he considered how bad cell phone reception was in the mountains.

Finn tapped Michael on the shoulder. "You have to leave now."

Michael shook his head and covered the phone with his hand. "I don't think so."

"This fire could be a distraction in an attempt to get to you."

"Finn, you're getting paranoid. Besides, Tim and Dana saw the guy who started it. By the description, I'd say it was the same asshole who arrived at Tim's door with the bloody knife."

Finn put his hands on his hips. "Damn. You need to leave."

Michael continued as if Finn hadn't given him an order. "He killed the police chief."

"And the chief's computer is missing," the gray-haired lady added.

Michael smiled at her. "This sweetheart is Shelly. Shelly, I'd like you to meet FBI Special Agent Finn Callaghan and his partner, Special Agent Kennedy Morris. They're friends of Tim's."

The older woman nodded and then held her phone to her ear, listened, and then said, "No, Hank. You're not coming back for your boat. It's a useless pile of junk. It doesn't float because it has a great big hole in the bottom."

Michael held an earpiece to his ear, listened, and then tugged off his headset. "There are a lot of elderly people who need help to get out."

A crackle came over the radio. "Shelly, it's Xavier. Officer calling for help, critical."

Shelly frowned and reached for the small black radio with a hand mic attached. "Xavier, this is dispatch. What's wrong?"

"Dana's in trouble."

"Go ahead."

"Zoe Harris has a gun on Officer Hayden. They're heading toward the fire on Molly's Mountain."

Shelly paled and pointed to Finn, asking silently for his help.

Finn answered with a nod.

"Back up is on the way."

Finn headed for the door. He stopped as he reached the front desk and faced Kennedy. "Stay with him."

She nodded. "Got it, boss."

He marched into a wall of choking smoke. The feeling of spiders crawling down his spine told him trouble was coming his way. He just didn't know where or how.

Chapter Forty-Three

Tim held his breath as his truck swung off the road and followed a trail through the forest. They tailed from a safe distance. There was a chance Zoe Harris hadn't seen them in the rearview mirror. It was a risk, one they had to take. Finally, Dana pulled over two hundred yards ahead.

The fire was close. The extreme heat caused beads of sweat to drip down his spine. The flames and wind shot the smoke high into the air, which meant it wasn't as thick on the ground next to the fire.

Officer Robinson skillfully parked their vehicle, being sure to hide it in the middle of a small copse of young Lodgepole pine.

Damn it. Tim could take Mrs. Harris out with one shot if he had his rifle with him, but he'd left it in Ben's cabin when he'd set it down so he could attack Moore. He'd have to make do with whatever was available.

"I'm going to need this." He raised his voice to be heard above the roar of the blaze and pointed to the Remington model 870P shotgun secured to the middle of the dashboard.

Officer Robinson shook his head. "It's not going to happen. I can't give up my shotgun to a civilian."

"I was a Ranger. I'm trained to move undetected through difficult terrain. I can get within touching distance of Zoe Harris without being seen." His gut twisted and cramped at the idea of Dana getting hurt.

"It doesn't matter. I still can't give you a weapon."

A cold vice tightened around Tim's chest. For the second time today he was terrified, not for himself, but for Dana. He'd just found her and couldn't lose her. With her, he saw the chance at a normal life, one where they would fight, laugh, and love. "Okay, here's what we'll do. I'll go around the front and draw her fire. You can then take her out."

"Have you ever done anything like this?" Sweat dripped from the young policeman's brow.

Tim wasn't sure if the officer was nervous or if he was reacting to the intense heat. "Yes, in Afghanistan. I'm going to approach from the front. You're going to walk toward them from the rear."

Officer Robinson drew his weapon and grabbed the door handle.

A knock at Tim's window made him jump. "Finn, dammit." He opened the door and climbed out of the car, his heart hammering in his chest.

Officer Robinson was out of the cruiser, gun drawn.

Tim made the introductions as the young officer holstered his weapon.

"What's the plan?" Finn said, getting to the point.

Tim assessed the terrain. He wouldn't have to be quiet. The wildfire was deafening. There wasn't much ground to cover, but he needed to get close if he wanted to divert Mrs. Harris's attention. "Give me a minute, maybe a minute and a half. I'm going to get in front of them and distract Mrs. Harris. You two come from the sides. The minute she points her weapon at me, you can take her out."

He took off running, blending into the forest, not giving the lawmen a chance to stop him. He was doing this whether they agreed or not.

It would've been much easier to hide if he'd been wearing a ghillie suit. The camouflage uniforms were designed to help snipers blend into their environment. Using the forest for cover, he circled around the women until he was ten feet in front of them. Then he got on his stomach and crawled through the undergrowth, ignoring the throbbing pain in his ribs. Blood dripped from his shoulder, running down his arm to his elbow. He ignored that too.

The ache in his chest lessened at the sound of Dana's voice. "So how does your husband having an affair lead to this?"

He wriggled closer, crawling through the dirt and under a huckleberry bush so he was within seven feet of them.

Dana stood in front of Zoe with her hands raised.

"He doesn't love her. He just wants her money and connections. He needs her to get ahead." Mrs. Harris's voice had risen to a shrill squeak. She sounded desperate, unbalanced.

Using a tree trunk for cover, Tim stood.

"I don't understand. What has Ben got to do with it?" Dana seemed calm, in control.

"He found some rare gold coins on Morgan's land. I heard him telling Jack. If I had those coins, I could sell them for a fortune, and then Paul wouldn't need her."

Ben had died because of some coins. Tim buried the knowledge and focused on Dana. He needed her out of the way so Finn could do his thing. He stepped out into the open. "Why would Ben tell my dad? He has Alzheimer's. He wouldn't understand."

Zoe jumped, a high-pitched squeal escaped her throat, and she swung the small handgun in his direction. "No, but I did. Somewhere on Wind Valley Ranch is a tin of rare gold coins. Ben stole some to pay his lawyer. I gave him devil's breath so he would lead me to them."

"So that's why you drugged him. You wanted control of his mind," Finn, weapon drawn, came from the right side.

Zoe pointed her Smith and Wesson at Finn. Her voice rose to a shout. "I'm not stupid. I did my research. Ben would've recovered completely. He might remember what I did, but he wouldn't be able to say anything because he'd stolen some, too."

"How did you get close enough to give it to him?" Officer Robinson closed in from the left.

She spun toward the policeman, waving the gun. "Don't come any closer or I'll shoot."

Dana held up her hands, telling them to halt. "No one's going to shoot you, but we need to know. How did you get close enough to administer the drug?"

Zoe changed her focus and aimed her weapon at Dana.

Tim's breathing hitched. He needed Zoe to hone in on him. "Answer the question."

She swung the Smith and Wesson in his direction. She seemed calmer, quieter. "It was easy. Ben always was a skirt chaser. I took lunch up to his cabin, flashed my breasts, and then blew it in his face. The stuff was working too, but then—"

"He died of a heart attack. Did you shoot the body?" Dana asked.

"No, I called Booley and told him. He knew what Paul was up to. He comforted me."

Tim took a step forward. He was amazed at how much information Zoe Harris was willing to share. He was also pissed that neither Finn nor Officer Robinson had taken her out. Had they forgotten the plan?

"Comforted you?" Finn raised an eyebrow in question.

"Nothing like that. I'm not a whore," Zoe wailed.

Dana moved in front of Tim. "So you called the chief and he came, found the gun, and shot the body?"

Tim wanted to grab her and push her out of the way, but a sudden movement might trigger Zoe to shoot.

"Yes, why'd you have to get the Granite City-Elkhead County Police Department involved? It was a Hopefalls matter. You ruined everything."

"Because Molly's Mountain isn't in Hopefalls." Dana's hands were now fisted and raised in a defensive position.

"Put the gun down," Finn demanded.

"You self-righteous bitch!" Zoe pointed her weapon directly at Dana.

"No." Tim rushed at them, desperately attempting to close the distance.

Dana seized the gun and pointed it to the sky.

Zoe struggled, but Dana was too strong. She punched the older woman. Blood spurted from her nose. She slumped to her knees, her hands covering her face.

Dana relieved her of the Smith and Wesson. In swift practiced movements, she released the magazine and then ejected the cartridge from the chamber. "Lady, you are bat-crap crazy."

Chapter Forty-Four

Dana, who was officially off duty, sat next to Tim. He was slouched in her chair at the police station. She had forced him to take her seat while she finished her paperwork. Her chair was softer and more comfortable than the visitor seat she was using.

The best way to describe him would be walking wounded. He was conscious, but he wasn't talking. His quietness bothered her because it was impossible to tell whether he was simply tired or if he was in too much pain to talk. She could tell by the way he sat that his ribs and back hurt, but he had refused to go to the hospital until she had finished her report on the day's events. She should've known he wouldn't leave her. This nightmarish day had done a number on both of them. Dana had experienced real toe-curling fear when Zoe had pointed her weapon at Tim. For the second time today, she'd been scared she would lose him. That fear had honed her feelings about him. He'd said they were in a relationship, and she'd resisted. But now, she was done fighting. She wanted to get to know him and see if this attraction between them could grow into something real.

The wind had changed directions, and now blew the inferno back in on itself. Denied of fuel, the wildfire was considered under control. Crews were still out extinguishing hotspots and flare-ups, but the residents could return home. The highway between Hopefalls and Wind Valley Ranch was closed. Tim wouldn't be able to return for a while.

She'd spoken to Logan again and had wanted to drive to Granite City to pick him up, but he'd asked her to wait. He wanted to ride back with Mia.

This had been the longest day of her life. The knife-wielding maniac who'd showed up at Tim's door had also murdered Chief Booley. Ben's cabin had been set alight, resulting in a wildfire. On top of that she'd shot Ethan Moore—the psycho with the knife. It wasn't the same as the first time she'd killed. She wasn't traumatized. She had no doubt that Moore intended to kill Tim and had reacted accordingly. She wasn't sorry for her actions. Maybe she'd feel differently later, but at the moment she was fine with it.

Zoe Harris had been the biggest surprise of the day. She'd admitted to accidentally killing Ben over some gold coins. Detective Ramirez had taken her into custody. They were on their way back to Granite City. Zoe would be charged with manslaughter at the very least. The only question that remained was how much the mayor knew about his wife's crime and if he'd covered it up. He had been at the cabin the day Ben's body was discovered, as had Booley. They knew Booley had shot the dead body. What role had Mayor Harris played?

Michael hobbled to the coffee machine. According to Shelly, he'd been a great help in organizing the emergency personnel. Special Agent Callaghan and his partner, Special Agent Morris, stood against the reception counter, watching them. Dana had no idea why they were still here.

The place looked like it had been hit by a whirlwind. Papers were strewn about the floor. Empty coffee cups overflowed the garbage until they, too, were heaped on the floor. And to make the chaos complete, Booley's office was a crime scene.

She patted Tim's good shoulder. "You need to go to the hospital in Granite City."

"The medical center in town will be fine."

"Granite City has better imaging equipment. Moore could have severed an artery or something." She pointed to the stab wound in his shoulder blade.

Tim grunted and then said, "He didn't."

"How do you know?" She didn't like the way he looked. Pain shadowed his eyes, every twitch and every movement, even the simple act of breathing made him wince.

"If he had, I would be dead by now." He squeezed her hand. "You knew I was there, didn't you?"

He didn't go into detail so she qualified his question. "When you were in the bush in front of me and Zoe?"

He nodded and sat up slowly, his actions stiff, careful.

"Yes, I knew you were there," she said. "The bush moved."

"Damn, I must be losing my touch." His face was still covered in dirt and soot, and a twig stuck out of his messy hair.

Dana ran a hand over her head, wondering if she looked as worn-out as Tim. Not that her looks were important right now. Logan and Tim were safe, and the town was out of danger. "Thank God the wind changed direction."

"Michael said it was arson," Agent Callaghan said. He obviously needed more details about the day's events. Details she didn't want to relive.

"I saw the fucker pour the gasoline over Ben's cabin. Oh, and he killed Booley." Tim held his left arm protectively across his ribs.

"Who was he?" Agent Morris asked.

Tim winced as he swiveled in his chair to face the room. "I know him as Ethan Moore."

Dana cleared her paperwork and sat on her desk, staring at the agents, wondering how much they knew about Ben's death and Molly's Mountain.

Callaghan smiled at her and then addressed Tim. "But you don't think that's his real name?"

Tim shrugged. "How should I know? I don't play cop, but whoever this guy was..." He paused, seemed at a loss for words.

"He liked to slice," Dana finished for him.

"What do you mean?" Agent Callaghan took out a notebook.

"Moore toyed with Booley before he killed him. It was nasty." Dana's stomach heaved at the memory of the butchered body and all the blood.

Agent Morris rolled Shelly's office chair over to the coffee counter, but instead of sitting in it, she pointed to Michael and then to the seat, silently telling him to sit.

Dana strolled to the percolator and poured herself a cup of coffee. "I think Booley was killed because he was blackmailing someone."

"What?" Agent Callaghan scribbled in his pad. "Why do you think that?"

Dana pressed her lips together. "Jack said he had to take Ben's guns away from him because he was drinking and planned to kill Booley."

Agent Morris joined Dana, helping herself to a mug. "When was this?"

Dana shook her head. "I've no idea, probably years ago. According to Jack, Ben wanted to kill Booley because he knew the name of Ben's mistress, which was a secret." She decided not to mention how Booley had tried to blackmail Mrs. Anderson. That was something she would only use if she had to.

"Knowing someone's secrets isn't the same as blackmail. Besides, if this happened a long time ago, why would someone kill over it now?" Agent Morris took a sip of her drink and grimaced.

"I don't think they killed over that. I'm pointing to a pattern of behavior. At some time in the past, Booley was prepared to blackmail Ben."

"And if he's committed blackmail before, he would do it again," Agent Callaghan clarified.

"Exactly. Then there's the messed-up office, and his laptop's missing." Dana pointed to the door, which was now secured with crime scene tape, probably Shelly's doing.

Callaghan shoved away from the counter. "If he was running, he might take his laptop with him." He opened the door to Booley's office and scanned the interior.

Michael turned on Shelly's computer. "You know a lot of computers automatically store to the cloud. If you have this guy's email address, I can access his accounts."

Dana jotted down the information and then moved to stand behind him. "You probably don't want to use this computer. It's on the intranet not the Internet. It's an independent system."

"Not a problem. I can switch the settings to the Internet and see if there's a wireless connection nearby. He pressed a couple of keys. A small white box popped up on the screen. "Hopefalls town hall Wi-Fi." He then clicked on a tab and a search window appeared.

Agents Finn and Kennedy crowded around Shelly's desk, watching Michael.

"That was way too easy. Could someone transfer police files to an outside source?" Dana was horrified. The police system was supposed to be secure, isolated.

Michael nodded. "Yep."

"Damn!" She'd have to see about safeguarding their electronic files.

Michael typed in the sequence of letters and symbols that represented Booley's email. "As long as I have his email address, I should be able to access all the accounts, pictures, and documents he has saved to the cloud. I'm in. What do you want to look at first?"

Dana was shocked. It had taken him less than thirty seconds to switch to the Internet and access Booley's private files.

She stared at Tim, who smiled back at her. "He's a genius."

"Does he have a photos folder?" Dana said, gathering her wits. Things were coming at her too fast to process. She needed to concentrate on one thing at a time. Right now, she wanted to know what her boss had been up to and why he had been killed.

Michael punched a few buttons. Pictures of Paul Harris exiting the Elkhead County Records Office flashed on the screen, followed by another shot of a deed showing the mayor's ownership of the mineral rights. There was a photo of Paul Harris in a compromising position with a woman with mid-length blond hair.

"I take it she's Lucy Portman." Dana pointed to the woman who lay on the bed, enjoying Paul Harris's sexual favors.

Agent Callaghan's head snapped up. "What do you know about her?"

"Paul's affair with Lucy was Zoe Harris's motivation for drugging Ben," Dana explained.

Tim raised his hand. "Are you investigating her?"

Agent Callaghan didn't answer. Instead, he looked to his colleague.

Agent Morris sighed. "Go ahead. Michael already knows. You need to warn Tim, who will probably share what he knows with Officer Hayden. So you might as well get it out in the open."

"We believe Mayor Harris is involved with a group of businessmen who call themselves the Syndicate. We think the Syndicate manipulate events to make money." Agent Callaghan stated the facts.

Tim stared at Agent Callaghan, his gaze unflinching, as though he was communicating with his friend using an unspoken language. "Were they involved with Marshall Portman's attack on Marie last winter?"

Michael stopped typing and turned in their direction. "The Syndicate ordered Portman to kill her and destroy her solar panel."

This was a lot for Dana to take in. "Whoa. What does this have to do with Hopefalls?"

Agent Callaghan straightened, pulling himself up to his full height. "We think Lucy introduced Paul Harris to Lance Ackerman. Ackerman convinced Harris to steal the mineral rights from Ben. Then—"

"Wait. Why just steal the mineral rights? Why not the land, too?" Dana needed to get all the details clear in her head.

Tim gave a soft whistle and then said, "Everyone would know that was a lie. Ben would never sell his land."

Agent Callaghan continued, "Anyway, Harris steals the rights and sells them to Ackerman who then mines the coltan and corners the market for electronic devices. All your cell phones, computers, tables, GPS, everything would be controlled by them."

"Look at this." Michael pointed to the computer screen. "Booley had pictures of the deed." Then there was a photo of a crumpled piece of paper, which showed Ben's signature copied over and over. There was another image of a receipt from an office supply store.

Agent Callaghan laughed and then said. "Here's our proof of forgery. Harris purchased forms that transfer property. Then he forges Ben's signature and files the form at the county recorder's office. That's all he had to do to obtain the mineral rights to Molly's Mountain. The mayor of Hopefalls is going to prison for a long time."

Agent Morris explained, "We suspected the mayor stole Molly's Mountain's mineral rights. There's no record of North having any bank accounts, and Harris didn't make a payment to him. But we can't prove Ackerman's involvement. He will walk away free and clear."

Tim's pain-filled gaze settled on Agent Callaghan. "Let's see if I've got this straight. The mayor effectively stole North's home. Then his wife accidentally kills him because she wanted the gold he'd found. And somewhere on Wind Valley Ranch there's a pot of gold. I can't believe I said that with a straight face. It sounds like a bad St. Patrick's Day joke."

Agent Callaghan nodded. "That about sums it up."

Dana paced the room, trying to figure out how it went down. She stopped when she got to Agent Morris. "Who is Ethan Moore?"

The two FBI agents stared at each other and then shrugged in unison.

"Once we recover the body, we might be able to get fingerprints or DNA to help us identify him." Dana rubbed her eyes. It would be a long time before she would be able to sleep through the night. The image of the freak with the knife was a nightmare that would be hard to banish. The only comfort she could take was that he was dead and couldn't hurt them anymore.

Chapter Forty-Five

Finn exited the Dumb Luck Café carrying a tray with three coffees. It had been a long day. Tim had gone to the medical center with Dana. It was clear that she was not only concerned for Tim, but that she cared for him. If someone had told him a year ago that his friend would fall for a cop from Hopefalls, he wouldn't have believed it.

Michael had come with Finn to Granite City. Leaving him with Tim wasn't the best decision Finn had ever made. He should've found somewhere better, a place where no one would look. Normally, Michael could've disappeared, lived below the radar, bummed around, and worked odd jobs for cash, but that just wasn't possible in his present condition. He needed a place to lay low for a few months, at least until he could fight again.

A man standing at the fountain caught Finn's eye. There was something familiar about him. He was around forty, wearing a suit. He had gray-streaked hair that was swept back and the distinguished handsome face of an actor.

Finn inched closer. "Are you Paul Harris?"

Harris nodded and switched his gaze to the police station.

Finn placed the coffees on a nearby table, his hand automatically covering his weapon. "We've been looking for you."

"I'm going to jail, aren't I?" His voice cracked.

Finn wondered if he was going to cry. "Yes."

Harris stared, blankly, seemingly lost in his own thoughts. His eyes were bright, almost feverish. He was a fragile man who'd made mistakes. Finn suspected he would be the fall guy for the Syndicate, but proving that might be difficult, if not impossible.

Finn inhaled. First, he needed to make a connection with Harris. Any attempt to strong-arm him might fracture his already fragile state of mind.

"Let's go inside. It gets chilly in the evening at this time of year." He pulled a cup from the tray. "Would you like a coffee?"

Harris took the cup and walked with Finn to the federal building.

"So where have you been hiding?" he asked casually.

"I was with Lucy at the Sharp's Inn and Resort."

That was Ackerman's hotel.

"Why were you staying at a hotel? She owns a house in town."

Harris shrugged. "She said she preferred to keep her home life separate from her extra-curricular activities."

Which translated to mean Harris was just the entertainment and not part of a meaningful relationship. "Where is she now?"

"I don't know. She took off. I woke up this morning and she was gone. I tried her number, but the line's dead, and I'm not allowed to contact her at work. Do you think she's in trouble?"

Finn almost laughed. He believed Lucy Portman was a survivor, who had strung Paul Harris along because she needed him for the Molly's Mountain mine, but now the deal had gone sideways, she had cut him loose.

Kennedy leapt to her feet as they entered the office. Finn shook his head, warning her to be quiet. Michael, who was seated in Finn's ergonomic swivel chair, began searching Finn's desk, probably looking for a video camera to record the interview.

Finn sat Harris down in a chair and pulled up another seat so they were opposite each other. Without a word, Kennedy set up the video equipment.

"Tell me about Molly's Mountain. Why don't you start at the beginning?" Finn suggested.

"Lance Ackerman and Lucy Portman concocted the whole thing to get the coltan."

"How did they know the coltan was there in the first place?"

"Some geology students stumbled upon it when they were doing a survey."

"What happened then?"

"Ackerman contacted me—"

"When?"

"About two years ago. He was interested in building a mine near Hopefalls. It would've created work for the whole town."

"Whose idea was it to forge the documents that transferred North's deed into your name?"

"Lucy's. She said the deal would be made with or without me. All I had to do was get the mineral rights. Ben would still have his mountain. We just wanted what was beneath it."

Finn glanced at Kennedy, who held her breath as she stared at Harris.

"Let's talk about the Syndicate." Finn doubted Harris knew much.

"I only know two members—Lance Ackerman and Lucy Portman."

This was his proof, a witness, and confirmation of the Syndicate's existence. Finn needed more. "How do you know about them? Are you a member?"

"No, Lucy mentioned them. She liked to talk while we had sex."

Finn winced at the image that swept through his mind.

Harris hugged his arms across his body as he rocked in place. "They're going to kill me, aren't they?"

Finn, mindful that the interview was being recorded, asked for clarification. "Who's going to kill you?"

"The Syndicate."

"We will protect you if you'll testify against them."

Harris nodded.

Finn swiped a hand in front of his throat, signaling for Kennedy to turn off the video equipment. He needed to call Deluca. He had to get Harris into protective custody immediately.

****

Michael winced as he fidgeted in Finn's ergonomic chair. He hadn't complained, but Finn could tell he was in pain. The trip to Salt Lake City, the mad drive through a wildfire, and now sitting for hours on a broken pelvis had made him sore.

Finn had tried getting in touch with Sinclair, but her phone had gone straight to voicemail.

Agents had arrived to collect Paul Harris. Deluca had assured Finn that the information on the former mayor's location would be known only by his superior in the Department of Justice and the agents in the U.S. Marshals Service assigned to protect him, which meant only the high and mighty would know of his whereabouts.

Maybe he should ask for the same consideration for Michael. Finn wanted his friend to be safe. Sinclair had seemed like the perfect option. She had her own resources with Child Seekers International, safe houses where women and children saved from the sex trade could hide until new homes could be found for them. But Sinclair wasn't picking up her phone, and they were out of time.

A knock at the door made him jump. He covered his weapon as Kennedy turned the handle.

Sinclair marched in, then stopped and stared at Michael. Her eyes widened for a moment before she turned her green-eyed gaze on Finn. "Sorry I'm late. I drove out to Tim's, only to find the road closed, so I came here. What the hell happened?

Finn stepped forward. "Wildfire. It's a long story. I tried calling. Did you turn off your phone?"

"I always pull the battery and SIM card from my phone when I'm relocating someone. It makes it harder to track me."

Michael grinned. "Smart."

Her gaze drifted over him, taking in his long hair, the awkward way he sat on his good side, and how he favored his left arm. Finally, she nodded in his direction. "We need to get going. We have a long drive."

Michael scrunched up his face as if he smelt something bad but didn't comment.

Sinclair answered anyway. "I know, but it can't be helped. I have the perfect place for you and a new identity. It won't stand up to much scrutiny, but it's not as if you'll be working and paying taxes. You'll be safe while you heal."

"Then what?" Michael's question was barely a whisper.

"Let's hope Finn catches the bad guys and you can go back to your life."

Chapter Forty-Six

Finn smiled at Kennedy as they entered the Sharp's Inn and Resort. They'd called ahead to make sure Ackerman was still in the building and had been advised he was checking out of his suite tomorrow morning.

They now had the results back from the Questioned Documents Unit, and those findings, along with Booley's images, proved the deed was forged and therefore the mineral rights to Molly's Mountain belonged to Ben North and would be left to his heirs.

Paul Harris was willing to testify that the syndicate was real, but he had no knowledge of their future plans. That could be a problem. He only knew about the Syndicate because Lucy had mentioned them, and that was hearsay. He hadn't witnessed the group firsthand or received instructions directly from them. A good lawyer would argue that Lucy had been lying to impress her lover. Although he could still go after Ackerman and Portman on the forgery, Lucy Portman had chartered a private jet this morning, her whereabouts unknown.

They had turned Harris over to the Justice Department and the U.S. Marshals Service this morning. He was now entering WITSEC, the protection program for threatened witnesses.

"Showtime," Kennedy muttered as she knocked.

Finn held up his credentials when Ackerman answered. "FBI Special Agent Callaghan and this is Special Agent Morris. We spoke a few days ago."

"I remember." Ackerman smiled, seeming relaxed and comfortable.

"We want to talk to you about your plans to mine Molly's Mountain."

"I only have a few minutes. That's all I can spare." He waved a hand as if swatting a fly. He didn't invite them in.

Finn eyed Kennedy. Interviewing him in this location wasn't ideal, but it was possible.

Kennedy withdrew a small recording device from her pocket and spoke into it. "I'd like to state for the record that agents Callaghan and Morris are interviewing Lance Ackerman in the Sharp's Inn and Resort."

Ackerman grinned and pointed to the device. "Son, you might want to turn this off."

Finn narrowed his eyes. "Why would I want to do that?"

"I was up late last night reading."

Finn said nothing. In his experience, it was best to let the suspect ramble on and hang themselves.

"It was a great story about a young man whose mother was single. It's kinda sad. She had him when she was fifteen, ended up in Chicago with no money. She started working as a prostitute. That was how she supported herself and her son, by hooking. She died of an overdose. Didn't she Agent Callaghan? You were fifteen. You were in the system for a year before you were fostered by a cop."

Finn flinched. His mom and his childhood in Chicago were part of his past, a part of him.

"What was it like knowing your dear old mom was turning tricks while you were watching cartoons. Did you meet the johns? Were they introduced as 'uncles'?" Ackerman made air quotes and then chuckled.

The implication hit Finn like a fist punching him in the chest. He grabbed Kennedy's arm. "We need to make some calls."

She didn't move. "No, we need to—"

"No, we have to go—now." He headed for the car, hoping she would follow. Ackerman's laughter echoed in the background, but that didn't matter.

"What the hell is wrong with you?" Kennedy spat the moment they were in the SUV.

Finn took a long, calming breath in an attempt to suppress his panic. "He has access to our personnel files."

She shook her head. "I don't understand."

"Do you have access to my file? No, you don't. He has someone high up. Maybe someone in the Justice Department."

"No, that's not—"

"Everything he said was true. Mom was a hooker. She died of an overdose when I was fifteen."

"But he could've found out—"

"Juvenile records are sealed, and I told no one. Not my friends, none of my colleagues. The only time I talked about my background was when I entered the FBI. I figured not telling them about something that big would come back to bite me in the ass."

"What does it matter where you're from? The FBI checked you out. You're in the clear."

"Who gives a shit about me? If they have someone with that kind of access, then they can find Paul Harris."

"Shit."

"I'll drive. You call Deluca." Thank God, he hadn't put Michael in witness protection.

Chapter Forty-Seven

Ethan sat in the overstuffed couch in Lance Ackerman's hotel suite wondering if he'd rip his stitches when he stood. That bastard Morgan had cut him deep and probably nicked an organ. Stopping the bleeding had been a bitch. He was running a fever, and his whole body ached. Or maybe the stab to his calf was infected. Then there was the scrape to the side of his head where the cop had shot him. Luckily, the bullet had only grazed his scalp. It had stunned him, bled a lot, and given him a pounding headache. Ironically, that had worked in his favor. Everyone thought he was dead, which meant no one was looking for him.

He reached into his jacket pocket and retrieved a bottle of aspirin. He popped two in his mouth and swallowed them without water. He'd have to go to the hospital and get checked out. He would claim he'd been knifed in a mugging, but first he had a job to do, one more murder to commit.

Ackerman paced the length of the room, his distended belly jiggling with every step. Ethan imagined slicing into all that fat but pushed away the impulse. He had a symbiotic relationship with the Syndicate, and he didn't want to do anything to jeopardize it. He would obey his orders to the letter.

Ackerman stopped and stared at him. "So you didn't get to plant the knife on Morgan, but you probably destroyed that stupid endangered shrub, or whatever it was, with the fire. That means we're still on the plus side."

Ethan nodded.

Ackerman sat in the chair opposite him, a tablet in hand. "Tell me about this Native American who got the drop on you."

"What's to tell? There were no distinguishing features, no scars. Black hair, brown eyes, tanned complexion, good looking."

"And he was sitting down the whole time?"

"Yes."

Ackerman flipped his tablet around. "Was this him?"

A handsome man wearing a dress shirt and tie smiled at the camera. The man he'd seen in Morgan's kitchen was scruffier, his hair longer, and he was thinner, but it was the same guy. "Yes, that's the one. Who is he?"

"My sources in Justice tell me his name is Michael Papin. Up until January, he was an Army CID agent who worked in their cyber division, using the alias Spider. The Syndicate suspects he's the man who infiltrated Marshall Portman's company. It wasn't until he surfaced for a meeting with the FBI in Salt Lake City that we knew his name. The reason he was sitting, instead of standing, is because Portman hit him with his car."

Ethan put a hand to his head. The bastard was crippled. He was weak and injured. That should've benefited Ethan. He'd turned and ran when he should've stayed and killed the son-of-a-bitch.

"This guy"—Ackerman tapped the screen—"is the biggest threat to our organization. He knows about us and has the computer skills to expose our plans."

"Shit, I could've had him."

"You mean you *should've* had him."

Ethan nodded. He never let pride get in the way of business. He'd screwed up. Now he had to deal with it. "You're right. Although I didn't know who he was, and I had no idea he was hurt."

"Then don't second-guess yourself. My sources tell me he's a genius who's more than capable of killing without hesitation."

Ackerman was right. Papin had the drop on him, but now Ethan knew what his target looked like. Sooner or later he would track down Michael Papin.

Ackerman stood and paced the room. "Like I said, Papin is a dangerous adversary. He had access to Portman's computer files. God knows what he dug up."

"You want me to go back and take him out?" Ethan inwardly groaned at the idea. He fucking hurt, and there was no way he could take on anyone, at least not today. Besides, he had other plans.

"Word is he's gone into hiding. My sources are trying to find out where."

"You think Morgan works for the FBI, too?"

Ackerman shook his head, making his chins wobble. "No, he's just a salesman. Tell me about him."

"He looks soft, but he's one tough son of a bitch." Ethan didn't want to go up against him again. Some people only fought to protect themselves. And most people posture before a fight, trying to make themselves bigger than they are. Most people avoided knives. They didn't like the idea of being cut, and there was no way to avoid the nick of the blade in a knife fight. But Morgan hadn't been scared of getting carved up; he'd expected it, accepted it. Ethan had seen it in his eyes. Morgan would've sliced his throat without a backward glance. Deep inside, the man was a cold, methodical fighter. Ethan respected that, and he would bet Morgan was as good with a gun as he was a knife.

"He was a Ranger," Ackerman said, as if confirming Ethan's thoughts.

"In that case, he's the best of the best. I tussled with a few Rangers back in the day, but this guy was exceptional." Although Ethan had never served his country, he had fought with a number of mercenary services. They'd given him a chance to hone his skills, but unfortunately they drew the line at indiscriminate killing.

Ackerman raised his eyebrows. "Was he that good?"

"Yes. He won't be an easy target."

"All right, let's forget about using Morgan to flush out Papin. I don't want to draw too much attention. I still have hopes of resurrecting the Molly's Mountain Mine. The

Syndicate have people digging into Papin's friends and family. If there's a weakness, they'll flush him out. In the meantime, I have another job for you."

"Lucy?" Ethan raised an eyebrow. This was his cue. Using the armrest, he levered himself off the couch and reached into his inside pocket for the syringe.

Ackerman, assuming he was about to leave, stood too. "You can't use your knife. It either has to look like natural causes or an accident."

The door to the suite slammed open. Lucy Portman strolled in. "I heard you had plans for me."

Ackerman's eyes bulged. "Lucy, I thought you were in New York."

Ethan used the distraction to plunge the needle into Ackerman's thigh.

He twisted, trying to grab at the injection sight. "What have you done?"

Ethan shook his head. "Sorry, I have my orders."

Lucy smiled as she stepped closer.

"They'll know it was murder." Ackerman stumbled but remained upright.

Ethan moved to stand in front of him. He wanted to see the life fade from Ackerman's eyes and revel in the power that taking a life gave him. "That's doubtful. This will look like an overweight man having a heart attack. I used potassium chloride, which has to be injected and is almost impossible to obtain. I had to buy your dose from a veterinarian. It's perfect because you're a diabetic so the medical examiner won't notice the needle mark And Unlike SUX, it leaves absolutely no trace in your body. Even if the FBI suspects we killed you, they won't be able to prove it."

Ackerman grabbed his chest, his face twisting in pain.

Lucy pointed in his direction. "I voted to let Ethan slice you. I hear that's how he gets his kicks, but the others wanted it to look like an accident. You got greedy. You stayed and tried to make the Molly's Mountain deal work when you should've cut and run. You even talked to the FBI, for God's sake."

"You gave Harris my number." Ackerman's knees gave way, and he crumpled to the ground, his massive butt in the air.

"Because you were already a dead man. I just needed authorization. The Syndicate will survive without you." Lucy smiled.

Ackerman made a loud wheezing sound as he struggled to breathe, and then everything went quiet.

Lucy opened her purse and pulled out a large vibrator. "I don't know about you, but watching someone die always makes me want to fuck."

Ethan understood the impulse. He'd felt it often enough, but he couldn't indulge her. A cold shiver wracked his body. His fever was getting worse. He needed to leave now, but he didn't want Lucy to know he was weak. The woman was as lethal as a scorpion. He took a step back, inching closer to the door. "I don't fuck women."

That was a lie. He'd had sex with plenty of women. Sometimes it was necessary, but he only enjoyed men.

"Pity." She waved him away. "I'll lock the door when I leave."

Ethan exited the room, not daring to turn his back.

Chapter Forty-Eight

Two weeks later

Tim stood shoulder-to-shoulder with Dana. He wished he could make this easier for her, but that wasn't possible. It was something she had to face. There was no getting out of it. Dana had been a wreck all morning. The woman could shoot a knife-wielding maniac, but the thought of public speaking filled her with panic.

Mrs. Anderson, the newly appointed mayor, cleared her throat as she strode to the podium. "I'll keep this short. I know you're all busy."

Shelly hustled forward carrying a Bible, which she held out so Dana could place her hand on it. Mrs. Anderson led Dana through the oath of office. It was a simple ceremony. Dana swore to defend the constitution of the United States, Montana, and the people of Hopefalls. Then her badge was pinned to her chest.

The town hall was packed with residents. All of them had come to witness the swearing-in ceremony of the new police chief. It hadn't taken long for the State Police to investigate. Eva was under arrest for killing Alice Hayden. That had caused a rift in town with Eva's family claiming she'd been wrongfully accused, but Tim wasn't worried about them. Most of the residents of Hopefalls supported him and were happy to have Dana takeover as police chief.

The State Police had also cleared Dana and Xavier of any wrongdoing. Many details of the case were still unknown to the public. Tim could've asked Finn but had decided against it. As long as there was no threat to Dana or Logan, he didn't need to know. The only thing that kept him awake at night was the fact that the police and FBI hadn't found Ethan Moore's body. Tim had shown them the exact spot where Dana had shot the freak. There were no charred remains, no body, and no trace.

A facial composite had been created from the descriptions he and Dana had provided. The Montana State Police were circulating the image, but so far no one had seen him.

As the ceremony ended, Joe Freeman approached him. "I'm sorry. I've been meaning to deliver this letter to you, but with everything…"

Joe didn't need to finish his sentence. Tim understood. The chaos of the last few weeks had thrown the whole town into disarray. Not only did they have to deal with the political fallout of their corrupt mayor and police chief, there was also the chief's murder and then Zoe Harris had been charged in Ben's death. On top of that, there was also the damage caused by the fire. Although the blaze hadn't reached the town limits, there was red fire retardant over most of the houses, and the smoke damage was extensive.

Joe passed him a plain envelope and a piece of paper. "I need you to sign for it."

Tim narrowed his eyes. In his experience, nothing good ever came in mail that required a signature.

The swearing-in was over. Dana was still busy. Everyone seemed to want to congratulate her and shake her hand.

He made his way to the back of the room, tearing open the envelope.

Dear Timothy,

If you are reading this, then I'm dead. I've been putting off meeting you because I'm a coward. Your father and I had our differences over the years, but I always respected him. I fooled myself into thinking you didn't need the money, but does that matter?

Last summer I was at my favorite fishing spot on the river when I saw something shining on the far bank, on your side. It was a can of coins. The dealer thought they were from a robbery committed by the Wild Bunch in 1901. I don't know if that's true. I'm just telling you what he said.

I sold six of them and got twenty thousand dollars a piece. I used the money to pay a lawyer to fight Third Estate Mining.

I told myself Jack wouldn't mind me taking them. Your father loves the land as much as I do. But a guilty conscience can be an awful thing. See, I never gave Jack a choice. It got so I couldn't sleep with the idea that I had stolen something that was rightfully his. Then I heard through my dear Victoria that you got power of attorney and were selling Wind Valley Ranch. I was furious. I stormed into Shady Pines thinking to give Jack a piece of my mind. I wanted to tell him what a bastard you are. But there is no Jack. The man I knew is gone, stolen by that awful disease.

Tim, I had no idea you were so broke. There are still a lot of coins left in that can. I left it where I found it. In my favorite fishing spot on your side of the river. I know you'll use the money for Jack's care.

Hopefully, I will find the courage to tell you in person. I'm not proud of what I did and I hope you can forgive me.

If you're reading this, then I died a thief and a coward.

I'm sorry,

Ben.

Tim folded the paper. The one thing they hadn't discussed since the fire was Zoe's motive for poisoning Ben. She'd said she didn't mean to kill him, and that was probably true.

Dana made her way to the back of the room. "What's wrong?"

He smiled. He loved how she understood him. "Nothing." He passed her the letter and watched her expression. Her mouth fell open as her gaze followed the words on the page. "We need to give this to Ramirez. It proves Zoe Harris's motive. She said she was looking for a pot of gold."

A sour taste filled his mouth. "Do you think this will become public?"

She nodded. "Yes. There's no way around it."

He kissed her cheek. "I'll be back later."

She grabbed his elbow. "Where are you going?"

He grinned. "Ben's favorite fishing spot." Then he strode out of the town hall, the prospect of finding a fortune in gold coins sending a thrill through his veins.

Epilogue

Two Months Later

Dana opened her eyes just a crack. Tim stood at the window, naked, staring out over the wild Montana landscape. It was a full moon, so even in the darkened room she could make out the slope of his back, his taut buttocks, and his shoulders. The two-inch scar on his left shoulder blade had healed. He flexed, stretching his spine, and shifted his weight from one foot to the other.

It wasn't unusual for him to wake and stand guard while she slept. She knew he was haunted by the idea that Ethan Moore was still out there. Normally, on nights like these, she'd reach for him, run her hands through the hairs in his chest to feel his muscled torso. That was all it took for them to go back to bed and make love, tangling the sheets in their quest for completion.

He had found what was being called the Molly's Mountain Hoard. The old rusted can contained over a hundred coins, all of them dating back to the mid-nineteenth century. There was speculation about their origin, but the prevailing theory was that they were stolen in a bank robbery and buried. Whoever buried them had either died before their loot could be retrieved or were never able to find it again.

Tim had set up a trust that would cover his father's medical bills. Then he had set to work remodeling the ranch. The bunkhouse was now a studio apartment. Logan loved it and had claimed it for his own. He had enough room for all his art supplies and privacy when Mia visited.

Dana tried not to think about what her son got up to in the bunkhouse. She had lectured him on birth control and then asked Tim to talk to him. Tim had refused on the grounds that Logan didn't want to have the sex talk from the man who was sleeping with his mom.

Dana had reacted with no tact, sensitivity, or charm. If they were to have a future together, then Tim was going to have to take on a parental role. Tim disagreed. He said Logan was a young man, not a child, and should be treated with respect. Tim wasn't and never would be his father, but he promised to always be there for her son.

It had been their first argument, and it probably wouldn't be their last. But of course, making up was always the best part of arguing.

She slipped out of bed and went to him. Even from a distance, she could feel the heat emanating from his body. He clasped her hand.

The stark moonlight cast harsh shadows across his face.

"There's something I want to talk to you about." He didn't look at her, but instead stared out at Molly's Mountain.

The tension in his spine and the fact that he refused to meet her gaze sent a chill down her back.

"I love you, Dana." He blurted the words before she could ask what was wrong.

"I love you, too."

"Marry me? I've talked it over with Logan and I asked his permission."

"You asked his—"

"Yeah, I know you don't want us to decide your life for you, but I figured he'd appreciate the gesture. The final choice is yours." He stared at the ground, avoiding eye contact, and she realized for the first time he was unsure. This confident, capable man had put himself out on a limb, uncertain of her response.

Somehow that vulnerability made her love him all the more. "Of course, I'll marry you. I love you."

Before she knew what was happening, she was in his arms and they were kissing.

He worked his way down her neck with licks and nips of his teeth. A familiar hum of excitement scattered down her spine. His thumb brushed her nipple, sending a shockwave through her. She jumped, wrapping both legs around his waist, reveling in the feel of his erection pressing against her vagina.

He caught her, his big hands caressing her butt. "Logan thinks we should live here. He has more privacy, and so do we, for that matter."

"That's good. I plan on making some noise tonight."

"I'm going to make you happy," he promised between kisses as he carried her back to bed.

She smiled as her hands stroked his firm body. "You already do."

Please help others find Fire Storm by leaving a review

About Marlow

After being thrown out of England for refusing to drink tea, Marlow Kelly made her way to Canada where she found love, a home and a pug named Max. She also discovered her love of storytelling. Encouraged by her husband, children and let's not forget Max, she started putting her ideas to paper. Her need to write about strong women in crisis drives her stories.

Marlow is an award-winning author, and a member of the Romance Writers of America.

FIRE STORM